NADINE LITTLE

Give the Devil Her Due

Divine Demons 2

LITTLE PUBLISHING

Sign up to my mailing list to get an exclusive bonus scene by scanning the QR code at the back of the book. Members of my mailing list get other free stuff and behind-the-scenes material.

Members are always the first to hear about my new books and discounts.

Join now!

'No one loses their innocence.
It is either taken
or given away willingly.'
Tiffany Madison

'Darkness cannot drive out darkness;
only light can do that.
Hate cannot drive out hate;
only love can do that.'
Martin Luther King Jr.

1

"Hey, Phin—has anyone ever said you look like a goth but dress like a rainbow?"

I smile at my best friend's teasing lilt. She tosses a grin over her shoulder while her hands are busy at the chrome coffee machine. Steam puffs towards the ceiling.

"You," I say. *"Daily."*

I tuck an escaped tendril of black hair behind my ear and glance at my outfit—red chunky shoes and tights, a jade skirt half-hidden beneath my apron, and a lilac top the same colour as the centre of my unglamoured eyes.

Not that any but my kin have seen those. And none of them are in Inverness, thank goodness.

I pop the little bubble of homesickness lodged in my chest. Has it really been six years since I saw another of my kind? My home of mountains and trees and our clan nestled within? Though I've learned a new term for that.

Cult.

"Remember I had to tell you what a goth was the first time?" My best friend pours milk into a cup, adding a flourish in the shape of a leaf. The name tag on her mauve shirt reads 'Harmony' above the smaller word 'Manager.'

She showed me on her phone before I even knew what a

phone was. This tiny device of noise and knowledge. She pesters me at least once a year to buy my own, but the things are too overwhelming. Intrusive. I like my landline in my house. It's shiny teal, and solid. I love the ringing clunk it makes when I drop the receiver on the hook. Harmony is the only one who calls me. I see her every day at work, so what do I need a mobile for? An immobile phone suits me fine.

"I remember," I say. "It won't be the last thing you teach me."

"Sweetie, that's because you grew up in a cave."

It wasn't really a cave. We had cabins. Electricity and running water. A garden, a hospital, a school.

Civilised, yet so many lies.

Harmony passes the cup to the man waiting patiently across the granite counter. He takes his eyes off me to accept the coffee, then his gaze returns.

People are so friendly in this town, the males especially.

I offer a smile, and he hesitates, his saucer clasped between blunt fingers. His lips twitch as if he might speak, though he stuttered a lot when I took his order.

Maybe he's shy. Harmony says I'm shy.

He ducks his head and clomps to a table at the front where the floor-to-ceiling windows look out on a tree-lined walk along the River Ness. Gold and russet leaves skitter on the pavement in the wind off the Moray. Goosebumps pebble my forearms, though the door to the cafe is shut, the interior warmed by chattering bodies and the comforting scent of coffee and cinnamon.

I sup the man's beatha—his life force—similar to how his friends are slurping on their drinks, but with more finesse. Caffeine in particular stirs a human's energy, and I siphon the excess. They don't even notice.

My method of feeding is better than the clan's. Less horrific.

This coffee shop has been my sanctuary in more ways than one.

Harmony wipes down her station and clears the carton of milk away, her braided ponytail whisking between her shoulder blades. I tidy the packets of cookies and shortbread next to the till, mussed earlier by a youngling—a *child*—with grabby hands. The bell over the door tinkles. A couple sweeps in on a lick of cold, wrapped in scarves, their fingers entwined. One woman kisses the other on the red tip of her nose. I watch them from beneath my lashes.

There are no same-sex relationships in my clan. A male selects a female and she becomes his Chosen, serviced by him alone from the age of sixteen, though he may service others. Her duty is to reproduce.

I shudder at the memory, forcing a smile as the women stop in front of me. They order coconut flat whites—my favourite—and a slice of chocolate cake to share. The taller of the two taps her card on the reader and steers her companion to Harmony's station.

"Damn," Harmony says, peering into the fridge. "Can you grab more coconut milk, Phin?"

She is the only one who calls me Phin. People tell me my name is beautiful—Seraphina—right before they shorten it to Sera, as if the syllables hurt their mouths.

"Sure," I say.

I plonk a generous wedge of cake on a plate and deliver it to the couple, now cuddling as they wait for their coffee. Harmony squeezes my arm as I slide past, my back angled away, just in case. I still marvel at the contrast of our skin, used to the shades of grey and ochre and red of my kind despite my time among the humans. She releases me quickly.

The brief touch is all I can allow, even from my best friend. I would love to let her hug me, as other friends do, but my glamour can only cloud the vision, it can't deceive the sense of touch.

One day I will show her who I really am—*what* I really am—and hope she doesn't run screaming.

It's what I miss most from my clan. Touch, affection. Playing and laughing, testing our powers, irritating our teachers. My childhood was a joyous one. It was at puberty that things started to go wrong.

I hook two cartons of coconut milk from the shelf in the storage cupboard and skip back down the short corridor past the staff room. The kitchen opens to the archway leading behind the counter.

"Thanks, sweetie," Harmony says above the purr of the coffee machine.

The female couple sits by the window, scooting their chairs close. Comfortable with each other. Gentle, too, I hope. I slice cake and grill paninis, humming a tune I heard on the radio, safe and content in my coffee shop.

I love my job. I love being able to wear what I want, go where I want, *do* what I want.

Goosebumps continue to prickle my arms. I check the air-conditioning panel, but it seems to be fine, warming the space against the autumn chill.

"Don't look, but that guy at the sofas is totally staring at you." Harmony wiggles her eyebrows. "And he is *hot*."

"Does he need a cold beverage?"

She hoots a laugh. "Phin, you crack me up. After all the poor sods pining for you, this one is worthy of attention. He could be your first boyfriend."

I resist the urge to peek over my shoulder, and scrub the grill instead, savouring the aroma of cheese and mushrooms.

"Do I need a boyfriend?"

"I'm not saying jump straight into bed—though, with this guy, I'd be tempted. Start with a kiss."

A shiver vaults up my spine.

Harmony's expression softens. "Seriously, sweetie, one of these days I'm going to set you up and you'll be thanking me for the rest of your life."

She sends me a bawdy wink, and I swat her arm.

"I don't need to be set up. I have everything I want—a best friend, a great job, my own house…"

I stop. I suppose the occasional cuddle would be nice. But he's human, so I'd have the same problem.

Harmony props her hip on the counter. "At least look at him and think about it. He hasn't taken his eyes off you."

I wash the grill brush with an exaggerated sigh and dry my hands on a towel by the sink. My gaze lifts from my fingers to the sofas nestled in the back, the chocolatey leather complementing the amber honey of the walls. A young family is engrossed in a picture book, their plates and cups abandoned on the low table. A man flicks his newspaper and licks his thumb before turning the page. A boy sits on the last couch, alone, an untouched coffee in front of him. Slim fingers clench on his thighs. Bronze eyes flash from a spill of brown hair, flickering like a tossed penny.

Harmony was right—he *is* staring at me. But it's not interest in his eyes.

It's hatred.

2

"Are you listening, Seraphina?"

I jerked my gaze from the sun-brightened window and blinked at the elder female drumming a talon on the desk at the front of the classroom. My wings twitched but I managed not to slap Cyrus, the male sitting next to me, like last time.

"Yes, Teacher," I said.

A snort ruffled my hair. Marrichar. Only she had a snout big enough to cause such a stir.

"Then what was I saying?"

I wriggled in my seat. "You were... telling us about... the Diviners."

"Specifics, please."

"Um..."

A scoff sent another blast of air across my back. My shoulders hunched. The female tutted and, after a final, disapproving tap on the desk, she spun to the blackboard and chalked another line of emphasis under the word 'Diviners.'

"Really, Seraphina, if you must daydream, save it for a class where you can be forgiven for your ignorance. Mating etiquette, perhaps?"

The room erupted in titters, and I sank low in my seat, cheeks blazing. Marrichar honked like the geese that collected on the loch. Teacher faced us until the noise faded, the chalk pinched between her fingers.

"You are all in your twelfth year," she said. "You are no longer younglings but close to coming of age. Soon you will be split into the duties that will protect this clan. Duties none of us should take lightly."

She dived into a lecture on the honour of male and female roles. My attention drifted to the window. A group of males in their sixteenth year mock-battled on the playground, their muscles straining, claws scouring dried mud and grass. The sun glinted on horns and scales.

Unlike our enemies, they didn't fight with weapons. A male's body *was* a weapon. A male's body also had another purpose. One we would be allowed to watch after class for the first time.

A funny feeling rolled through my stomach.

Would I birth a warrior or a female when it was my turn to be mated? Odds were it would be the latter, given the higher proportion of females born compared to males.

Teacher clapped, and I jerked my eyes from the glass. "Let's return to the real subject of our lesson, shall we? Who knows how to tell if a Diviner is near?"

Rumps shuffled on seats in the silence. I stuck my hand up.

"Yes, Seraphina?"

"Their beatha is different to a mundane human's. Cold. Their focus even raises goosebumps."

Teacher offered me a smile. "What else does their life force do?"

"It pollutes silver and makes it toxic to us. They use the material in their blades."

"Well, thank goodness you listen to some of my lessons."

"Why do they hate us so much?"

Her smile turned sad. "To them, we are monsters."

My wings flared in indignation. Cyrus ducked. Growls and hisses filled the classroom.

"Humans are cruel and arrogant," Teacher continued, "Diviners more so. Don't think that because most of them are female, they will be lenient. Their only goal is to slaughter us all. They do not spare our young, yet they call *us* evil."

A shiver danced down my spine. Thank goodness I probably wouldn't meet one. They murdered our warriors, but they wanted us. The females. It was why we were told never to stray beyond the loch. The world wasn't safe outside the clan.

"How can they call us monsters when we've done nothing to them?" I said.

"They cannot control us and that makes them afraid. Humans kill what they're afraid of."

I shook my head. I wished they'd leave us alone. Humans had spread over the whole planet; why couldn't they leave a little slice for us to live in peace?

Teacher glanced at the clock behind us. "There's half an hour left. practise your glamour and your abilities. But no broken windows this time, please, *Marrichar*."

My turn to snigger. I masked my wings and changed my lilac and violet eyes to a human blue. I took a deep breath, centring myself, and the classroom blurred into horizontal streaks of colour. Vertigo swooped in my belly. The colours settled. Warm wind teased my hair against my cheeks. Grass between my toes replaced the wooden floorboards of the classroom. I waved to the males on the playground. Two collided and fell in a tangle of limbs. I turned my back to hide a giggle and caught Marrichar scowling at me through the window, her snout fogging the glass. Her eyes were a soft shade of grey, like spring clouds.

I'd told her they were pretty, once. She'd pushed me in the mud. The others said she was jealous because I was slim and delicate and human-looking, and that was prized in a female. A human-looking male would be an embarrassment. Marrichar might have more characteristics of a male with her snout and hump, but she had strong hips. She'd probably birth many warriors. She should be happy.

She might be a little jealous of my ability, too.

I teleported once more and walked around the compound—birthing hospital, dining hall, greenhouse. I avoided the sunken amphitheatre, too nervous to peek. I wasn't allowed to go there yet. Marrichar sniffed when I appeared in the classroom, careful to return to my assigned corner.

I'd been warned many times of the dangers of teleporting into furniture or walls or another of my brethren.

The clock struck four, and Teacher wrangled us into a group.

"Everyone to the amphitheatre. We don't want to be late for your first ceremony. This will be a day you'll remember for the rest of your lives."

Her eyes misted and she marched out the door, forcing us to scramble to keep up.

She was no longer invited to participate in the mating ceremonies. Tests had discovered she was barren. Such a horrible word. Like all elders, she relinquished her name with her fertility. Though her name was beautiful—Éabha. Was giving it up another loss along with her ability to reproduce? She was still a valued female, able to teach and care for us when the others became too heavy with young.

The amphitheatre—set back from the compound in a glade

among the pine trees and off-limits to younglings except for special events—was a tiered oval of trampled grass stepping down to a floor of black marble that sparkled with flecks of quartz. A dark slab sat in the centre.

Officially, this was the first time I'd seen the revered space. Unofficially, I'd snuck here in my eighth year because I was curious. It had been empty at the time, and I'd soon got bored.

Seven females at their most fertile point in their cycle stood barefoot on the black marble, wearing white robes that ended mid-thigh. Éabha ushered us to the lowest tier, and we shuffled into a nervous clump. I tried to hide at the back, but a sharp elbow nudged me forward. The rest of the amphitheatre was empty, almost echoing, a circle of blue, summer sky above.

My heart slammed against my ribs despite my attempts to calm it. I focused on the female closest to me. Her head was bowed, her eyes on her feet. She curled her toes against the marble, her fingers petting her tail.

Maybe this was her first ceremony as a Chosen.

A leathery flap disturbed the peace. A male crested the outer rim and swooped to the floor, his silver-scaled wings spreading wide. I settled my own wings, so different to his— the skin black and red and delicate. Silver hair fell past his jaw and tangled in the spines on his shoulders. A simple cloth covered his sex, and I yanked my gaze upward to meet striking topaz eyes. His lips curved, sending a tingle to my toes and a blush to my cheeks. Marrichar grumbled behind me. The male's attention shifted to his Chosen, the female in the centre, and she dropped to her knees, her forehead pressed to the marble.

"I am honoured by your choice," she murmured.

Sharp, black hooves struck stone and the noise battered

the amphitheatre. A huge figure descended, muscles rippling under dusky, toffee-hued skin. Thick horns arched from his skull. He towered over the female closest to me, though she was tall. Taller than me. My head would barely pass the male's bellybutton.

She started to lower herself. "I am honoured—"

Thick fingers manacled her biceps and hoisted her onto the marble slab. She yelped in surprise. The male ripped his loincloth free, and spread her legs. Marrichar purred over my shoulder, but my stomach clenched.

He was too big. He couldn't possibly fit…

He rammed himself inside her, and she screamed. Biting her lip silenced the sound, but the echo goosepimpled my skin like the glare of a Diviner. The massive male thrust hard, rocking her body on the slab.

"I am honoured," she moaned, her voice pained. "I am honoured. I am honoured."

The male raised his head, his powerful hips pumping, and crimson eyes locked on mine. My knees wobbled.

I should be pleased by his attention. He was a strong male. His offspring would be great warriors.

Unease gripped my throat and I tasted real fear for the first time—metal and bile.

I was vaguely aware of several males entering the amphitheatre, but my focus was locked on the tears sparkling on the female's cheeks. Her white-knuckled hands gripped the edge of the slab, but the brute ignored her. The slap of flesh on flesh filled the amphitheatre and drowned out the noise of the other mating couples. I couldn't drag my eyes away to see if their rutting was as horrific as this spectacle, but their sounds weren't pleasant. Groans, whimpers, moans. The male's hot stare drilled to my core. My nails bit my palms, my fists shaking.

The male tossed his head, and grunted, sunlight glinting on grey tusks. His hips ground once, twice, against the shuddering female. When he pulled free, his organ was slicked red. He licked his lips, his gaze lingering on me, then he walked away. A burst of dizziness fizzed in my skull at the fading clomp of his hooves.

The female slid gingerly to her feet and hobbled to the edge of the amphitheatre, her tail curled protectively around her leg. Her hands clutched her stomach. Blood stained her thighs.

This was the mating I was to look forward to once I reached maturity? I glanced at my brethren, but instead of terror on their faces, their eyes sparkled with fascination, cheeks flushed, mouths parted. Cyrus touched himself while he watched the other couples finish.

Maybe I'd be paired with a gentler demon. A *smaller* demon. Like the silver-winged male.

I glimpsed him streaking into the sky. His female seemed tired, but there was no blood.

Please, *please* let me be his Chosen.

The brute would kill me.

3

There's a Diviner in my coffee shop. How could I have missed the signs? The goosebumps. The cold. I've grown complacent among the humans. Forgotten what I was taught.

Not everything my clan said was a lie.

I realise I'm staring at the boy. The *man.* His bronze eyes burn into mine. There's no sign of a knife, but his black combat trousers have deep pockets. A grey, fleece-lined jacket is folded next to him on the couch. His long-sleeved top hugs his shoulders, chest, and stomach, highlighting the muscle.

He's trained his whole life to kill demons like me. I'm trained in how to make the perfect espresso.

Hardly a fair fight.

"Wow, Phin. Try not to drool on the muffins."

Harmony's voice tugs my gaze to her amused brown eyes. My heart gives a solid kick and starts beating again. The clink and murmur of the coffee shop replace the buzzing void in my skull.

"What?" I say.

"That throbbing feeling? That's lust, sweetie. Go quench it in his lap."

"*What?*"

"Okay, maybe talk to him first." She winks, and nudges

13

an elbow into my arm. "Save the lap dance for when you're alone."

This conversation is making my head spin, not helped by the chill of the male's hatred burning a hole in my back.

"What's a lap dance?"

"Phin, you're so sweet and innocent. I love it. Guys will eat you right up."

This guy might. His stare reminds me of the nature documentaries Harmony and I watch at her house. A lynx stalking its prey. The eyes are the same.

I gulp. "I'm going to clean the kitchen."

"Wait! He's coming over. At least give—"

I scuttle away and hide under the stainless steel sink, willing my pulse to slow before it chokes me. Voices murmur through the doorway. The bell tinkles. I wait another minute, then slink back to the counter.

Harmony greets me with a fond smile. "You should have talked to him."

That's the last thing he would have wanted. He wants to slide his knife into my beating heart and turn me to ash.

I pick a piece of dust off my tights. "What did he say?"

"Well, first of all, his voice is as hot as the rest of him. Husky. A hint of danger. A wisp of mystery…"

"You got all that from his voice?"

She sticks her tongue out. "He asked how long you've worked here and if you'll be working tomorrow. Weirdly, he also asked if I've noticed any customers going missing. Maybe he's a police officer. Perhaps he knew your great-aunt when she worked in immigration."

She slips from behind the counter to clear the tables and I trail after her, barely noticing the basin in my hands and the weight of the crockery she piles into it. A brief flare of grief aches behind my ribs at the mention of Maggie.

Of course, she wasn't my great-aunt.

"Oh, and he wondered what time we were closing," Harmony says, scrubbing at a stubborn coffee stain.

My fingers go numb. Dirty cups scrape together as I struggle not to drop the basin.

Will he be waiting for me—hiding in the shadows, ready to pounce?

I glance nervously out the windows at the gathering dusk. Streetlights flicker on and shine on the sluggish water of the river. The coffee shop slowly empties. Blackness presses against the glass. At five on the dot, Harmony shoos out the last of the stubborn customers and flips the sign on the door.

"Come on, I'll walk you to the bridge," she says.

"You don't have to. I, um, forgot to check the stock. You go on ahead."

"Don't be silly. Do it tomorrow. You're lucky I'm such a laid-back boss."

She holds the door open. The bell tinkles cheerfully. Pulling my collar up, I force a smile to match hers and step outside. The brackish wind ruffles my glamoured wings, and I press them tight to my back.

So much for waiting until Harmony was gone and teleporting straight to the safety of my house. Maybe I can do it from Infirmary Bridge. No one should see me in the dark.

She chatters as we walk, but her words drift away like the lazy river on my left. My eyes scan for movement, for Diviners crouched behind parked cars or pressed against walls, their blades swirling like the night. My muscles tremble with adrenaline. I jump at the rustle of leaves.

They won't attack me here. They can't. Not with Harmony as a witness.

She stops and gestures me onto the suspension bridge, the white cables glowing in the dark. "I'll wait until you get half-way."

"Thank you," I choke out.

"See you tomorrow, Phin."

I hope so.

My shoes clomp on the decking panels. The wind moans between the trusses. Harmony waves the two times I look back. She's finally gone on the third, disappearing down a street heading away from the river. I release a breath and glance around, preparing to teleport. A figure approaches from the opposite bank, hood pulled up against the chill.

Darn humans are everywhere.

I press close to the railing and squint at the figure, my steps hesitant. Shadows cloak his face beneath the hood, but the size and shape suggest it's a male.

Is it the Diviner? Surely he has more important targets. Our fearsome warriors, for example. I'm just a demon who works in a coffee shop. I don't hurt anybody.

The male draws nearer. Goosebumps slither up my spine, and my feet stutter to a halt.

"I've never killed a female before," the Diviner says, drawing a knife from the sleeve of his coat.

Harmony was right—his voice is husky. Full of menace.

Should I call for her? She won't be far. But what if it puts her in danger?

"Maybe we should capture it," a woman says behind me.

I gasp and spin around. Another male and a female block the path, their blades out, the silver metal cloaked in swirls of black. The woman's pale hair dances in the wind, her body as bulky as the man beside her.

"It might tell us where its breeding clan is," she continues, her lip curled. "Look at it. I doubt it's as difficult to handle as the males."

I squash my fear into a tight ball that sits heavy in my stomach. I squeeze my eyes shut. Breathe in, breathe out. Picture my living room with its cosy fireplace and colourful knickknacks. My body grows lighter. A wave of dizziness rolls from my head to my toes.

"What the fuck is it doing?" the woman yells, though her voice is faint.

A hand clamps on my shoulder and shatters my concentration. I start to turn, my wings spread, and a searing pain flares under my shoulder blade. I yelp and leap forward, tripping over my feet and landing on my hands and knees. The rough decking panel scrapes my flesh. The boy stands above me. My blood looks dark on the tip of his blade.

"You stabbed me in the back!"

"Actually, I tried to stab you in the heart," he drawls, "but you moved."

My skin burns where his knife touched. Dampness spreads under my clothes. Tears clog my throat.

I've never felt pain like this. Nothing worse than bruised knees as a youngling, quickly tended by sympathetic females with healing abilities. If I was brave, I got ice cream.

Had I stayed in my clan, the agony would have come in my sixteenth year.

"Aww, Jace, you made it cry," the other male says.

The Diviner—Jace—glares at me, hood thrown back, his face hard and unforgiving. As cold and cruel as the rest of his species.

"You suck the life from people," he spits. "Spare me the crocodile tears."

"I haven't killed anyone," I whisper.

My back throbs. Nausea roils through my belly and sways the bridge under my knees.

"Like fuck you haven't," Jace snarls. "It's all you monsters do."

"I'm not a—"

He strides towards me, his teeth bared. With another yelp, I scramble away, but his hand bunches in my jacket and hoists me upright. He slams me into the railing, mashing my wound against the unyielding metal. I cry out, but his expression doesn't change. His knife stabs for my throat. I grab his forearm with both hands.

No one has ever touched me like this. Manhandled me. As younglings in the clan, we played—sometimes roughly—but no males were permitted to touch a female. No one would dare.

The icy bite of the Diviner's proximity tingles in my fingertips. He smells spicy and sweet—of cloves and blackberries. His beatha is intoxicating, swirling around me and nibbling at my senses, stronger than anything I've encountered before.

I could drink him down. All of him.

But I'm trying not to be that monster.

"Quit playing with it, Jace," the woman snaps. "We've been out here too long."

The man chuckles. "Yeah, this is embarrassing. It's just one female."

"Shut the hell up," Jace growls.

He strains against my grip, crushing me into the railing and forcing another cry from my mouth. His friends laugh while he fights to slit my throat, his grip on my jacket throttling me.

I've tried so hard to be good, but they don't care.

Jace releases his hold on my coat to go for a two-handed grip on his knife. In the second he stops pushing against me, I place a palm on his solid chest. Heat builds and bursts outwards, the pulse of energy sending him sailing back. He clangs into the railing on the opposite side of the bridge. Startled eyes meet mine as his tall body teeters on the edge, booted feet pedalling at the air. He flips and topples out of sight, splashing into the river.

My hand flies to my mouth. I take a step towards where he disappeared before I realise what I'm doing.

Furious shouts erupt from his friends. Their feet thunder on the decking panels.

I turn and run.

4

Stars prickled the velvet sky above the amphitheatre. Flaming posts sent flickering light into the bowl. My bare feet shuffled on cold marble, reminding me of the female two years ago. Her pain as she was rent by the sheer size and roughness of her mate.

Please, *please* let me be the Chosen of the silver-winged male. Felecior. Even his name sounded gentle. Not like Avzameth.

The brute.

His female—Deirdre—hadn't fallen pregnant from that first mating. He'd rutted with her fourteen more times before their pairing was successful. Thankfully, I hadn't been forced to watch any of them.

Marrichar's thick fingernail prodded me in the ribs. "Avzameth will choose me. I have the body that will honour him. Your puny frame wouldn't satisfy such a powerful male. He will choose me."

I hoped he did.

Teacher Éabha cleared her throat from behind us on the tiers. Marrichar wrinkled her snout, but shut her mouth. Thirteen others, all the other females in my class, stood beside me, watched over by the elders—the infertile adults—of our clan. A hush fell as we awaited the arrival of the males for their

20

selection. My heartbeat seemed loud in the quiet. I rubbed my palms on my simple, beige tunic.

No one else looked afraid.

I heard his footsteps before I saw him. Horns pierced the horizon. In a flurry of wings, tails, and claws, ten males assembled on the base of the amphitheatre. Avzameth was the largest.

Teacher had said the selection could get heated when males chose the same female and refused to concede. They would fight until one submitted and the victor claimed his Chosen prize when she came of age.

Avzameth had a reputation for killing his opponents.

The males paced and assessed us with burning eyes. I bowed my head, as I'd been instructed. Talons clicked on stone. An owl's tremulous call drifted from the pine forest above.

"What's your name?" The voice was soft, with a slight lisp.

My gaze jerked up. Felecior smiled encouragingly at me, his silver wings settled against his back. A tightness in my gut eased.

"Seraphina," I whispered, my voice as shaky as the owl's call.

"A beautiful name for a beautiful female."

Heat flared in my cheeks. Felecior chuckled.

"Seraphina, I choose—"

There was a grunt and a burst of heat. A massive shape blocked the torchlight, throwing me in shadow.

"This one is mine," Avzameth growled, spittle flecking his tusks.

My stomach dropped to my feet. Felecior, shouldered aside, raised his eyes up, up, and up to Avzameth's snarl. His wings rustled. I searched his face, hoping for defiance, possessive anger. Something passed through his topaz eyes. An apology?

No.

Pity.

He nodded stiffly to Avzameth and backed away. I clamped my lips on a protest. Voicing a refusal would be shameful. This was an honour. An honour…

I remembered Deirdre's pained cries.

I was going to be sick.

"Two years cannot pass quickly enough, my Chosen," Avzameth said, and licked his puffy lips.

I dropped my gaze to his black hooves, the edges rimed in mud. My skin crawled under the weight of his attention.

I didn't want him to touch me. I didn't want to become another screaming, quivering female, torn by the size of his organ.

Two years was too soon.

His hooves struck marble and his heavy tread faded. I stared at my toes, willing my legs to stop trembling. My heart felt like it was trying to crawl up my throat, and I wanted to cry. But no one else was unhappy. Even Marrichar bragged about her mate. Excited voices washed over me. Éabha congratulated me and I managed a smile, though I was too hollow to bask in her praise. I slipped away, avoiding the feast of roast pig and spring vegetables.

I was no longer hungry.

Deirdre met me in the woods, waddling across the needles and pine cones. Her tail arched over her shoulder, tangling in her red hair. The light from our camp gilded her cheek and left the rest of her face in shadow.

"Avzameth," I blurted before she could ask.

Her expression faltered, but it was steadied by a bright smile.

"He is a great warrior. A fertile male. You have been truly

honoured."

"But he's… And I'm…"

I waved at myself. There was a hint of breast and hip beneath my beige tunic, but my figure was petite. Lithe. Easily broken.

"What if it hurts?" I murmured.

It was the closest I could come to voicing my fears when I wanted to shout and scream that I didn't want him. *I* didn't want *him.*

Deirdre's sympathetic pat nearly released my tears. I blinked to clear them.

"It *will* hurt, Seraphina," she said, not unkindly. "But the pain is a small price to pay for fulfilling our duty. For this gift he's given me."

She rubbed the bulge of her belly. Her skin glowed in the darkness amongst the pine trunks. She looked… content. She threaded her arm in mine and we strolled the perimeter.

"Will you travel to another clan after the birth?" I said.

The majority of females chose to leave afterwards. Some went to clans in other countries. The elders encouraged it to broaden our gene pool, and when other clans were struggling to maintain their population. My mother had done it right after I was born.

I didn't even remember her face.

"No way," Deirdre said. "I know it's uncommon, but I'd like to raise my youngling. To watch them grow up, like my mother did for me until she travelled after her fifth birth. And you're here."

She rested her head on mine for a second. I watched the stars through the gaps in the canopy. We walked in silence, listening to the snuffle and skitter of night creatures. My panic and fear settled to a niggling ache in the pit of my belly.

Maybe everything would be okay.

Deirdre gasped and stumbled away. Her hands gripped her stomach. Fluid coated her legs and dampened the ground.

She lifted her head. "Seraphina! It's time!"

I supported her to the birthing hospital, pine cones stabbing my feet in my haste. Healers lowered her into a chair and wheeled her up the ramp into the wooden building. I moved to follow, but a firm hand on my shoulder stopped me.

"This is as far as you go, youngling."

"But…"

"She will be cared for."

The female disappeared through the door, leaving me alone on the grass. A bolt clunked into place. I fidgeted from foot to foot.

They let us watch the mating ceremony—horrifically painful as it was—why not the birth? Shouldn't they prepare us for that, too?

I glanced around, but everyone was at the feast, the invitation opened for all following the selection. I centred myself and teleported to the hospital's roof—the interior of the building was a mystery to me and too dangerous to risk.

A metal ventilation duct curled upwards. I padded along the wood and tested the screws fastening the grill, wishing I had talons like so many of my brethren. Like Avzameth. A brief teleport took me outside the dining hall, the inside filled with conversations and moving bodies. I sneaked into the kitchen, swiped a knife, and teleported back to the birthing hospital. A wave of dizziness weakened my knees, my energy depleted.

The tip of the knife scraped against the screws. They loosened easily and scattered around my toes. I carefully placed the grill on the ground and climbed inside the darkened maw of the duct. Metal squeaked under my weight, but I kept my movements slow, gliding on my belly towards light and the sound of voices, my wings tight to my back yet still brushing the sides and the ceiling. Another grill opened up on my right down a short tunnel. I held my breath, and peered through the slats.

Deidre lay naked and strapped to a trolley by padded restraints at her wrists, her legs bent and in stirrups. Two elder males bustled around the room. Metal instruments clinked on a tray. The female who'd stopped me from entering scrubbed her hands at a sink, a patch of red and green scales covering the back of her neck and disappearing under a blue gown. Deirdre's belly rippled like the flank of a cow bothered by a fly.

"Why must our duty always be the sore one?" she panted to the female at the sink, though the female didn't respond. "A male's duty seems much more pleasurable."

She directed her wobbly smile to the other elders, but they remained silent, preparing instruments and a canister of gas attached to a face mask. Both males had fangs and elliptical pupils, their blue gowns hiding multiple humps on their shoulders. Deirdre groaned, tossing her head, the cords in her neck straining.

"It's getting worse. Should it be getting worse?"

Her voice was nearly as pained as when she'd rutted with Avzameth.

I wanted to comfort her. Hold her hand and tell her to breathe. Stroke her dishevelled hair. The demons in the room were as warm as a bucket of ice.

The female dried her hands on a sterile towel supplied by one of the males, and bent between Deirdre's splayed legs.

"You have to push," she said.

Deirdre nodded rapidly, her breath whooshing in and out. "Is it almost over? I'd like it to be over now, please."

She bleated a laugh, then gritted her teeth to bear down. Garnet blood gushed between her thighs and pattered on the floor. The female raised her gaze to the two males, and something passed between them.

Deirdre keened. "This feels wrong. This isn't... I can't..."

Her scream battered the room. I jumped, bashing my head on the side of the vent. Deirdre's stomach bulged, as if her young was pushing its fingers against her flesh from the inside. She shrieked and struggled against the restraints. A male slipped a mask over her mouth and nose, muffling her screams. Condensation flared on the inside of the plastic with her heaving breaths. The female moved to Deirdre's side, placing firm hands on her chest as she writhed.

Shouldn't she be trying to pull the youngling out?

Deirdre's eyelids fluttered, her head drooping. Her skin tented again, further this time, and her eyes snapped open. Her piercing wail hollowed my stomach, and I jammed my hands over my ears. Mercifully, her body went limp. I released a shaking breath.

Giving birth looked even less enjoyable than mating. No wonder we were not permitted to watch.

A wet sound filled the silence left by Deirdre's screams. More garnet blood flowed, streaking her sides instead of gushing between her legs. Something slim and black emerged from her stomach. I blinked, not understanding. Three more appeared—long and sharp and glistening in the light.

Was something... *stabbing* her from under the table?

The elder demons quietly watched the appendages slide

from Deirdre's gut. Blood poured to the floor. The salty smell caught in my throat.

A male sighed. "I was hoping she would make it. She was birthed from my seed."

"We do what we must," the female said.

The black blades stretched upwards from Deirdre's belly. Reaching. Then they slashed down, shredding her flesh with another wet ripping sound. My fist plugged my mouth, smothering a cry of horror.

Not blades. *Claws.*

A mewl shivered from the bloody mess of Deirdre's abdomen. The female peeled Deirdre's torn skin wider and reached into the cavity. She slid a slick ball of black talons free and cradled it in her arms. The youngling uncurled, bathed in the blood of its mother, and kicked its stubby legs. Five-inch claws sprouted from every finger and toe. The female cut the cord connecting the newborn to Deirdre, spun on her heel, and strode from the room, her bare feet leaving prints in the blood. One of the males turned off the gas canister, and the quiet hissing faded.

Shouldn't they be stopping the bleeding? Though it *was* slowing. Garnet dripped from the edge of the trolley to join the large puddle on the floor. Deirdre's face was so pale, her eyelashes appeared bright red against her cheeks. The condensation cleared on the inside of her mask. I waited for her next breath.

And waited.

Tears blurred my eyes. My fist struggled to muffle my sobs.

"Such a waste," the same male said. "Maybe we should cut them out early."

"We cannot risk the survival of the young. No matter what."

With another sigh, the male draped a sheet over Deirdre's body. They wheeled her shrouded, collapsing figure away, leaving streaks and footprints and an empty, blood-spattered room.

5

I take my first sick day from the coffee shop in six years. The two days after that, I wasn't working anyway. No one can comment on my hiding, though I sometimes pop in for a coffee on my days off if Harmony is working.

But not this time.

I duck my head and pull my woollen hat down tighter, my eyes zig-zagging behind my sunglasses as I hustle across Ness Bridge. On my first day back, the morning is bright and clear, frost glittering on the pavement, so I don't look out of place. The route adds six minutes onto my usual ten-minute walk, but I'm avoiding Infirmary Bridge.

Did I drown the Diviner? Jace. Humans are fragile, even Diviners. If his friends managed to pull him out, he could still have succumbed to the cold.

I hope not. I don't want him to die. I don't want anyone to die.

"Phin!" Harmony unlocks the door and greets me with a warm smile. "How are you feeling? I missed you."

She called me every day to ask how I was, and brought me soup on the second day. Soy noodle. It was delicious. I felt guilty siphoning some of her beatha, but the postman doesn't come frequently enough for me to drink from him. I barely

29

have enough energy to hold my glamour. That, more than courage, forced me to the coffee shop.

And I refuse to be driven from a job and a life that I love.

I return Harmony's smile. "I missed you, too. And I'm feeling all better. Must have been your soup."

She squeezes my arm and ushers me into the warmth, flipping the sign on the door.

"Are you sure? Your outfit is a little more, ah, *subdued* than usual."

I'm wearing a honey-coloured wool jumper, and a black skirt and tights. My shoes are also black, though the laces are rainbow. It's not much of a disguise, but I'm less obvious at a distance.

"I'm sure," I say.

"Glad to hear it, sweetie."

The smell of coffee relaxes my muscles, though a spot of tension remains between my shoulder blades. It stays as morning turns to afternoon. I jump every time the bell tinkles, my gaze whipping to the door, expecting furious bronze eyes and a troop of Diviners. The familiar routine of making coffee, slicing cake, and bussing tables soothes me. I draw beatha from the customers, careful not to take too much from a single person despite my hunger.

Only once have I felt so woozy from a lack of energy—six years ago. I'd resigned myself to dying. The alternative was too awful to contemplate.

I have a mushroom and spinach panini for lunch in the staff room, tucked on the sofa, feet curled under me, reading my latest romance novel borrowed from the library.

Demons don't fall in love. Male demons have no concept of *making love*. The mating ceremony is a world away from the sex scenes in books, though I tend to skip those. I still don't believe anyone can enjoy having that… *thing*… rammed inside them. But pairing off and finding love is a human milestone. Perhaps the most important one.

I slide my book into my bag beside the envelope of cash Harmony gives me every month. The other staff get slips of paper. She's done it that way since she first hired me, even though I have an identity now. A fake one, but still.

I check my jumper for crumbs, and rejoin Harmony at the counter. She grabs my arm and twirls me around, her eyes sparkling.

"He's here! He's been here the last three days, but I wanted it to be a surprise. He's *so* got the hots for you. You have to talk to him."

My pulse freezes for a second, then ping-pongs into my mouth. A wave of cold sweeps to the base of my spine, and goosebumps erupt on my arms. I don't have to turn around to know he's watching me.

What a fool I am. Of course the Diviners won't leave me alone. I should have run away the minute I'd healed myself.

But I like it here. I ran away from home once before. I never expected to find another. A place to belong. To be free and (almost) myself. A place to feel safe.

Will I ever have that again or will I always be hunted? Like a monster.

"You need to get over this fear you have," Harmony says gently, probably mistaking my silence for shyness instead of despair. "Talk to him. Take him a muffin. He won't bite."

No, he'll just stab me.

"Harmony, I don't think—"

Her hands clasp my shoulders. "Seraphina van Ize, you

will go up there and talk to that man because you are smart and beautiful and I want you to be happy. The poor guy will worship you. And if he doesn't, I'll throw his arse out."

Somehow, I find myself walking towards the Diviner, muffin in hand, my shoulders hunched. His eyes flash as he watches me approach. I stumble up the two steps onto the raised platform opposite the counter. He's wearing black combats and boots again, his jacket draped on the back of his chair. His maroon hoodie hugs his shoulders and biceps and brings out the striking colour of his eyes.

Eyes that are currently glaring at me.

"My friend thinks you like me," I mumble to his half-empty cappuccino, "so I have to pretend to talk to you. Here, I brought you a muffin."

I thrust it out. He cocks a brow.

"You have friends?"

I frown at him. "I'm a lovely person."

"You're not a person."

I glance around, but no one is close enough to hear our conversation over the other chatter. Harmony gives me an encouraging thumbs up from behind the counter.

"Just take the stupid muffin," I sigh.

I plonk the baked good in front of him since his hands haven't moved from his lap. His eyebrow climbs higher.

"It's bran," he says.

"You stabbed me in the back," I hiss.

"And you tossed me in the river. I think we're even." He gives me a casual scan from top to toe. "Plus, it doesn't look like you're suffering."

"I healed myself." I eye the chair opposite him. "Are you going to knife me under the table if I sit down?"

"Depends. How many people died so you could heal?"

I lower myself slowly into the seat, never breaking contact with his fierce gaze.

"None," I say.

He pops a piece of muffin in his mouth, wrinkles his face, and shoves the rest away. A silver bracelet flashes on his wrist. He tugs his sleeve down before I can read the inscription.

"I find that hard to believe," he says.

"That's your prejudice, not mine."

His brow hikes upwards again. "It's experience, not prejudice."

He reaches for his cup, and I can't stop a flinch. He smirks, taking a sip, his brown hair flopping into his eyes. His focus drops to the tag pinned to my apron.

He snorts. "*That's* your name?"

"You were expecting it to be Beelzebub? Or would you prefer Satan... Jace?"

He starts at my use of his name, then shakes his head.

"I don't care what you're called, princess."

I copy his signature move and raise my eyebrow. "Princess?"

"As in, princess of darkness." He squints at me. "What exactly are you hiding under your glamour? Let me guess— elliptical pupils and ugly bat wings."

My *beautiful* wings flare in outrage, though he can't see. To a Diviner, my glamour shimmers like the air above concrete on a hot day. It's how they know what I am. And our attention feels like a prickle of heat, whereas theirs is an icy tingle.

I shiver and hug myself. "Are you always like this?"

"I think I'm being pretty civil. You're still alive, aren't you? For now."

I push a crumb around the tabletop. "I'm not hurting anyone.

Can't you just leave me alone?"

"Why *are* you alone? Female demons don't usually leave their nest."

Nest. Like we're insects. Pests.

"I have my reasons," I say stubbornly.

Jace thrusts forward. I twitch away, but not before catching his strange clove and blackberry scent.

"Tell me where it is and maybe I'll leave you alone."

I cross my arms. "I'm not going to tell you. I will *never* tell you."

Not that I remember exactly where it is. When I ran away, I flew for two hours in the dark. All I know is it's somewhere south. And the clan may be… not what I wanted, but that doesn't mean the Diviners get to slaughter them all. Some of them are innocent.

Jace smirks. "Brave words when you're all on your own out here."

"I'm not on my own. I have a friend. A best friend who will kick you out if you're not nice to me," I finish smugly.

I remember Harmony is watching, and uncross my arms. Jace throws her a salute.

"Does she know what you are?"

"I… haven't told her yet."

"And what happens when she's horrified that you're a monster?"

"I'm not a monster," I say hotly, but my ire fizzles and I stare at my hands in my lap. "I hope… she won't be horrified, but if she is… I'll have to find another place to live."

Sadness clutches my chest. The fear of losing Harmony, of being rejected, is the main reason I haven't told her yet. The guilt from doubting her doesn't help.

"Is that before or after you kill her?" Jace sneers.

My head snaps up. "I've been here for six years and haven't killed anyone."

"I don't believe you."

"Again—your prejudice."

"We'll have to agree to disagree on that one. You were obviously raised in a bubble."

I stand as slowly as I sat. The Diviner tracks me the whole way. He takes another nonchalant sip of his coffee.

"Are you going to leave me alone?" I say.

"It's not up to me, princess."

"Goodbye, Jace." I pause with my back to him. "I'm sorry I tossed you in the river."

His icy focus drills between my shoulder blades on the short walk to where Harmony is practically bouncing behind the counter.

"So?" she says. "What's he like? Are you going on a date?"

The Diviner shrugs into his jacket, his hoodie rising to show a line of stomach. He walks like a hunter—graceful, confident, strong. His predatory gaze stays on me until he reaches the door. The bell tinkles.

"He's a little intense," I say.

"Oh, come on! What's a little intensity for a guy that hot? Those shoulders. That butt…" She fans herself with a handful of napkins. "You could be happy together."

"He's the last person who would make me happy," I mutter.

6

In my fifteenth year, I met a human for the first time. A mundane human.

Not that I'd met a Diviner, either. Teacher had shown us plenty of footage of them in action, though, and the results of their cruelty. The smoking remains of a breeding clan they found in Switzerland had stayed with me, ash scattered everywhere. They spared no one, not even the younglings.

Humans, I'd heard, were just as cruel to each other.

"Listen class, this is very important," Éabha said, interrupting our quiet reading period. "Today, we're having a visitor. One you must use your glamour on at all times. Seraphina, the elders have requested you be the one to make him feel welcome."

My head snapped up. "Me?"

"Of course perfect little Seraphina gets the special assignment," Marrichar muttered behind me.

"Go to the playground," Teacher said. "He arrives soon."

My chair scraped on the wooden floor. Curious gazes followed me to the door, and I ducked my head. My bare feet stuttered on the steps, then padded on damp grass from a brief, autumn shower. A cold wind whipped my tunic around my legs.

Soon it would be time for shoes and tights. The adults didn't seem to feel the cold, happy to walk through snow in bare feet.

Two elders waited for me on the playground near a dirt path that led down the hillside to the loch. The same two elders in the room when Deirdre gave birth. Their fangs and humps were glamoured, their pupils round rather than elliptical. I copied their example and masked my wings, turning my eyes a human blue.

The day after Deirdre's labour, after I'd spent the night shaking and crying silent tears in my cot, they presented the new youngling to the clan, Deirdre's blood cleaned from its talons. They'd told us she was tired, but recovering well, and that she planned to travel to a new clan. That she was excited about it.

How many times had they lied to us? How many females had died? More than half the kin my age had absent mothers, though the ones who remained had had several younglings. I'd been told mine travelled to another clan. I didn't have claws or fangs, but maybe I'd killed her.

What else had they lied about?

"Thank you for joining us, Seraphina," said the elder who'd suggested cutting younglings out early to save the mothers. Deirdre's sire. His name had been Zev, when he was fertile. I'd asked. I'd wanted to know the names of the demons who'd let Deirdre die. "We know it's been a hard year for you, but we thought it would be a treat to show our special guest around the camp. You're also by far the best at holding your glamour."

He gave me a pleased smile and I struggled to match it.

A hard year? He had no idea.

They'd thought my withdrawal was because I missed the fictional Deirdre supposedly gallivanting around her new clan.

But I was grieving. Grieving the real Deirdre, her ashes buried in the woods somewhere. I'd burned with the need to tell the females they risked their lives with each pregnancy. I wrestled with the betrayal. What would happen if I told the truth? Our numbers would dwindle. The Diviners would hunt us to extinction.

This was our fate? Did all the elders know? They must. They kept this awful secret so females would continue to give birth.

We were taught it was an honour. But it was a death sentence.

"Now, listen closely, Seraphina," the other elder said—Kalyan. "Our guest is human. He knows nothing of demons, so we must pretend we are like him. We do not want to frighten him before the feast tonight. Do you understand?"

I nodded, confused.

Why had we invited a human to our clan at all? If he glimpsed something he shouldn't—a youngling unable to hold their glamour—wouldn't his information lead the Diviners right to us?

"Tonight's feast celebrates the beginning of your journey into adulthood," Kalyan continued. "You are but a few weeks from your sixteenth year, are you not?"

Each passing day clenched my stomach with worry.

I managed another mute nod. Zev gave me a soft—pitying?—smile.

"You must be excited for your first mating," he said.

I would never have sex. What was there to look forward to? The tearing pain of Avzameth's thrusts, then my own youngling slashing its way out of my belly.

I wished I were born a male.

Thankfully, before I had to craft a lie of my own, the elders turned towards the trees. A human dressed in a black robe and trousers emerged from the pines, accompanied by another elder. A white collar circled his throat. He picked his way carefully, his shiny black shoes slipping on cones and slick grass.

"Seraphina, this is Father Benjamin," Zev said.

Father? Whose father? My sire had been killed in battle. Apparently, he'd had wings like my own.

"Hello," I mumbled.

The man held his hand out between us. I flicked a panicked glance at the elders.

What was I supposed to do?

"Take his hand, Seraphina."

I touched his fingertips. His palm slid against mine, slightly clammy. He clasped our hands together and moved them up and down before releasing me.

Must be a human custom. How strange.

"Seraphina—that's your name?" His green eyes were gentle, his smile showing a crooked front tooth. "A seraph is the highest order of angels, second only in importance to God Himself."

"What are angels?"

"One of many wondrous things I can teach you. Though, I confess, I am more excited to see the artefact your family contacted me about. Travelling from Fort William to Mallaig, then incognito in a private boat has made me feel quite the spy. I was disappointed to bypass Inverie. It's the most remote village in Scotland—the UK in fact—yet you have yourself hidden away further still."

"Why don't you show the Father around, Seraphina?" Zev said before I could query the unfamiliar place names. "Ask him questions. We will come find you in time for the feast. And the artefact revealing. Don't stray too far."

The three elders bowed to the human and strode away. My cheeks flushed at his undivided attention. I stared at my toes wiggling in the grass.

"You could start with your school," Benjamin said helpfully. "I've heard you're all home-schooled here."

I took him to the cluster of classrooms, though most seemed empty. Only my class pressed their faces against the glass to watch us pass. Benjamin waved to them, and they hid.

Everyone younger than fifteen appeared to be absent. It reminded me of a trip we would take every few years—a hike along the loch valley, then camping. We would roast marshmallows on a bonfire and scare each other with stories of Diviners. Was that where they were? Perhaps I was too old to go now. A fledgling adult.

I avoided the death hospital and amphitheatre, leading Benjamin to the dormitories, dining hall, greenhouses, and farm. While I petted my favourite goat, he told me angels were spiritual beings with wings who served his god.

I had wings. Did that make me an angel?

We went on my favourite walk through the woods to the viewpoint over the loch. Benjamin perched on a stone and fiddled with something in the pocket of his robe. A string of beads spilled out.

"What is that, Benjamin?" I said.

"*Father* Benjamin," he chided. He pulled the object from his pocket and held it out. "This is my rosary. It guides me in prayer."

The beads were carved wood in bronze and gold, and smelled faintly of nutmeg and cinnamon, the surface smooth under my fingertips. Larger brass balls separated the wooden beads, with woven brown cord in between. A single line of beads ended at a cross—a crucifix according to Father Benjamin—where a human seemed to be nailed with his arms spread.

Teacher wasn't exaggerating when she'd said humans were cruel.

"It's pretty," I said.

"You can have it." Father Benjamin curled my fingers around the rosary when I tried to give it back. "If you ever need someone to talk to, He's always listening."

Would his god listen to my fears about sex? To the horror I'd seen in the birthing hospital? Would he tell me what I should do? Without Deirdre, I'd had no one else to talk to.

"Thank you," I whispered.

"Here, let me put it on."

Father Benjamin looped the rosary over my head and it settled around my neck, the crucifix hanging between my breasts. He patted my hair. I stroked the rosary, the beads warm.

I'd never had something of my own, except my toothbrush. Everything else was shared between the adults and younglings. Would I be allowed to keep it once Father Benjamin left?

"What's it like out there?" I said, emboldened. "I've never left this valley."

Father Benjamin described his village—Fort William—his church, his work. He tried to tell me about his lord and saviour, but they were not as interesting as the human world.

"You should let the Lord into your heart, Seraphina, while you are young and pure," he said. "Before the devil tempts you to sin. Only faith in the Lord can keep you on the straight path."

"What is the devil?"

"He is a creature with horns, bat wings, and the hindquarters of a goat. He not only lacks goodness, but has a conscious will against God, His word, and His creation. The devil will entice you towards evil."

Evil. Father Benjamin thought demons were evil. Monsters. If I showed him my wings, would his fascination turn to repulsion?

He tried to engage me in further conversation as the sun set, but I withdrew into myself, watching the light fade over the water. The elders found us in our silent walk back, darkness gathering between the pines. They strode ahead with Father Benjamin and he chattered about the artefact. A lump of carved stone I'd never seen. Would Éabha know what it was? We paused on the edge of the amphitheatre, the tiers nearly full with adults, elders, and younglings in their fifteenth year, all cloaked to appear human.

"Oh, wonderful, you gathered everyone together," Father Benjamin said. "May I conduct a sermon? It seems only fitting to talk about God's love if it truly is a Celtic cross you've unearthed."

Kalyan nodded. "Of course, Father. This feast is held in your honour. Come."

Unsure if I were to follow, I trailed the group. Shadows coalesced as we descended, the flames on the torches of the upper rim dancing against the velvet sky. I hesitated on the tier where my classmates stood, Marrichar glaring balefully at me. Her eyes narrowed, and I realised I was playing with the beads on the rosary around my neck.

I didn't like this place. Nothing pleasant had happened to

me here.

Father Benjamin beckoned with his hand. "Come, Seraphina. I'd like you at the front."

I stopped on the lowest level, my bare toes touching the marble where it ended in a border of grass. A brief scan confirmed I was surrounded by males. I ducked my head, though they made space for me, careful not to touch. A shudder zipped up my spine at the weight of Avzameth's gaze from across the circle.

Father Benjamin walked to the marble slab in the centre and turned to survey the crowd. His eyes rested on me. He opened his mouth to speak. Avzameth clamped a huge hand on his shoulder. Father Benjamin gave him a puzzled frown.

"Can I help—"

Avzameth dropped his glamour, revealing horns, tusks, and cloven hooves. His talons pierced Father Benjamin's robe.

Now I saw why they mistook us for the devil.

Father Benjamin, his face bleached white and his mouth agape, touched his fingers to his forehead, the centre of his chest, his left shoulder, then his right shoulder. He jerked against Avzameth's grip, and the talons sank deeper. Avzameth hoisted him easily onto the slab and pressed him flat with a hand on his neck. Father Benjamin's wild gaze flew around the amphitheatre where everyone had dropped their glamour. His eyes fixed on me, my glamour in place, my feet frozen to the ground.

"Seraphina, please—"

Avzameth raked his claws from throat to stomach, shredding Father Benjamin's robe and some of his flesh. Blood, black in the moonlight, glided down his heaving ribs.

"Our-our Father, who art in H-Heaven, hallowed be thy

name..."

Avzameth pulled an elaborate knife from his breechcloth. Father Benjamin's words faded to a rapid wheeze. I wanted to shut my eyes, but I stared at the cursed slab and the further atrocity about to be committed upon it. The rosary bit into my palm. A drop of garnet blood plopped onto my foot.

Father Benjamin sought to pry Avzameth's fingers from his neck. "Wait—please. Wait a minute—"

The blade plunged down. Father Benjamin shrieked. Avzameth stabbed the knife into Father Benjamin's chest and yanked it sideways in a gout of blood that splashed on the marble. The male jammed his arm into the wound with a sickening crack of bone and the rip of flesh. A sharp tug rocked Father Benjamin's limp body. His head flopped, his gentle eyes glazed and staring at me. Avzameth shoved a dripping hunk of tissue aloft, and the amphitheatre erupted into howls.

Something staggered me and the crowd, invisible but potent. It appeared to have radiated from Father Benjamin's body. Energy fizzed through my veins and burned in my muscles, blasting my glamour away. My wings stretched, slapping the males on either side of me, though they were too busy writhing in ecstasy to notice.

I felt like I could fly to the moon.

The euphoria faded at the sight of Father Benjamin sprawled on the slab, his blood still pattering on the marble, his face slack. Dead.

"Remember this moment," Avzameth growled, his crimson eyes scanning my classmates' tier before alighting on me. "This is what it means to be adult. From your sixteenth year, you must feed on beatha—human life energy—or you will weaken and die. Their death is our sustenance. This is why they fear us—they are no longer the apex predator."

Horror numbed my lips and swept to my toes.

This was why we were hunted—we slaughtered humans and bled them dry like a chicken on a hook. No wonder the Diviners hated us.

No, I couldn't. I *wouldn't*. No other creature would die so I could live. The price was too high.

"And this is how we will defeat our enemies." Avzameth tore a mouthful from the heart. The tissue crunched between his tusks. A smirk twisted his lips. "With the blood of the lamb."

I looked at my brethren. Not a single face was aghast or revolted. A greedy light sparkled in Marrichar's eyes. My stomach roiled, threatening to rebel and splash my sickness on my toes.

I couldn't stay here.

My clan was *not* safe.

I'm careful over the next week, teleporting to and from the coffee shop after my intense talk with the Diviner. His friends come in a couple of times—the stocky male and female—sipping their coffee and glowering at me, but Jace is never with them.

Has something happened to him or is this his way of leaving me alone like I asked?

Harmony tries to coax me out in the evenings. I make excuses until she finally insists.

It is my birthday after all.

She drags me to the cinema at Eden Court—a grey building of angles and glass, with a large sycamore out the front shedding copper leaves right next to our coffee shop and Inverness Cathedral. I half-watch a romantic comedy, my eyes scanning the darkened theatre for glaring Diviners, though my skin remains goosebump free. I walk Harmony home afterwards, though she protests.

"I'll phone when I get in," I say to mollify her as she hesitates on her doorstep.

"I really wish you had a mobile, Phin. What if something happens to you on the way? It's getting late."

"I'll be careful, I promise. I'll stick to the main roads."

She kisses me on the cheek. "Happy birthday, sweetie."

She got me a beautiful blue bag with rainbow tassels. It sits at my hip, the strap across my chest, matching my navy jacket, skirt, and tights, my top red with glittering sequins.

It took me a while to get used to giving and receiving gifts. There are so many human customs to learn.

Harmony waves, and shuts the door. Restless, I head south instead of straight home. The air is crisp and fresh, promising frost. Harmony won't expect my call for at least half an hour and I've been cooped up over the past week.

Night time is my favourite. The energy is different—more untamed and expectant. The world holds its breath, waiting for the return of the light.

I teleport to the other side of a wrought-iron, curlicued gate, the spikes at the top painted gold. The cemetery spreads around a wooded hill. I say hello to Maggie's gravestone, then walk into the trees and perch on a stone bench, the clearing at the summit containing larger tombs.

It's peaceful here. Like my clan in its wooded valley when they weren't sacrificing humans, giving birth, or mating. Small critters shuffle in the undergrowth. My breath puffs white and drifts towards the stars.

What am I going to do about the Diviners—hope they get bored and give up? Show them I'm not a threat? Like Jace said, I'm all alone out here. No warriors to fight them off and keep me safe, though the thought of returning to my clan to plead for help fills me with dread. What would they think of me? How would they treat me? Will they force me to mate with Avzameth as if no time has passed? Assuming he's not died in battle by now.

I rub my palms on my tights, ruffling the material above

my knees. The night creatures have fallen silent, the trees blocking any sounds from the city.

It's like I'm the only soul left alive.

I shiver and slide off the cold stone. My shoes crunch on leaves. Before I can close my eyes and concentrate, a shadow slinks around the side of a tomb. A huge shadow. Horned. Crimson eyes glow in the black.

"If it isn't my Chosen, returned to me," Avzameth growls.

Every part of me freezes—blood, breath, limbs. My glamour falters at the wave of terror.

Avzameth straightens from his stealthy crouch and stalks towards me, branches cracking under his hooves. A jagged scar runs from the corner of his left eye to his upper lip, twisting his face into a permanent sneer.

He must have been too late reaching a healer. Or didn't bother at all.

His massive body bathes me in heat as he stops in front of me. My heart batters against my ribs, trying to escape since the rest of me can't move. I stare at Avzameth's muscled stomach without blinking.

When did I last breathe? I need to gather my wits and teleport to safety.

"I thought it unlikely the rumours of a female in Inverness were true, but I hoped. Still so pretty." Talons catch in my hair. Avzameth sniffs loudly. "And still pure. I have waited so long for this day. Present yourself to me, my little runaway."

I remember Deirdre—her scream of agony, the blood. He ignored both, and thrust to his own release, then left her to hobble away.

My gaze drops to the huge bulge in his loincloth.

It will rip me to pieces.

I shake my head, my hair whipping my shoulders. My vision goes white, and my knees wobble.

If I faint, will he take what he owns? I am his Chosen, but it was never my choice.

"Present yourself, Seraphina," he says.

He grunts at my hesitation and reaches for me. Images of Deirdre hoisted aloft and pinned to the slab flash through my mind. I swipe at his giant hand, miss, and slap the horrifying organ he wants to split me with. He roars and curls around himself. His fury electrifies my stalled muscles. I stumble for the path, half-blinded by tears, my breath finally coming in tortured gasps.

"I will have what's mine!" Avzameth bellows.

The ground shudders beneath my feet as he thunders after me. I run and run and run, too afraid to think, though I know I'm forgetting something. I burst out of the trees and sprint between the gravestones.

The city lights seem a million miles away. Like every human in the world has disappeared.

I trip on a flat stone hidden in the grass and scrape my knees on the gravel path that winds through the cemetery. I scramble to my feet, Avzameth's heavy snorts powering me on. Skidding around a monolithic tomb, I collide with something warm and solid. Hands grip my upper arms.

"Nice wings, princess," Jace drawls.

Oh, right—my wings. I could have flown from Avzameth instead of scurrying away like a panicked mouse.

I shove at Jace's chest. "Run! We have to run. He's coming—"

"Where? Where is—"

"Oh, this is a fortuitous day," Avzameth chuckles. "Reunited with my Chosen *and* I get to slay a Diviner."

Jace sweeps me behind him, as if he's forgotten I'm a demon female and not a human needing his protection. My fingers pluck at the back of his grey jacket.

"I'll be the one doing the slaying," Jace says. "Why else do you think I'm here?"

I pull on his arm. "Jace, no—he's too strong. We have to run. *Please*."

"You should listen to my Chosen," Avzameth says. "One human on their own is no match for me."

"I'm not alone. The others are"—Jace frowns and scans the empty cemetery—"around."

Avzameth laughs. "Foolish boy. Your allies could be three metres beyond and still not see us. Nothing will disturb this battle or the prize I will claim after."

His hungry gaze rests on me cowering behind Jace.

"Stay here, princess," Jace says.

"Jace, no—"

Jace prowls towards Avzameth. Two blades appear in his hands. He throws one in a blur, but Avzameth bats it away with a hiss. They circle each other, feinting, testing each other's skill. Jace looks tiny compared to the demon, but he's fast, dodging and blocking and slicing with his knife. Garnet blood splatters the grass.

Maybe he *can* win.

Avzameth seems to falter. Jace closes in, but the demon's meaty arm parries his blow and knocks the second knife from his grip. It clatters off a headstone and vanishes into a pot of plastic flowers. Avzameth wraps a hand around Jace's throat and hoists him into the air. Jace chokes, his legs kicking. My breath locks in my chest.

"No human can kill me, foolish boy." Avzameth's sneer

crinkles his scar.

Jace draws a third knife from the pocket of his black combats and stabs the demon's arm. Avzameth howls. Jace falls to his knees and one hand, struggling to breathe. His silver bracelet flashes on his wrist. Avzameth bunches his fist above the stooped Diviner.

One blow will shatter his skull.

I launch myself at Avzameth, flapping hard to gain height. I claw at his eyes, avoiding his sharp tusks and horns and wishing I had talons. His arm swings out and sends me flying. I thump onto the grass, rolling until I slam side-on into a gravestone. The granite bruises my ribs and punches my breath out. Winded, I struggle upright, my hair tangled over my face.

"I will deal with your disobedience later, my Chosen," Avzameth growls.

Jace is back on his feet, circling the demon. I watch anxiously, my side throbbing.

Can Avzameth feed on Jace's beatha where it swirls around him, heightened by the battle, or can he only feed from taking his life? Am I the only one who can survive on small portions? Has anyone from the clan ever tried?

Jace manages to cut Avzameth a couple more times before the demon halts him with a powerful kick to the ribs. The crack of bone seems to echo. Jace swallows a groan, teeth gritted, favouring his injured side. Avzameth dodges his next blow, slapping the blade from Jace's hand. The knife skitters to a stop at my feet and I dance back, blackness swirling along the blade. Avzameth's huge fist thuds into Jace's temple. My stomach clenches at the awful noise. Jace hits the ground on his back, blinking and dazed.

Avzameth raises his cloven foot. "You are not the first Diviner I've crushed into the dirt. Nor will you be the last."

I can't watch him kill Jace. One human slaughtered in front of me is more than enough, even when *this* human tried to kill me. Can I blame him? I've seen how monstrous my brethren are.

Stomach lurching, I scoop his knife from the grass. The handle sears my palm, and I bite my tongue on a shriek. I force myself to tighten my grip instead of hurling it away, and propel into the air. I race towards Avzameth. The blade stabs at his neck. I scream at the pain, at the thought of Jace's skull trodden into the mud. At the image of Avzameth claiming his victory and burying himself inside me, then dragging me back to the clan, torn and bleeding. Hot blood drenches me and sludges in my eyelashes. My hand burns. Avzameth howls, trying to swat me, but I swoop and dive, stabbing. Always stabbing. I stab until the blade sinks into the grass in a puff of ash. I blink at the smouldering pile that used to be Avzameth. Dust sticks to the blood on my clothes and coats my knees.

My birthday present from Harmony is ruined.

Smoke wisps from my hand. I pry my flesh from the handle of the knife, revealing a mess of blisters and burned skin. My stomach heaves and I vomit into the ash, choking on tears and bile. Shaking, I cradle my hand to my chest and crawl to Jace through red, flickering flames and the tang of burnt chlorophyll. His eyes are closed and blood oozes from a nasty gash on the side of his head, sticking a clump of hair to his temple.

Voices drift from somewhere among the gravestones. Jace's pocket vibrates. As soon as it stops, it starts again.

How long until the Diviners find us now that Avzameth's

cloaking magic is gone? What will they do to me? I need to go, but I can't leave Jace here, injured and vulnerable. He may have been more concerned with killing a demon male, but he still tried to defend me. What if his kin don't find him in time and he dies, alone in the grass? What if they find him, but his healers can't fix the damage?

I carefully run my good hand over him, memorising the feel and weight of his body. Shoulders, solid chest moving as he breathes, firm stomach. He's so smooth and unadorned compared to a demon male. Boring, really. I hesitate at the slimness of his hips, his long, muscled legs. His black boots end mid-calf and are scuffed at the toes. His jacket lies open, his dark top twisted to show a line of skin above the waistband of his combats.

The voices grow louder, breaking my assessment.

"Where the hell is he?" a female says—likely the stocky woman with pale hair. "I'm sick of babysitting him when he just fucks off whenever he wants."

"Jace!" yells the male.

I curl myself around Jace, letting the voices fade. A swoop of vertigo and a streak of colour. A rushing in my ears. Beneath my knees, the lawn turns to the spongy cushion of my purple sofa, the upholstery immediately ruined by blood and ash. I scramble off Jace's prone body, turn a lamp on, and check I haven't miscalculated the teleport, leaving a hand or foot behind. He looks intact. His beatha flares where he's hurt— head, chest, and a multitude of smaller sparks for scrapes and bruises. Lamplight brushes his forehead and stretches shadows beneath his sharp cheekbones.

I take a couple of steadying breaths and crouch next to him, resting my fingertips on the side of his face. Warmth builds in my palms. Closing my eyes, I focus on the icy crackle of his beatha.

My healing ability was the last to develop. Teacher Éabha said I was very fortunate. Most demons get one ability, maybe two, and healing is rare. A female trait. Another reason why we're kept so close to home.

Marrichar was livid.

I coax my energy into Jace. A starburst fracture marks the blow from Avzameth's heavy fist. Deeper, the brain is bruised, blood collecting under the bone. My forehead wrinkles. Deeper still, there's an area of wrongness—a haze, unrelated to his battle wounds. Whatever it is, it would take more energy to heal than I have. Maybe even death energy.

I shudder and lean closer, my eyes squeezed shut. Jace's skull knits together. The bruising fades, the blood reabsorbed. Swaying on my knees, I direct the last of my strength to his broken ribs—three in total—keeping the bare minimum for me to function without passing out. His breathing eases and he slips into restful sleep rather than unconsciousness. I slump on my heels, lightheaded and weak, my injured hand throbbing.

I'm not working tomorrow, but I'll need to go out and scavenge beatha. The burn has tightened my tendons, curling my fingers into claws.

And it hurts like a motherfucker, as Harmony would say.

Shoot. I forgot to call Harmony.

I shuffle to my shiny teal phone on the table beside the couch, my bag leaving a trail of blood and ash on the carpet, and wedge the handset under my chin, dialling one-handed.

"Seraphina van Ize," she answers, "I was about to call the police."

I mumble an apology and a pitiful excuse about streets being closed for roadworks. She wishes me a good night after another couple of minutes of me struggling to string words together. I rest my cheek on the table and listen to the dial tone. Jace breathes quietly beside me.

I've never had a male in my house before. Harmony would be ecstatic.

Leaving a smear of blood on the handset, I drag myself upstairs to the bathroom. The contents of my not-so-new bag scatter on the floor—money, lip balm, hairbrush. No make up, though Harmony teases me about that, too. I dunk the bag in a bath of cold water.

Maybe a good soak will take the demon blood right out.

Garnet swirls in the water. My hand pulses. I scrub the mess from my face half-heartedly and plod downstairs, shedding my coat and shoes. In the kitchen, I run water over my burns and try not to whimper, then wrap my hand loosely in clingfilm. Jace continues to sleep the sleep of the newly healed. I drape the blanket from the back of the couch over him.

How will he react when he wakes? Should I barricade myself in my bedroom? I'm too tired to go back upstairs.

I light the fire, my skin cold to the touch, and curl on the rug in front of it. Jace's profile is the last thing I see before my eyes slip shut.

8

The horror of Father Benjamin's death propelled me into the air, though it was the power from his beatha that filled my wings and sang in my blood. The flames from the torches around the amphitheatre dwindled to specks in the darkness.

No one saw me leave. I'd weaved through the writhing crowd and slipped into the trees to fly from the only home I'd ever known.

Tears froze to chips of ice on my cheeks, but no chill pebbled my skin.

Was this why adults were immune to cold? Because they gorged on the energy of human deaths?

I climbed towards the stars. In the vastness of the sky, I teleported in short hops, desperate to flush the beatha from my system, even if it brought my own death quicker. Three trips had been my maximum. Now, I felt no fatigue after five. Ten.

The power was dangerously addictive.

Lights from human abodes peppered the blackness of the land below me. I travelled for miles into an unknown world. My muscles cramped, unused to the exercise despite the energy boost. A larger illumination sprawled on my horizon, separated by a strip of darkness—a loch or a river. I swooped down to the edge, avoiding the sweep of lights on a moving metal conveyance. I glamoured my wings and eyes and crept through the human city, my back hunched, expecting a Diviner to spring from every corner. The thoroughfares were empty. Hushed. Perhaps it was late for humans to be out.

Everything was strange and concrete and smelled funny.

What should I do—find a corner and curl up like a sick goat, waiting to die? How quickly would I fade?

Black letters on a white metal rectangle driven into the frosted ground read 'Holm Road.' Was this the name for the ribbon of concrete where lumbering things with wheels trundled along—a road? I walked to a large circle with the statue of a green serpent in the centre, and took the right path. Dores Road. I scurried on the grass between trees set in unnatural lines, disliking the roughness of the concrete tracks under my feet. I stared at lights mounted on poles, most the same colour as the bulbs in our cabins, but others flicking between red, amber, and green. Brick buildings, the windows dark, stretched on and on to my right.

So many humans crammed in one place.

A large hedge forced me to walk on the concrete. I wrinkled my nose until the grass and trees returned. The road continued forever. Buildings crowded in on both sides, none of them made from wood like the cabins back home. I breathed easier when trees towered above me but, too soon, they were replaced by more brick buildings. The path became Island Bank Road; nothing to mark the change bar the words on metal at the side. I walked and walked and walked. The soles of my feet throbbed on the hard surface. I passed a structure with a curved roof over the path. The words read 'Bus Stop' below a picture of a long, wheeled object.

Was that a bus?

Beyond the stop, a break in the low wall led to a white metal bridge across a wide river. I followed it onto a wooded island and happily wriggled my toes in the dirt of the path. I sat on the grass, content to listen to the water and rest my weary muscles. A mallard, disturbed by something on the opposite bank, gave a disgruntled quack. I watched the dark sky slowly lighten, and pondered my future.

Would I live to see my sixteenth year? Avzameth had said we needed to feed regularly once we reached adulthood. Would food and not sacrifice sustain me until I was sixteen, as it had up to now? That gave me a couple of weeks at least. I just hoped it wouldn't hurt once I started to weaken.

When the sun peeked through the branches behind me, I stretched my legs and returned to the main thoroughfare, continuing north. More wheeled contraptions zoomed up and down the road. Humans strolled on the paths, their bodies completely smooth. No scales or wings or humps. They gaped at me, their bland-coloured eyes sweeping from my tunic to my bare legs and feet. None of them were dressed like me, though some of the females wore skirts or pieces like my tunic, but clingier. All of them had shoes. So many different kinds of shoes. Where had they got them all? When a pair of humans tried to approach, I ducked my head and scurried away.

I wasn't very good at blending in.

A wave of homesickness hit me already, tightening my throat. I wanted to see my own kind—their fangs and claws and tusks. Marrichar's scowl. Teacher's smile of praise when I got her question right. But I couldn't go back, not to a short life of pain and human suffering. My life might be even shorter out here, but at least it was my choice.

Though how many females of my clan would die because I'd been too cowardly to stay and tell them the truth?

I swallowed the guilt and hustled away from the stares of humans to a path beside the river. With nothing else to do, I kept walking, looking glumly over the water. The track forked, smooth concrete continuing straight and a wider path of small stones branching off into a semicircle. A fence surrounded areas of flowers all squashed together.

Why were humans so fascinated by shoving nature into unnaturally geometric shapes?

Opposite the corralled flora, there was a stone pillar with a crucifix on top. My fingertips stroked Father Benjamin's rosary around my neck. I rejoined the concrete path and crossed a large bridge that spanned the whole width of the river, questing deeper and deeper into strange territory.

A scent teased my nostrils the further north I went—like roasted nuts and caramel. I followed my nose to a building nestled on the edge of a tree-lined space beside a huge stone structure. Words above the entrance said 'Ness Coffee Shop' in swirly script, the front wall and door composed entirely of glass. A bell dinged when I entered. The air smelled heavenly and filled my belly with warmth. Humans sat at tables, talking and laughing, drinking from mugs. Others approached the counter and a metal machine that pinged when a drawer opened. A human waved a rectangle of plastic at a smaller machine next to it.

The bell behind me tinkled, a blast of cold air ruffling my tunic. Some of the humans were staring at my bare feet. I shuffled forward to get out of the way of the humans entering the coffee shop, and joined a line past a glass case of cakes. The female at the counter couldn't be much older than me.

She had kind eyes and a braided ponytail. I found myself in front of her with no idea what to do.

She smiled and said, "What would you like?"

A badge pinned to her shirt read 'Harmony.' I wanted a little harmony right then, but I doubted that was what she was asking. She gestured to the board on the wall over her shoulder. It was a massive version of the menu we had in the dining room, stuffed with foreign words and a mixture of English.

Milk! I knew what milk was. And tea. That was all we had in the clan—black or green or flavoured. Coffee must be some other kind of beverage.

"What do *you* like?" I squeaked.

Someone sighed loudly beside me. The female—Harmony—scowled before directing a gentle smile at me. She listed off a stream of mysterious items—Americano, latte, chai. My eyes got wider. Parts of me wanted to flee, but the place smelled lovely and the warmth was comforting. I also wanted the human to like me.

"Is this your first time?" she said. "You look quite young."

I nodded rapidly.

"In that case, try the flat white with coconut milk. It's divine." She punched buttons on the big machine. "That'll be £3.75."

What was a pound? And seventy-five what?

Panic swirled in my stomach. I flexed my toes against the floor.

If I ran, would the humans chase me?

Harmony looked at my tunic, leaning a little further over the counter. A frown knitted her brow. She glanced from my bare legs to my face, then swept her gaze over the space behind me.

"Do you need me to call someone?" she whispered.

What did that mean? Was she going to shout for somebody? No one here knew me.

I shook my head.

"Are you hurt?"

Another head shake.

"Are you safe?"

I opened my mouth. Closed it. "It feels… safe here," I murmured, matching her soft tone.

"Okay," she said, then said it again. "If you wait over there, the barista will prepare it for you. I hope you enjoy it."

Little worry lines crinkled her eyes and mouth. I slinked to the space at the end of the counter. A large chrome machine whirred and hissed. I whispered the new words, "Barista," and, "Latte." A male at a nearby table frowned at me. I flushed and dropped my gaze. I waited for yells of, "Demon!" and, "Alert the Diviners!" but the humans continued their conversations. Their beatha buzzed in the air.

The female at the noisy machine pushed a white cup of brown liquid towards me. "Here you go. You ordered the muffin, too, right?"

"Um…"

"She did." Harmony appeared and nudged the plate closer to me. "Coffee and a muffin."

I carefully carried the cup and plate to an empty table facing the counter. Curious stares tracked my bare feet. I tucked them under the chair and focused on my mug, willing my blush to fade.

The attention of humans was unsettling.

I sipped the coffee. A burst of sweet coconut and chocolatey nuttiness almost knocked me off my seat. Harmony grinned at me from behind the counter and I returned it, savouring another delicious mouthful.

Had I completed a human right of passage?

The coffee shop was amazing—comfortable and warm, relaxing music, friendly atmosphere.

I took a huge bite of my muffin.

And a purveyor of tasty goods! This place was a refuge.

Harmony kept watch over me, when she wasn't serving humans or glancing at a slim, rectangular device in her hand. She even put it to her ear once before hastily tucking it in her pocket. I stayed until stiffness forced me from the chair. A couple of hours ago, Harmony had refreshed my coffee and slid me a sandwich. She hurried to me at the tinkle of the bell above the door.

"Come back anytime," she said. "I mean it, okay? You're safe here."

How many coffees could I drink in this wonderful place before I weakened and died? I needed to find out what three pounds seventy-five was so I could give it to Harmony when she asked on my return.

I walked back down the river and across the bridge. The sky darkened towards evening. A drizzle started, plastering my hair to my head. The warmth and acceptance of the coffee shop drained to leave anxiety and weariness.

I had nowhere to go. Should I wander the roads, returning to the coffee shop each day for a small slice of heaven? I needed shelter. Somewhere to rest. A night of no sleep had left me woozy.

An indignant voice drifted from the path beside the river. Light from a pole bathed an older human female and what could be a youngling, though his jacket hood was pulled up against the rain. The elder gripped the strap of a bag while the youngling tugged on it. She thwacked him with her umbrella, scattering water droplets. The male yanked hard and the female dropped to her knees. The youngling sprinted right for me, the bag clutched to his chest.

"Oot ma fuckin' way," he growled.

My wings, still glamoured, flared protectively. The male dodged around, but the bone of my wing caught his throat. He scrabbled at the air, lurching backwards and thumping onto the path. The bag flew from his grip and bounced onto the wet grass. The elder struggled to her feet.

"Thief!" She waved her umbrella menacingly. "Police!"

The youngling leaped upright and darted past before she could give him a poke, disappearing down the path. I scooped her bag from the grass and held it out.

"Thank you, dear," she said. "You tackled that ruffian like a pro."

Her white hair had escaped from her bun and stuck to her cheeks. Her thick, maroon duffel coat was buttoned to her neck, the knees of her trousers wet. She rummaged in her bag and offered me a wad of colourful paper.

"For your trouble, dear."

I waved the papers away, though she tried to argue. Reluctantly, she put them back. Her pale eyes lingered on my feet.

"Where are the rest of your clothes?"

"This is all I have."

Her gaze rose to my face. "Have you run away from home?"

"Yes," I rasped, struggling to swallow an upwelling of emotion.

She nodded once. "Come with me."

She strode down the path, heading south, sprightly for an elder who'd taken a tumble. I hesitated, then followed. Where else was I going to go? She led me on the reverse of the route I'd walked last night. After ten minutes, we crossed Island Bank Road to a large house within a walled and wooded garden set back from the thoroughfare.

She held the red door open for me. "What's your name, dear?"

"Seraphina."

"My name is Margaret van Ize, but you can call me Maggie. Now, let's get you something sensible to wear, eh?"

9

A dark shape stands over me, silhouetted against soft lamp-light. I gasp and jerk into a sitting position, wings arched, my clingfilmed hand cradled to my chest. Daylight seeps around the border of the closed curtains, the fire burned to cold ash at my back.

"Princess," Jace says, "where the hell am I?"

His hands are empty—no sign of a knife. Maybe he lost them all during the battle with Avzameth.

A demon can hope.

I swallow my pulse. "You're in my house."

"Why?"

"I brought you here."

"You *carried* me here?" His gaze sweeps across my hunched form and circles the living room, pausing on the stained couch.

"Teleported," I say.

"Tele…" His attention zips to me. "Fucking hell."

He steps back. His heels hit the sofa and he sits hard on the cushion. I manage to breathe normally again, though his proximity prickles at the nape of my neck. He rubs his face, mussing his hair so that it flops over his forehead. He frowns at the dried blood flaking onto his fingertips. A cautious hand prods his temple, his ribs.

"What did you do?" he says, his bronze eyes accusatory.

It seems Diviners only know how to be hateful, not grateful.

I wilt under his stare. My fingers pick at the torn material of my navy tights.

"I healed you," I whisper.

"Who did you kill?"

My head snaps up. "I didn't kill anyone."

"Did you kill that demon?"

"I…" My mouth shuts. "He was going to kill *you*."

Jace watches me until I look away. Goosebumps flare on my arms.

"I think we need to talk some more, princess," he says.

An alarm peals from his pocket. He hooks his phone out and snorts at the screen.

"Great. Thirty-seven missed calls. Can I get a glass of water?"

I blink at him. "Um, okay."

Jace shrugs free of his jacket. I walk to the kitchen, trying very hard not to scuttle, especially when he follows. I turn on the lights, brighter than the lamp in the living room. The walls are a cheery yellow, the window ledge crowded with orchids in ceramic pots. I tug the blinds over the window and French doors, cutting off a view of the frosted garden.

"Distrustful, princess?"

I ignore Jace's smirk and open a cupboard, sending a string of beads on the handle swinging. Without thinking, I reach for a glass with my right hand. Pain crackles to my shoulder. I brace my uninjured palm on the counter at a wash of dizziness. Jace appears at my elbow, and I flinch.

"You're very jumpy," he says.

"There's a Diviner in my kitchen."

"You brought me here."

He reaches past me for a glass, and I slide a little further from the heat of him.

He's not as hot as a demon male, but it's still noticeable. Still disconcerting.

"I'm trying to decide if that was a really silly idea," I say.

He runs the tap and fills the glass. Three red and white capsules appear from one of his many pockets. He swallows them with a mouthful of water, but pauses before taking another drink, catching me staring. He frowns and steps closer. I slide along the bunker but come to a halt, trapped in the corner. One wing brushes my utensils holder, scattering wooden spoons, spatulas, and tongs across the worktop. Jace stops a few inches away. I'm very aware of the dried blood in my hair, the rest of me smeared in more blood, and ash.

Jace cocks his brow. "Your eyes are purple."

"Lilac and violet," I sniff.

He makes a, "Hmm," sound and sits at my round table, sipping his water. Candles float in a rainbow bowl in the centre. My muscles are starting to get wobbly from all the bursts of adrenaline whenever Jace gets close to me.

He nods at my clingfilm-covered hand. "Why didn't you heal yourself?"

"I used all my energy on you."

He watches me for a long time in silence. I squirm under the intensity.

"Do you want a coffee?" I say to break the quiet.

"Sit down, princess."

"My name is Seraphina."

"I'm not calling you that. Sit down."

I sidle to the chair opposite him and lower myself. It reminds me of our conversation in the coffee shop. My forced offering of baked goods.

"Then I'm going to start calling you *prince*," I mutter to the tabletop.

He smirks. "Yeah? Well, if you're the princess of darkness what am I the prince of?"

"Prince of being annoying or… prince of hating bran muffins."

"Bit wordy." His expression sobers. "Tell me how you're the only demon I've heard of that doesn't kill its food."

I shudder at the thought of Father Benjamin—his gentle eyes glazed, the horror of his final expression. The awful yet glorious rush of power.

"I didn't know it was possible at first. When I ran away, I was sure I was going to die."

"You ran away?" When I lift my gaze to his, he continues. "Was it because of that monster yesterday?"

"Avzameth."

Jace makes a face. "Right."

"He was part of it." I play with a loose edge of clingfilm. "Why are you the first Diviner I've seen in six years? The way we're taught, I expected you to be skulking in every shadow."

Jace snorts. "Your males prefer Aberdeen to Inverness. Better hunting ground. We were tracking your friend—Crystalmeth or whatever—after he slaughtered a pub full of people."

A shiver races down my spine. I avoid the glare Jace is no doubt directing at me. The pain of my injured hand is a suitable distraction.

"Get back to the energy thing," he says in his husky voice.

I smother another shiver. "It took a month for me to weaken.

I went to the coffee shop every day and they gave me a job. I tried…I tried not to take any energy, but I was starving. Dizzy. My heart was racing. I couldn't take a deep breath. I thought I was going to turn to ash right there on the pastries." I stare at my hand clenched on the table. "So I took a drink. A tiny sip of beatha before I stopped myself. The person didn't even blink. I did it again. Nothing. Then a different person, and another and another until I was full."

"Beatha—that's what you call it? Sucking the life from someone." Jace wrinkles his nose.

As if it's any different to him stuffing himself with a McDonald's. Cows die for that. Though the shape of Jace's body suggests he's not one for unhealthy eating.

I return to staring at my hand. I'm not sure what I'm looking for in his face anyway. It's not like he can understand.

"Humans give off beatha." I quirk my mouth. "Especially when they're caffeinated. I drink the excess."

"Am I giving stuff off now?"

I focus on his beatha. It's strong despite the rigours of his battle with Avzameth. Tingly. Calling for me to have a taste.

I nod at him.

"Use it," he says.

"What?"

"Heal your hand. But let me see." He pins me with a stern look. "If I feel even a wee bit woozy…"

"You'll what—brain me with a frying pan? You lost all your knives yesterday."

"Why would you think that?"

I barely stop myself from ducking to check under the table. "You have a knife?"

"I carry spares."

"You are a terrifying male, Jace."

His lips twitch. "Yes, I am."

I sigh. This is a bad idea. I unwrap the clingfilm from my hand. Jace winces at the sight of the swollen and weeping flesh. My stomach rolls a little.

"How did you manage to keep hold of my knife while it was doing that?" he says.

"Stubbornness."

He chuckles, then schools his expression, jerking his chin at me. His fingers grip the edge of the table. His gaze bounces between my face and my burned hand.

I sip his beatha.

Oh, wow, it's potent. Like drinking ice water and electricity, leaving a hint of cloves in my nose. It sizzles to my belly. I'm vaguely aware of sprawling in the seat, head tossed back.

That's not good. What if Jace thinks I'm sucking him dry?

My eyelids flutter. I herd the energy towards my wound. Scorched flesh heals and smooths together. My skin buzzes happily.

A hand wraps around mine. I gasp, my eyes snapping open. Jace leans across the table and traces his fingers along my newly healed palm. The tickling caress sends a different kind of tingle to my belly. I squirm in the chair.

"You all right, princess?" That intense bronze gaze meets mine, his fingers continuing to stroke. "You've never tasted a Diviner before? I hear the energy is like nothing else."

That last is said with a dollop of bitterness, but I'm finding it hard to concentrate. He's still touching me. Gently. Fuzzy moths flick their wings and flutter all around my stomach. My smile feels… goofy.

"You taste nice," I sigh.

"I taste *nice?!*" he says, affronted.

"And you smell like a fruit pie."

Shut up, Seraphina. Please shut up.

"A fruit…?" Jace lets go of my hand. "Are you drunk?"

I hum what may be agreement. My eyes seem to have closed again, my wings flopped to the floor.

Harmony made me try alcohol. It didn't taste as nice as Jace's beatha. The effect wasn't as delightful, either. It's tempting to take more. Just another sip.

No. Jace is not someone I can feed from without permission. He's too dangerous.

"Where's your breeding clan?" he says.

I crack open one lid. "I'm not that drunk, Jace."

"Worth a shot." He huffs a breath. "You weren't lying about the energy thing."

"I tend not to lie."

"You lie about what you are every day."

My wings flare. "Hiding so I don't scare people is not lying."

"Prickly on that subject, are you, princess?"

He is definitely the prince of being annoying. Are all Diviners like him? Frustrating and… maybe a little fascinating.

I run my fingers through my hair, forgetting. Brown flakes drift to the table. My hair is crusted to my scalp, the ends tangled. Jace isn't much better—blood clumped at his temple, dirt on his combats—though he's not also wearing the ash of Avzameth.

I can't believe I killed him.

"If you don't want coffee—or breakfast—I'm going to go clean up." I stand. The chair scrapes the floor, so it may have been a little abrupt. "Stay here."

Look at me, ordering a Diviner around. Harmony would

wonder where shy Seraphina has gone. I wonder myself. Jace seems to bring out a side of me I didn't know existed.

"Am I a prisoner?" he says, his brow cocked.

"Do I look like I could hold you here?"

"You're stronger than a human."

"I'm not a warrior, Jace. I work in a coffee shop."

"So, I can leave?"

"Um…" I glance at the clock. It's only 9am. "After dark."

"After *dark?*"

"I don't want you to see where I live. I'll teleport you somewhere quiet later."

"Yeah, once when I was out of it is enough. I'd rather not do it awake."

"Unconsciousness can be arranged," I say.

A sound rumbles in his chest. He chuckles, a slow grin lighting his face and sparking in his eyes. A sensation like dizziness washes to my toes.

"Princess?"

"What?"

"Stop staring at me."

My cheeks heat and I frown at my stockinged feet. Jace's phone vibrates. He sighs and slaps it on the table without answering.

I peek through my lashes. "Aren't you going to let them know you're okay?"

"I will." He crosses his arms and looks me up and down. "As soon as I know what the hell I'm going to say."

"You could tell them the truth."

"They won't believe me."

"They were looking for you—when you were… indisposed. They sounded angry. Complained about babysitting you.

What did they mean?"

Jace shifts in his chair and levels me a cool look. "I think I'll have that breakfast now. And decaf coffee."

10

Jace deigns to let me wash the blood from my hair before I feed him. Who knew Diviners were so accommodating?

I close the rest of the curtains in the house, shuttering us in perpetual twilight. Hopefully, he won't peek while I'm out of the kitchen, but it's not like I can stop him.

I lock myself in the bathroom. My birthday present from Harmony floats in a soup of brown water. I wrinkle my nose, and drain the bath. The bag may be salvageable if I throw it in the washing machine. The shower hisses on, chasing the rest of the diluted demon blood down the plughole. I brush my teeth while I wait for the water to heat. I bin my torn tights. My fingers hesitate on the zip of my skirt.

It feels funny getting naked knowing Jace is in my house. I've never been naked near a male. They weren't allowed in the female dorms or within twenty metres of them. Even during the mating ceremony, females kept their robes on. Jace is downstairs, sitting at my kitchen table. Unless he's crept up and has his ear pressed to the door.

My heart speeds. I strip off my clothes and step into the bath. Water patters on my wings and glides down my shoulders and chest, swirling grey at my feet. My hands slide from my ribs to the curve of my hips.

I've seen naked males. Demon males. Jace is nowhere near Avzameth's proportions, but he has broad shoulders, a slim waist, and long legs. Does he make his females scream and bleed when he ruts with them?

I scrub my hair, my body. I picture Jace in the room under my feet.

Can he hear the water? What is he thinking?

I'm naked and vulnerable. A little excited. I'm not sure what I'm anticipating. It must be Jace's beatha. The effects are still scrambling my reactions.

I turn off the shower and dress in violet leggings and a lilac top that's as light and floaty as gossamer. All my clothes are adapted for my wings with slits or gaps in the back, some held together by Velcro or hooks. The top and leggings bring out the colour of my eyes, especially with my black hair slicked back, my face pale. I stretch my dark wings in the fogged mirror and the breeze stirs the slits in my top, the material tickling my skin.

Like Jace's fingertips tracing across my palm. I really should tell him he's not supposed to touch me.

Though I'm no one's Chosen now.

He's sitting in the same position—palms flat on the table, the triangle of his fingers and thumbs framing his phone. He glances up at my entrance, his eyes flashing through his hair where it's fallen over his forehead. His gaze tracks from my head to my toes, lingering in between. My pulse ping-pongs between my chest and the base of my throat.

"You don't dress like a demon," he finally says.

"I have a tunic if that's what you prefer."

He smirks at my dry tone. "Is that what females wear? Your males seem to like armour and scraps of cloth. Not exactly shy, are they?"

I let my focus wander from his tight, black top to his combats. I may pause longer than is polite on the span of his shoulders and chest. The only skin he's showing is his face, neck, and slim hands.

"Are *you* shy, Jace?"

He quirks his brow. "Why did you save me, princess?"

I walk past him to busy myself at the coffee machine. Turning my back on him helps settle my heartbeat.

He's not exactly a relaxing male to be around, though I've yet to meet one who is. They all make me tense.

"I didn't want you to die," I say. "I don't want anyone to die."

"I tried to kill you."

I send him a look over my shoulder, stretching my wing out of the way. His gaze flits to my lower back where the material of my top shifts.

"Maybe I wanted to prove you wrong," I say.

"You're proving something." His eyes meet mine, and goosebumps wash down my arms. "I'm not sure what yet."

I concentrate on grinding beans, filling the kitchen with the wonderful aroma of coffee. It never gets boring. Smells like home—my human home—and safety.

Will it stay safe? If I can sway Jace, can I get him to convince the other Diviners to leave me alone? He's here in my kitchen, listening to me, intense but not threatening. Though the Diviners aren't alone in hunting me; Avzameth said he'd heard a rumour about a female in Inverness. Are other demons searching for me? Will they punish me for killing him, especially when it saved a mortal enemy?

One advantage of living in the clan—life was a lot simpler.

"Are you sure you want decaf?" I say to Jace. "Nothing

stronger?"

"Caffeine is bad for me," comes the terse reply.

I wait, but nothing more is forthcoming.

"Do you want to clean up before breakfast? Bathroom is at the top of the stairs."

"That demon—Avzameth." Jace pauses. "He called you his Chosen. What is that?"

With the coffee machine churning, I heat oat milk in a pan and add porridge. Jace waits with the patience of a lynx. I slide him his decaf in a mug that says 'I'm a happy go lucky ray of fucking sunshine.'

Another present from Harmony.

Jace snorts and takes a sip. "Nice cup. But now who's being shy?"

"I'm trying to decide how much to tell you."

"Tell me all of it."

I pour my fully caffeinated coffee into my favourite cup— two dragons, one lilac and one blue, touching hands, their tails curled around each other's. I push a steaming bowl of porridge topped with sliced banana, strawberries, and blueberries to Jace and reclaim my seat opposite him.

I flick a small, ceramic jug. "I don't have cow's milk, only oat or coconut."

"You're a vegetarian demon?"

"I believe the term is vegan."

Jace laughs. "You are unreal, princess. Now, stop avoiding my question."

Why is he allowed to avoid mine? This is my house. Surely I have host privileges. Oh, and let's not forget I saved his life.

"A female's duty is to bear young," I say. "A male can select as many females as he wishes, but a female mates with only one unless he dies in battle. Chosen means Avzameth chose me as his mate."

Jace chokes on his coffee. "But he was…"

"I know."

"And you're…"

"I *know*."

"Christ, even I would probably—" He waves his spoon. "Never mind. You ran away before you had to…?"

"Mate with him? Yes." I chew a mouthful of porridge—sweet and oaty. Sadness wells at the memories of Deirdre. "I saw him with another female. She was taller than me. She couldn't help screaming. And there was so much blood. I never want to experience that."

"You've never had sex?"

I shudder. "Sex is for male pleasure only."

"I think you're hanging around with the wrong people, princess."

I tilt my head. "Do *your* mates bleed and scream?"

Jace coughs and thumps his chest. His eyes start to water. I jump up and thwack him between the shoulder blades until he spits out a blueberry.

"You're quite candid, for a virgin," he wheezes.

"We learn of mating from an early age. It is our duty. We can watch the ceremonies until we're old enough to participate."

"Yeah, I think human and demon sex is a little different."

We eat in silence for a few minutes. Jace seems unable to meet my gaze, which is unusual for him and a respite for me.

"So no bleeding and screaming?" I say.

"Fucking hell, princess." He rolls his eyes to the ceiling. Wipes his mouth. Shifts in his seat. "Bleeding—no. Screaming? Well… not all screaming is because of pain."

"Screaming can be good?"

His gaze lifts. His cheeks are flushed, his eyes dark and hot.

"Screaming can be *very* good," he says, his voice a husky purr.

My wings flare. Whoops. I gulp and duck my head, hiding my own blush.

How did we get on this topic? And what, exactly, does a male do to get good screaming?

I bite my lip to avoid asking the question. We finish our breakfast and I top up our coffee, ushering Jace into the living room.

How to keep a Diviner entertained for a few hours? At least the days are short.

"Looks like I ruined your couch," he says, eyeing the soot- and blood-smeared upholstery.

"Don't worry about it."

I flip the stained cushions while he disappears upstairs to use the bathroom. Five minutes and he returns, face free of dirt, wet strands of hair sticking to his cheekbones. He's blotted some of the mud from his clothes, too. Not that I have anything for him to wear if he were covered in more than mud. My stuff is way too small and I don't think he'd be happy with one of Maggie's cardigans.

"I really have to stay here until dark?" he says.

"Am I not being a good host?"

"It's… You're… Never mind."

He sits on the couch. I curl up on a chair beside the fireplace. Sitting next to him would be too intimate.

"How do you afford this place on a barista's salary?"

His gaze roams from the fireplace to the TV on the wall to my teal phone and the purple couch set. The curtains are still closed, the lamp bathing one side of his face and shadowing the rest.

"It was my great-aunt's," I say.

He gives me his signature raised eyebrow of polite inquiry.

"Not my real great-aunt, obviously." I smile at the thought of Maggie. "I stopped a young—a youth—from stealing her bag on my second night in the city. She invited me to stay with her. She taught me so much. I think she was lonely. We lived together for two years before she died. Everything is paid for from a trust she set up. I buried her in the back garden."

Jace splutters coffee on the clean side of my sofa cushion. "Is that legal?"

"It was her wish. She has a gravestone in Tomnahurich Cemetery. I visit sometimes. That's partly why I was there last night. She looked like this sweet elder, but she had people—'contacts' she called them. They made her documents so I could get a job and she could be buried where she wanted. That's her." I nod to a picture on the fireplace mantel showing a woman with grey hair in a bun, standing proud in a black uniform, cap tucked under her arm. Shiny metal decorates her shoulders and hat.

She tried to get a picture taken of us together, but my glamour always messed with the photos, leaving blurry parts and reflected light. Same with all the images Harmony captures on her mobile.

Maggie also taught me new words. Words like human trafficking, black market adoption, and illegal immigrant.

"Did she know what you are?"

"No. You're the only human who knows what I am." I stare at my hands in my lap. "Hiding gets exhausting sometimes."

"Tell me about it," he mutters.

My raised eyebrow receives no response. Maybe I should stop telling him things until he shares more.

"But if you hadn't run away from your breeding clan, you would've had to mate Avzameth?" Jace continues. "Couldn't you say no?"

"It's an honour. I would've been the first to refuse. It would've been… shameful." I finish my coffee to give myself a minute. "It wasn't the only reason I ran away."

Talking to Jace is freeing. Harmony is my best friend, but I haven't told her the whole truth. I tried talking to Father Benjamin's god, but he never talked back. Jace now knows more about me than anyone. He might as well know everything. I tell him about horrific demon births and Father Benjamin. The lies used to control us.

"Does that make me a bad person?" I whisper to the empty coffee cup clasped in my hand.

"What, running away?"

I shake my head at Jace. "I didn't warn them—tell them they might die during birth. And now I know we can survive without killing humans for their beatha, shouldn't I share that?"

"Do you want to go back?"

"I don't even know where it is, except the name of a nearby village. *Don't* ask me what it is," I say when he opens his mouth. He smirks at me instead. "What if they don't believe me? What if they already know about the beatha and don't care? What if they… hurt me?"

Father Benjamin mentioned the name of a village, one he was disappointed not to visit on his journey to the clan. I assume it's local.

Jace scrubs his face. "This is a lot to process, princess."

"Okay. But do I still look monstrous to you?"
He raises his gaze. My heart does a little wobble.
"I don't fucking know," he says.
"Well, that's better than 'yes,' I suppose."

11

The day passes quickly in the company of a Diviner. He doesn't even try to stab me.

I make us sandwiches for lunch with pickle and vegan ham. Jace wrinkles his nose, but seems pleasantly surprised when he finally takes a bite. I give him the tour of the rest of the house—three bedrooms, a study, and a dining room. He slides me a look at the rosary hanging from my bedpost.

It feels taboo, showing him where I sleep.

We end up back in the living room, Jace sitting on the floor, leaning against the sofa, and me cross-legged on the rug in front of the fire, the flames warming my wings. Flickering light dances across his face. He rests his forearm on his bent knee. The silver bracelet flashes on his wrist.

"What is that for?" I say, nodding at it.

He glances at the curtains. "It's getting dark. I should go."

"You avoid my questions yet ask me a million? Is that a you thing or a Diviner thing?"

All I know is he lives somewhere called Tomatin, which is south of Inverness, but he travels a lot, staying in rented accommodation or Diviner-owned properties. He hates Aberdeen and drives a bright-blue Honda Civic, which is still parked near the cemetery somewhere. Oh, and he likes something called a PlayStation.

"I'm not avoiding anything, princess," he says. "And you also ask a million questions."

"So answer this one."

"Are all demons this pushy?"

"Are all Diviners this evasive?" I frown at him. "*You're* also pushy."

He heaves a sigh and snaps out his arm, yanking his sleeve higher to reveal a smooth, muscled forearm and the shiny bracelet. I hesitate, but he doesn't move, watching me intently. I crawl half the distance, then pause.

"I'm not going to bite, princess," he drawls.

My heart rate climbs the nearer I get to him. I crouch at his feet, my body tense, wings curled. He just stares, his eyes unsettling. His pulse jumps in the hollow of his throat, so maybe he gets nervous at proximity, too, though you can't tell by looking at the rest of him.

The bracelet has a chain and a rectangular plaque, the weight pulling it to the underside of his wrist. I hook it around with one finger and rest it on top, careful not to touch him. There's an inscription. Lots of unfamiliar terms: epilepsy, phenobarbital, zonisamide. The words 'Allergic to diazepam,' are inscribed in smaller script at the bottom.

I sit on my heels. "What does it mean?"

"I get seizures. These are the medications I'm on. And diazepam makes me quit breathing." Jace tugs his sleeve down and tucks his arm to his chest. "Happy?"

"Is this why your friends mentioned babysitting?"

"Can't have a Diviner who's a danger to others in battle wandering around alone. And a danger to himself. Half of them want me to retire, but it's not like you can just *stop* being a Diviner. The other half won't touch me—like epilepsy is fucking contagious. They all think I'm going to have a fit during—" He huffs, scowling at my curtains as if he can bore right through to the world beyond. "And this is why I don't talk about it."

The area of wrongness in his brain—this must be it. The epilepsy. And the pills this morning—his medication.

"Have you always had it?" I whisper, unable to tame my curiosity despite the angry set of his jaw, the hunched shoulders.

I stay very still in case movement makes him lash out. He slices a glare at me anyway.

"Oh, this is where it gets hilarious. A demon did this—picked me up in the middle of battle, flew higher, and dropped me." Scathing bronze eyes scan my back. "He had wings like yours, though they were bigger, and grey. Horns like a sheep. I hope the fucker is dead."

"When did… it happen?" My breath hitches as his furious gaze meets mine.

I should probably stop asking questions, but I can't help it. Maybe I *am* pushy.

"A couple of years ago. Guess I'm lucky I didn't get complete brain damage." He barks a laugh. "A wee bit of brain damage is enough to ruin my life."

He leaps to his feet. I scuttle away, but he ignores me and paces across the carpet, hugging his elbows.

"And so if I don't sleep enough, eat enough, have too much alcohol or caffeine, get stressed out, I have a seizure. You know what people don't like? A Diviner who drops during a fight and starts fucking twitching. I've only done it once, but they never let me forget."

He was impressive in his fight with Avzameth. Should I tell him that?

He keeps pacing.

"Jace." I repeat his name until he looks at me. "Sit down and take a deep breath," I say in a calm voice.

To my surprise, he actually does it.

Harmony wouldn't recognise me if she saw me now, and not just because of the wings and inhuman eye colour. *I* don't recognise me.

"Do you want a cup of tea? Or I could let you… out. It's dark enough."

Jace shoves his fingers in his hair. "Christ, that means teleporting, right? Let's get it over with."

"You're not going to argue?"

He gives me the side eye. "I'm tired. Just tell me what to do."

I motion him up. He watches me warily and shrugs on his jacket. I stand in front of him, close enough to have to tip my chin to meet his gaze.

"I need to touch you," I say.

The nerves are back. This was so much easier when he was unconscious.

He nods, and I step into him. I hug him, pinning his arms to his side, my head on his chest. He's solid and warm. Soft in places. His heart thuds under my ear, the rhythm steady. Comforting. His ribs expand against my arms when he breathes. His clove and blackberry scent fills my nose.

"Are you sniffing me, princess?"

"Ssh, I'm concentrating."

"Sure you are."

I tuck my wings in tight. "Don't move."

I close my eyes. Remember the feel of him, the weight of

him. The length of his body. I embrace the vertigo and picture our location—red brick cathedral, scattered trees, the coffee shop nestled on the edge of the car park. The carpet changes to crunchy grass under my bare feet. Jace staggers, and I release him. He leans his rump against the cathedral wall and plants his hands on his knees.

"Yeah, let's not do that again." He sucks air in and out in a puff of white. "Fucking hell."

The side of the cathedral and the high wall opposite hide us from view, nothing around us but trees and grass and the soft gloom of evening. A car rumbles on a nearby street. I glamour my wings and eyes. Jace squints at me.

"I hate when you do that."

"My glamour?"

"It wavers. If I stare too long, it makes me dizzy."

What do you know—he's a font of truths now. It only took one to get him started.

I hug my bare arms, my skin goosepimpled worse than under a Diviner's glare. My toes nip from the chill of the ground.

"Are you cold?" Jace says. "Demons don't get cold."

I shiver to prove him wrong. "I think it's the energy thing— less potent in small doses. I get cold. I'm probably not as sturdy or as strong as a demon with… different eating habits."

Jace straightens and pats himself down. "Well, princess, this has been fun."

"Wait." The word slips out.

He cocks a brow.

"I have to tell you something."

The brow hikes higher. I drill my big toe into the solid ground.

"When I was healing your skull fracture—"

"I had a *skull fracture?!*"

"—I could sense there was something in your brain. Something wrong. I think… I think I could heal it, but—"

He stalks close and I squeak, scrabbling until my back hits the wall. He traps me between his arms, his palms on the brick, his face inches away.

"What the hell are you saying?"

"It wouldn't be easy," I wheeze. "It would take a lot of beatha. Maybe all of it. Or most of a Diviner's."

"Could you use mine?"

I manage a tiny shake. "It would deplete my energy and yours. Your body would struggle to produce its own after such a healing. I don't know if it's possible to transfer someone's beatha to yours as a replacement. We'd need a third party."

Jace groans and shoves away from the wall. "Why would you tell me this, princess? I'm not letting you kill someone and I can't exactly ask another Diviner. 'Hey, Ellie, would you mind if this demon sucked on your beatha to fix my epilepsy?' Not gonna happen."

"I'm sorry," I mumble.

"Next time, princess, keep it to yourself."

He turns to leave, hands stuck deep in his pockets.

"Wait," I blurt.

He bows his head. "Christ, what else have you got to torture me with?"

"Will you tell the other Diviners to leave me alone?"

Seconds tick by. Jace keeps his back to me. Anxiety and guilt churn in my stomach.

"I'll try," he finally says, and walks away.

12

I mulishly go back to normal—working at the coffee shop, nights out with Harmony—but stay cautious and teleport as much as I can. Thoughts of Jace flit through my brain during the quiet moments.

No wonder he hates demons, and not just for their human-killing tendencies. His condition seems to isolate him from the rest of the Diviners. How hard is it for him? Do the others think he's less of a warrior? I think he's a great warrior. He held his own against Avzameth for longer than any demon male, going by Teacher's stories of Avzameth's battles during mate selection. He didn't even hesitate to challenge him, or retreat like Felecior.

I scrub coffee stains from the counter top, distracted by images of furious eyes, the curve of a shoulder, slim hips. His husky voice. The way he purred when he talked about good screaming…

I shiver, and scrub harder.

It's just gone 5pm. Harmony had a dentist appointment, so she left early and no one else is working today. The lights behind the counter are the only ones on, the rest of the coffee shop in shadow. Darkness presses against the glass at the front.

The bell above the door tinkles. My head snaps up, my heart in my throat.

I definitely locked that ten minutes ago.

"Your turn to run, princess," Jace says.

He's wearing his usual black combats and grey jacket. I have black tights, but the rest of me is yellow, orange, and red.

Harmony said I look smoking hot, which I assume is better than a rainbow.

Before the door can shut after Jace, four other Diviners pile inside—three females and a male, two the couple from the bridge.

Five Diviners. *Five.*

I start to hyperventilate.

The bulky female—the Ellie Jace mentioned?—shoves past him. "I swear to god, Jace, if you don't cut this crap, I'm getting you banned from hunts."

"It's not my fault you're slow, Ellie," he drawls.

The four Diviners advance towards me and range themselves on the other side of the counter, a knife in every hand. Jace stays at the back, his hands empty. He shrugs when my wide eyes alight on him.

What does that mean—sorry, I tried or sorry, I never tried at all? I didn't expect a declaration of friendship, but the sting of betrayal fogs my eyes.

"Come with us or die," Ellie says. "Your choice, demon."

I can't seem to stop looking at Jace. "Come with you?"

He gives a tiny shake of his head. Ellie frowns over her shoulder, following the line of my attention.

"Are you dense?" she says to me. "We have things we want to talk about. Questions that need answering."

I didn't mind talking to Jace. It was kind of nice. But I

doubt the talking these Diviners want to do will be anything as pleasant. And I'd rather not trap myself with a whole bunch of them.

One semi-threatening Diviner is enough.

Ellie sighs. She flicks her arm. I yelp and duck. A knife thunks into the wall. Shouts spill over the counter top. I scrabble on hands and feet into the kitchen, then bolt left for the corridor. Footsteps slap behind me. My shoulder blades itch, expecting the burn of a knife between them. I barge into the toilet and slam the door, twisting the lock so hard, I hurt my fingers. Something thuds on the other side—fists or a body. The wood rattles in the frame. I back away and sit hard on cold porcelain.

"Open the goddamn door, demon," Ellie snarls. "You're only making it worse for yourself. There's nowhere to go."

Nowhere to go? Jace must not have told them about my teleportation or the little ride he went on. Did he tell them anything?

"Oliver, kick the door down," Ellie says.

Is that the stocky male? Why doesn't Ellie do it herself? She's sturdy.

I ignore their voices and stare at the sign on the door showing the fire escape routes. The words blur. Blood rushes in my ears. I bounce onto the couch in my living room, the cushions clean after multiple applications of water, vinegar, and washing-up liquid.

If the other Diviners don't know about my teleportation, they do now. The toilet has no windows and they're currently bashing down the only exit. I picture their faces when they see I'm not there. Jace's smirk. Or maybe he's disappointed.

Who knows what he's thinking.

How will I explain the busted door and knife slice to Harmony? It seems the Diviners are going to keep harassing me at work. I suppose 'live and let live' was too much to ask for since my brethren slaughter when they get peckish.

I don't want to leave. I *won't*. This is my city, too. I can't spend my life running from what scares me.

I prowl my house for the rest of the evening, unable to sit still or concentrate. The TV holds my attention for a minute, my book—five at the most. I stay awake all night, but no one comes.

Jace doesn't know where I live. He didn't peek when I was out of the room. Or he did and couldn't recognise his surroundings from the view through my windows.

A foolish part of me hopes he knows and just chose not to tell.

13

Revolution on Church Street is Harmony's favourite nightclub. You can have dinner in their restaurant upstairs, a cocktail or two in one of the bar areas, then dance on the ground level. I like the leather armchairs in a basement room that has shelves of books, the roof a curve of exposed brickwork.

I hope Diviners have no time for a social life.

Harmony grabs my hand. "That's enough rest. Let's boogie."

I groan, but allow myself to be levered out of the comfortable seat. The chiffon layer of my sleeveless, royal-blue dress swirls above my knees. My loose hair falls straight over the lace bodice, a satin belt cinched at my waist in a bow. My wings are bound to my back as tight as I can make them, which hurts, but it's effective for the inevitable jostling from humans on the dance floor.

No one's run screaming yet.

I struggle to keep up with Harmony on the stairs. She insists on me wearing heels, and this pair are tall, black, and strappy. I have to keep sipping beatha to stop my poor foot bones from aching. My shoe concession avoided the make up Harmony always wants to smear on my face.

We reach the ground level. Everything is red velvet and mahogany, with more exposed brick. The bass thuds in my

93

chest. Harmony clears us a space in the corner, my back to the wall.

She knows what I like.

We jig under the twirling, coloured lights and the sparkle of a disco ball. I smile at Harmony. She's so free with her body, dancing as if she's the only one in the room. Happiness personified. It's why I keep coming with her even though all the humans and the gyrating make me uncomfortable. Males watch from the sidelines with greedy attention.

"It's happening tonight," Harmony yells without opening her eyes, her arms held above her as she sways to the beat. Her dress is burnt orange and complements her skin. Her dark hair is also loose, flowing in tight waves around her face and bare shoulders.

"What is?" I say.

She cracks open one eye and it twinkles in the lights. "Your first kiss."

I scrunch up my face. She laughs and shimmies as the music shifts to something fast and electric.

"Plenty of eligible bachelors here if you won't pursue the hottie from the coffee shop. You know, he hasn't been around in a while. I bet he was devastated." She nods towards the edge of the dance floor. "What about that guy? He's definitely checking you out."

I follow her gaze. The male is shorter than Jace. Blocky. His shoulders are the same width as his hips. A trimmed beard covers his jaw and disappears into his dark hair. He's not as disciplined as Jace, his muscles soft beneath his shirt and dress trousers. No pockets.

Where does he keep all his knives?

I shake my head at Harmony.

She tugs on my hair. "My fussy little Phin. What about him?"

A male in a tight, white t-shirt flexes beyond a cluster of humans. His muscles stretch the material, his veins popping under his skin. Sweat shines on his wide forehead, more veins at his temples.

I shake my head harder.

Harmony grins. "Just kidding. He'd squish you."

I make the mistake of catching the eye of the blocky male. He smiles and starts pushing towards us.

"Um, I'm going to the bathroom," I squeak at Harmony.

"Okay, sweetie. Hurry back. I love this song!"

I leave her twirling, and duck behind the press of bodies.

One advantage of being short and slight—slipping unseen through a crowd to escape the notice of questing males.

The human mate selection process is less regimented. More chaotic. Nightclubs and pubs seem to be their amphitheatre of choice. The only similarity is males approach females, though I have witnessed the brazenness of some females. They can also say no. The method appears to be successful, given the number of couples pressed into dark corners, hands everywhere, mouths locked.

The sight of them always causes a little flutter in my belly before I drag my gaze away.

The bathroom at the back is unusually quiet. Of people. The music thrums through the walls and vibrates in the soles of my feet. My shoes clack on the tile floor. I splash water on my flushed cheeks and check my glamour. A single frosted-glass window, wedged open a tiny inch, lets a lick of cold air into the room. Goosebumps race across my shoulders under the lace.

Rough hands grab my upper arms. I gasp, and a foot sweeps my legs. A weight slams me to the floor on my front. I toss my head to clear the hair falling over my face. Two females manacle my wrists and pin my palms flat, crushing flesh against bone. A body straddles my rump, my skirt rucked up past my waist.

They can see my underwear!

I struggle and buck, but it only gets worse.

"Thought you were clever, didn't you?" Ellie sneers from my back. "Well, you made the wrong choice, demon."

I strain my neck to see over my shoulder. Behind the hunched shape of Ellie on top of me, an unfamiliar Diviner leans against the door, arms crossed, her expression bored. *Bored!* Ellie waves her knife at my nose, the blade swirling black. I flinch, but have nowhere to go.

Not this time.

"Wait. Please." I think of Father Benjamin. Avzameth ignored his pleas. Why would a Diviner be any different? "I'll come with you. I won't run."

"Too late for that, little she-bitch," Ellie says. "Can't have you flitting off whenever you want. Teleportation—are you fucking serious? We should have killed you weeks ago. How many people have you murdered since then?"

"I haven't killed anyone," I say, tired of repeating myself.

The Diviners laugh.

"Sure, a humanitarian demon. That makes sense."

I bite my lip instead of asking where Jace is. If I tell them I spoke to him, will he get in trouble? Or is he here, guarding the other side of the door?

"Why won't you believe me?" I say, my voice thick with frustration.

Ellie slices me a cruel smile. "Let's give you something to really whine about."

Bruising fingers clamp my wings and the shock blasts my glamour away. The Diviners pinning my wrists curl their lips in mutual expressions of disgust. There's a rip, and my wings flop free from their bindings. Relief zips to the ends of my fragile bones. Then Ellie grabs my humerus and pulls my wing straight.

I hiss at the discomfort. "I just want to be left alone."

"So did your victims," Ellie snarls.

Her knife slices delicate tissue. I shriek and jerk my hips, trying to toss her off. The blade scorches and shreds my wing. My screams bounce off the tiled walls, swallowed by the music outside. Ellie moves on to the next, turning both my wings to ribbons. I beg and howl and thrash, my flesh on fire. Dizziness and nausea clash in my belly. The back of my dress is sodden. Garnet blood stipples the floor. Ellie bunches my hair in her fist and yanks my head back.

"I will spit in your ash, demon," she says.

Desperate, I blast my power into my hands even though they're pressed to the floor.

I can heal a broken arm or two. I can't heal death.

The hold on my wrists slips as my body sails upwards. Ellie and I collide with the ceiling. Gravity slams us to the floor. Ellie's weight pummels the air from my lungs and worsens the agony of my wings. She bounces off and tangles with one of the Diviners knocked on their rump from the force of my escape. I scramble for the window, woozy from pain, half-deafened by my own screams, gasping for breath, but my ribs are locked. I leap for the glass. Another blast from my palm shatters it outward. Shards left in the frame gouge my arms and legs and tear my dress. I crumple into an alleyway, scraping the skin from my hands and knees. The fresh zap of pain weakens my limbs, everything hazy.

I want to curl up and sob. Or faint. Fainting would be good. But I have to get away.

I lurch upright and limp for the end of the alleyway and the lights of the main road. I'm missing a shoe. Covered in blood. Unglamoured. The only thought in my brain is *run.* Run, run, run.

I crash into a warm, solid wall. Spicy and sweet. A dark silhouette blocks the light from the road only a few paces away.

"We have to stop meeting like this, princess," Jace says.

I try to speak, but I'm too dizzy. I wheel backwards out of his arms. A streetlight blinds me. I can barely stay on my feet.

"What the fuck?" Jace growls.

"Please," I manage. "Don't kill me. Don't let them kill me."

My knees buckle. Instead of the sharp kiss of concrete, arms scoop me against a firm chest and the rapid thud of a heart beneath muscle and bone. Blackness furs the edge of my vision.

Jace says something, his husky voice rumbling in my ear. The meaning is lost, but right at the end, right before I lose consciousness, I swear he calls me Seraphina.

14

Gentle hands shake me awake.

Maggie? She never comes in my room, always respectful of my privacy and my aversion to being touched, though that's a lie. I'd love for her to touch me, hug me. Wait. Maggie's been gone four years. Did I stay the night at Harmony's? We were at the club—Revolution. Did I drink too much? That must be why everything hurts.

"Come on, princess. You need to heal yourself."

I gasp at the voice and nearly inhale a pillow, my nose pressed into it. I jerk my head to the side, sprawled on my front on a spongy mattress, the covers tucked around my waist. The movement stirs my wings. Sharp agony sizzles in all directions. Every part of me stings and burns. A whimper slips out.

"Easy," Jace says. "Try to keep still."

I finally focus on him leaning over the bed, his hair mussed. Lamplight and shadows soften his face. There's a smear of blood on his cheek. My blood—brown now, instead of garnet. More blood streaks his blue, long-sleeved top.

He matches my dress.

The clock on the bedside table reads thirty minutes after midnight. An hour has passed since I was attacked in the bathroom. But how am I staring at *my* clock and *my* bedside cabinet?

My accusatory gaze flies to Jace. "You peeked."

The words are croaky, my voice rough from screaming. Another thing that burns.

It takes him a second to figure out what I'm talking about. Then he smirks.

"Of course I peeked. I'm a Diviner. We're not very trusting."

"What about the—"

"I didn't tell them where you live."

I ease out a breath. Warmth blooms in my stomach and throat.

He didn't betray me. He couldn't stop them from harassing me at the coffee shop or stalking me to the club, but he helped where he could. He rescued me.

I remember the feel of his arms. The worry in his voice.

"You called me Seraphina," I say slowly.

"You were pretty out of it, princess. You must have imagined it."

I manage a half-smile. "I know what I heard."

"Suit yourself." He flaps his hand at my recumbent position. "Use energy from me. You can't stay like this."

I carefully tilt my head, moving as little of my body as possible. Bandages wrap my hands and arms, covering the scrapes from concrete and glass. My legs are bundled under the duvet, but the slight restriction at knee and calf says I'm bandaged there, too. Butterfly sutures hold my shredded wings together, each one neat and even.

The thought of him treating my wounds, caring for me while I was unconscious, sends a confusing tingle right to my core. My throat tightens, as if I might cry.

"You…" I lick my lips and try again. "You bandaged me up."

"Just returning the favour. At least this time, it wasn't me who ruined your upholstery."

I laugh, then wince.

Jace waves at himself. "Heal."

"I'll need more beatha. I don't know how much…"

"Do you want me to beg, princess?"

His smirk makes me breathless, though I'm sure it's just the pain of my injuries. Not him or the way he's looking at me.

"Okay," I whisper.

"Okay—you want me to beg?"

I grin. "Not necessary. I'll take it."

He flops on the bed without his usual grace, jostling me on the mattress. I suck in a breath.

"Sorry," he mutters.

He's turned towards me, one leg bent and tucked under him, the other foot planted on the floor. I scan his face, puzzled, but he's controlled his expression and gives me nothing. His pulse jumps in the hollow between his collarbones.

I shut my eyes and drink him down. He tastes *so good*. I writhe on the bed, too distracted by the electric thrill of his beatha to feel self-conscious. My flesh knits together. My heart beats faster. Heat blazes from my skin. I love being full of Jace, surrounded by his energy. It's exhilarating, wild, dangerously addictive—

Thump.

My eyes snap open. Jace is on the floor, his eyes half-lidded, his breathing shallow. Erratic. The bracelet flashes silver on his bared wrist.

"Jace!" I yelp. "I took too much!"

He was right. What a horrible, soul-sucking monster I am.

I drop to my knees beside him. My skin buzzes, wonderfully healed, but I feel sick rather than refreshed. My hands flutter over him.

What have I done? Have I pushed him into a seizure? I looked the term up after he left since it was as unfamiliar to me as epilepsy and phenobarbital.

He lies completely still. No convulsions or rigidity. His chest hitches with each inhalation. I place my palm on his centre, and his heart thuds much too slowly. I coax his beatha out of me, as if I'm trying to heal a wound, but it dissipates with nowhere specific to go. It does the same even when I put both hands on him and visualise him waking up, breathing normally, glaring at me for being careless.

"Jace, I don't know what to do."

I shake him. His heads lolls. A tear rolls down my cheek.

I have to do something. I can't let him die. I can't.

I like him.

There must be a way to give beatha back. That's what healing is—guiding energy into a body to seal flesh and bone and sinew. When I take it, it's like drinking. Breathing, almost. Maybe I have to breathe it back into Jace.

I plant a hand beside his head. My fingers skim his jaw—so smooth—turning his face towards me. His eyes remain closed, his lips parted. His shallow exhalations barely caress my skin.

"Sorry, Jace," I mumble. "You're not going to like this."

I suck a gulp of air, lean down, and place my mouth on his. Breathing out, I release beatha into him. It sinks deep, and I taste salt. The relief sways to my knees and leaves my head light. I inhale through my nose without breaking contact and direct more energy as far as it'll go. His breathing deepens. His lips are so soft on mine.

This is probably not what Harmony meant by my first kiss happening tonight. I'm sure kissing unconscious boys doesn't count. Plus, we're not moving our lips like the couples in Revolution.

Harmony! I left her at the club! She must be panicking. I haven't heard the phone, but I bet she's called twenty times. She may be a second away from barging through the door since she has a key, though me abandoning her without an explanation is not normal behaviour. She's probably in the nearest police station, demanding a search party, dogs, helicopters.

I'll call her as soon as Jace opens his eyes and tells me to never touch him again.

Muscles tense underneath me. My heart skips. I start to pull away, ready to babble an explanation. In a burst of movement, Jace rolls me onto my back. His weight pins me.

Uh-oh. *Now* he's going to kill me.

There's a flash of bronze, then his mouth is on mine, his hands buried in my hair.

He's not killing me. He's *kissing* me.

His lips are no longer soft. They're hard, insistent. *Demanding*. Reeling, I try to copy the glide of his mouth.

Oh holy wow… *This* is kissing? This I could get used to.

Harmony will be ecstatic.

Harmony! I have to call her. I have to—

Jace licks the seam of my lips, and my thoughts scatter. My mouth pops open in surprise, and he slides his tongue inside. It curls against mine, stroking, licking. Electricity—like the taste of his beatha, the taste of him—zips to my fingers and toes. I can't describe what's going on in my belly. It's hollow and churning, as if I'm nervous or excited or scared. Maybe all three. My pulse is swollen in the base of my throat. I can't breathe, but it's a good suffocation. Like good screaming.

My heart rate triples.

Jace is heavy between my legs, his long body sprawled on top of me. My dress is rucked up to my waist. My fingers are clenched in his shirt. His hands control my head, the kiss merciless. Inescapable. Not that I want to escape. Heat flares from his mouth on mine to expand in my chest, and lower, to where he rests between my legs.

Is this the throbbing feeling Harmony was talking about? Lust? It's fantastic.

Darn it—Harmony. I keep forgetting...

Jace moves, rubbing his body against me and deepening the kiss. A groan slips from me to Jace, and he purrs low in his throat. His hips rock, gliding the muscled ridges of his stomach against the silk of my panties.

Has he seen them? No male has ever seen my underwear. They also match my dress.

Jace shifts, arching slightly. His sex—his *erection*—is as solid as the rest of him. Each thrust tingles to my belly and flares heat to my toes. My pulse has migrated to where he's pressed against me and it throbs with each grind of his hips, pressure building in my gut.

"Jace," I moan. "Something's happening. I don't know... I don't—"

"Just go with it, princess."

His voice is strained, his eyes dazed. There's a flush on his perfect cheekbones.

My hips rise of their own accord, meeting Jace, matching his rhythm. He groans this time and the noise isn't frightening. It makes me want to go faster, harder, to feel the slide of his skin against mine, the smooth heat of his body. There's an emptiness inside me.

The pressure swells. The friction… I hold my breath. My stomach muscles tighten. Shiver. The sensation peaks and spills through me, stealing control until I find myself squirming beneath Jace, mewling into his mouth. A wave of heat and euphoria leaves me limp and blinking. Jace shudders and stops moving, resting his forehead on mine, breathing hard.

He whispers, "Fuck, that was hot."

His eyes are dizzying this close, though that may be the effect of what he did to me.

"What was… What is… What…?"

His lips curve. "That was an orgasm, princess."

He props himself on his elbows, his hair falling across his forehead. The movement presses him firmly between my legs, his erection still so solid. My eyelids flutter. A little aftershock of the… orgasm… zings through my body.

"Di-did you…?"

"It takes more for a guy. Unless he's a virgin." Jace cocks a brow. "I don't think you're ready for that, though, do you?"

Demon males chase their pleasure whether their Chosen are ready or not. Jace seems ready. His combats and a scrap of silk are all that separate us. Unless he's wearing underpants. What are they like on a human male?

I gulp. Jace growls and kisses me, catapulting my settling heart against my ribs. He uses his whole body—lips, tongue, teeth, his fingers kneading my scalp, his hips torturing my sensitised core. Begging noises flutter up my throat.

How do human females resist this? How are they not kissing all the time? Rubbing up against each other?

Jace shoves himself up, panting again, his cheeks flushed. "Shit—fuck—stop it," he says.

He seems to be talking to himself since I'm too stunned to do anything. He climbs off me and holds out a hand. When I just blink at it, he gives me a smile that rolls through my stomach and weakens my knees, despite the fact I'm lying down.

"You need to take your dress off, princess," he says.

"I-I do?"

His smile widens, but it's no less dazzling. "It's ripped and covered in blood."

He crouches, grips my hands, and hoists me to my feet, catching me when I wobble. I sag into his chest, savouring the strength of his arms around me, the smell of him, the thud of his heart.

Hugs are wonderful.

Orgasms are wonderful.

He leads me to the bathroom. My pulse surges with each step, hammering by the time my bare feet hit the tiles and Jace twists the water on above the bath. He glances over his shoulder. He chuckles at whatever he sees on my face.

"I'm not getting in the shower with you, princess," he says. "Unless you ask nicely."

My cheeks flush. "Um…"

He smirks and walks past while I'm gathering my wits. Steam puffs towards the ceiling.

"Wait," I say as he's shutting the door.

"Changed your mind already?"

He really must stop grinning at me. I can't think.

"Harmony. I need to call her."

"Your best friend from the coffee shop? The one who'd kick me out?" At my nod, he says, "Better make it a quick shower then, princess," and shuts the door.

15

I shower quickly, confused, restless, my heart racing. It's like I'm ill—my skin flushed, an ache in the pit of my stomach. And lower. Thoughts of Jace—his mouth on mine, what he can do with his body when we're fully clothed—make it worse.

My first kiss *and* my first orgasm. I have to tell Harmony.

The dress and the bandages join my ripped tights in the bin, still there after our battle with Avzameth. I wrap a towel around myself and crack open the door. No sign of Jace. I tip-toe to my bedroom, my pulse rushing in my ears and drowning other sounds. The sheets and pillowcases have been stripped off the bed, leaving a surprisingly unstained mattress. I dry my hair and dress in a hurry, half-fearing Jace will walk in and half-wanting him to. My top is a clingy material changing from crimson to deep maroon at the hems and floppy cuffs, the back open with criss-cross straps. The black skirt hits above my knees, the tights a silky pair of hold-ups that Harmony got me.

She said they'd make me feel like a goddess. And guys like them.

Maybe I should have put my pyjamas on.

I sit on the edge of the bed until my breathing steadies, then slink downstairs. A gurgle of water comes from the kitchen. I head for my teal phone in the living room, guilty for waiting ages to call Harmony.

She must be so worried.

"I've put a load of stuff in the washing machine," Jace says, and I jump. "At least I know the bloodstains will come out of my jacket."

"You've had blood on your jacket before?"

He props his shoulder on the door frame. "Course I have, princess."

Definitely a terrifying male.

I dial Harmony's number. Goosebumps prickle up my arms. Jace stands behind me, close enough to feel the heat from his body. My wings brush his chest. I swallow hard and grip the handset, trying to concentrate. It rings once. Jace traces a fingertip along my bare shoulder blade, and I suck in a breath. He draws a swirling loop across my spine to my other shoulder. My wings go a bit floppy. Two rings. The tiny, tickling caress starts a throb deep in my belly. My muscles quiver. I lean into his touch.

"Seraphina?" Harmony gasps, her voice choked.

"Harmony, I'm so sorry…" I trail off. What can I say? I didn't think to come up with an excuse for why I disappeared. Is it time to tell her the truth about Diviners and demons? Jace can collaborate my story.

He continues to stroke my back, that one fingertip eliciting a surge of sensation.

"Sweetie, I was worried sick. Are you okay? Are the police there?"

"The police? Did you call them? I didn't mean to—"

"Oh, god, Phin, please tell me he's not still with you."

"Who—Jace?"

How does she know about Jace?

The questing fingertip pauses at the nape of my neck. I bite my lip on a whimper of protest, though, even when he's not touching, his proximity is enough to cause a pleasant tingle.

Harmony sobs into the phone. "Get away from him, Seraphina. He's mentally unstable."

"Jace?" I say stupidly.

"The police found me when I was searching for you in a panic. Undercover detectives. They've been tracking him. His name is Jace Mulholland—the guy from the coffee shop. He was stalking you. He's dangerous, Phin. He kidnaps women from public spaces, takes them to their own homes, and abuses them. *Tortures* them." Her breath wobbles. "Run out of the house right now."

Jace is very still at my back. Not touching.

"Was one of the police a stocky woman with short hair?" I say.

"I don't know. I can't remember. That's not important." Her voice drops to an angry hiss. "They should have been there by now. They told me to go home, wait for an update."

"Harmony," I say slowly, "did you give them my address?"

"Of course I did! Do you think I want you raped and murdered?"

"Fuck," Jace whispers.

"The only reason I didn't call was because they told me not to—it could tip him off," she continues, oblivious to my horrified silence. "It *killed* me, Phin. I've been sitting here imagining all the awful things he might be doing to you."

My hand is numb and cold on the handset. Jace wraps his fingers around mine.

"Hang up, princess. We have to go."

"Is that him?" Harmony screeches. "Listen to me, you sick fuck—if you harm one hair on her head, I will shove your balls so far up your arse, you'll be tasting nuts til Christmas."

"She sounds lovely," Jace drawls.

"Harmony." I have to shout her name twice before she'll stop describing Jace's bloody emasculation. "They lied to you. They're not the police. Jace isn't dangerous. Well, okay, he is… but not to me. Uh, anymore."

"Hang *up*, princess."

"We're coming round," I say in a rush, wrestling with Jace as he pries the phone from my ear. "I have so much to tell you. Don't trust—"

A huge crash echoes from my hallway. I yelp and drop the phone. The handset clunks on wood, then swings on its coiled cord between the table legs. Feet thunder on the floor. Diviners pile into my living room.

"Fuck," Jace says.

16

"I knew your brain was scrambled, Jace, but this is getting ridiculous."

"Shut up, Ellie," Jace growls.

Ellie sneers and stands in a formidable line with the other three females who attacked me in the bathroom. My wings tuck tight to my back in shivering remembrance. Jace keeps his body between me and the only door, blocked by the Diviners. He retreats us towards the curtained window. Harmony's tinny voice yells my name in increasing tones of urgency from the slowly swinging handset.

"I also knew you were having trouble getting lucky, but a goddamn demon? That's fucking desperate."

"Shut *up*, Ellie."

"Yes, Eloise, that's enough," a new voice says from the doorway.

A woman strides into the living room, as stocky as Ellie—or Eloise. There's a resemblance in the harsh features, though her hair is a pale-streaked red rather than ashy blonde. Her blue jeans match her t-shirt, which says 'Can I pet your dog?' Three males enter behind her, one the male from the bridge, all large and muscled. Jace seems to be the slim one of the group.

There are eight Diviners—sorry, *nine*—in my living room. I'm dead.

"I'm glad to see you're not too far gone to confront your own people with a Dyrnwyn in hand," the new woman says. "There may be hope for you yet."

"Hello, Rose," Jace says stiffly while I'm puzzling at the unfamiliar word.

Is that what they call their weapons? What a mouthful.

Every person is holding a knife except for Rose and Jace. And me, obviously. One case of second-degree burns was enough.

Rose calmly walks closer, scoops up my handset, and places it gently in the cradle, cutting Harmony off mid-expletive. The phone rings immediately. I'm the only one who flinches. Rose yanks the cable from the wall.

"Now, Jace," she says in a soothing tone, "I can understand why your white knight complex may have gotten confused— I grant you, she looks delicate and lovely—but she's still a demon. People have died for her to be standing here, as if butter wouldn't melt."

What is she talking about? What's a white knight? And why isn't the butter melting?

"She hasn't killed anyone," Jace says, and my heart melts, never mind the butter. "I tried to tell you about her. You wouldn't listen."

"I *did* listen. I listened with growing concern. Then I called your doctor to ask them to prescribe you a different medication as you were clearly hallucinating."

Ellie snorts, but Rose cuts her a glance and she schools her face back to its typical sneer.

"Your behaviour is erratic—unexplained absences, disappearing during hunts, consorting," Rose continues. "I'm in two minds what to do with you. I've been as lenient as I can after your accident."

"It was hardly an accident."

"True. It was a loss for us all. You were a great fighter, Jace. It's been tough watching you struggle."

"I'm still a—" He sighs and pinches his nose. "Can we get back to the issue here? You need to leave Seraphina alone."

I *knew* he could say my name. It sends a little thrill through me.

Until the rest of the Diviners scoff, much like Jace when he first learned it.

"That thing is no angel," Ellie sneers.

"Thank you, Eloise," Rose says drily. "We all have eyes. But the demon is not the issue. She will be dealt with. I just don't know what I'm going to do with *you*, Jace. This is very disappointing."

I choose to ignore whatever horrific scenario being 'dealt with' implies. Is Harmony on her way over? I imagine she sprinted out of her house as soon as my phone was cut off. She could be here in half an hour. Will they harm her?

"She doesn't hurt anyone," Jace says. "She works in a coffee shop for Christ's sake."

"Where I'm sure she stalks potential victims." Rose waves her hand. "Enough. This is not the time or place to argue. You're both coming with us."

Jace retreats another step, bumping into me and blocking my view of the looming Diviners. He slides me a look over his shoulder, all cheekbones and slitted eyes.

"What are you waiting for?" he hisses. "Get out of here, princess."

"I'm not leaving you," I hiss back.

Ellie gags. "Did he just call it 'princess'?"

"I thought you would be difficult, Jace," Rose says with a mixture of exasperation and pride, "so I came prepared. Oliver, if you would? Try not to hurt him."

"Wait!" I yelp. "Don't hurt—"

There's a pop. Jace grunts and staggers. I grab his arm, spinning him to face me. A puff of red feathers on the end of a metal cylinder sticks from his shoulder. The stocky male holds some kind of long-barrelled gun.

"That better not be fucking diazepam," Jace growls.

He yanks the object free and tosses it on the carpet. Red blood beads on a wicked needle. He turns his back to the Diviners, shielding me with his body. His hands grip my shoulders, his bronze eyes blazing into mine.

"Teleport, Seraphina. I'll be fine."

I shake my head.

"Stubborn, princess," he says. "Why did you have to be stubborn?"

He blinks and drops to his knees, his hands falling to my waist. He struggles to focus on me. His thumbs flex on my hips.

"Jace! Are you—*ow!*"

One of the poofy red things spears into my shoulder with a sharp stab of pain.

"I'm assuming you're more susceptible to sedation than your males," Rose says matter-of-factly, "though I'm happy to move to blunt force if that's not the case."

I throw my metal needle next to Jace's. A tiny, garnet circle marks my top, almost lost in the crimson material.

"Please don't hurt him," I say. Or try to. My tongue seems

thicker than normal.

"Shit," Jace sighs, and flops on his face.

Rose raises her gaze from his body. "Worry about yourself, demon. You've done enough."

Everything goes a bit wobbly. I blink, and I'm on the floor next to Jace. His dark lashes brush his cheekbones, his expression relaxed as if he's sleeping. A lock of hair has fallen across his forehead. His lips are parted, his soft breaths tickling across the carpet.

He's beautiful.

I reach for him, but someone grabs my hand before I can touch his face.

Then the world goes dark.

17

My dreams smell of damp stone and cloves. Voices echo. My body is unable to move, like when you lie in the bath as the water drains—that heavy, sinking feeling. My tongue sticks to the roof of my mouth. A lick of nausea swirls in my belly and tickles the back of my throat.

"Why is it taking so long to wake up?"

"She got the same dose as Jace, Eloise. There's a disparity in body size."

"This better not be permanent," Jace growls.

His voice is further away than the other two. It loosens something in my chest to hear it. I try to bend my arms and legs. Pain pinches at wrist and ankle. My wings refuse to flap, the sensation similar to when I bind them to go clubbing with Harmony.

Harmony. I haven't exactly eased her worries. What is she doing now? Contacting the real police?

"I think it's coming round," Ellie says.

"*She* is not an *it*," Jace barks.

"And *you* are a fucking *simp*, so excuse me if I don't listen to a word you say."

"That's enough, Eloise."

I blink. Blink some more. The world is a strange variation

of grey. Grey arching stone, grey metal bars, a light that hurts my eyes. I squint at two shadowy figures.

"Princess?"

His worried voice comes from elsewhere. His familiar frame is not one of those standing in front of me. They're both stout and female.

"Jace… I'm"—I glance at my hands cuffed to the arms of a metal chair—"okay?"

"Now would be the next-best time to leave," he says.

He seems to be in a room to the left of me, though I can't see him beyond the stone. Is he in a cell neighbouring mine? Everything is rock—the walls, the floor, the ceiling, even the corridor that stretches from left to right on the other side of the bars. The air is cold. I crane my neck, and gasp. Behind me is the stocky male—Oliver. Behind him, there's a single bed with a bare mattress, and a metal toilet and sink.

What is this place? Diviner jail?

"If you attempt to teleport away, demon, we will hurt him," Rose says, still calm and matter-of-fact.

Jace snorts. "No, they won't."

"His comfort is in your hands," Rose says firmly. "So what'll it be?"

I tilt my chin. "I'm not leaving him."

"Aww, the little she-bitch has the hots for you, Jace. You must have mesmerised her with your cock."

"Ellie," Jace sighs, "shut the fuck up."

Ellie sneers and crosses her arms. Muscles bulge beneath her leather jacket. She scans me from top to toe and her lip curls higher. Next to her, Rose is only in her t-shirt, despite the chill.

"How do we break your spell on him, demon?" she says.

"My spell?"

She clicks her tongue, as if I'm being difficult, and pulls a mobile phone from the pocket of her jeans. Her finger taps the screen. Ringing echoes in the small space.

"Good evening, Rose—or I suppose it's morning now. How can I help?" The voice sounds like an older female. Soft and authoritative. Sheets rustle.

"Sorry to disturb you so late, Marianne." Rose holds the phone in front of her face. "We're having a problem with one of our members and his sudden attraction to a demon. Your recent experience could be useful."

Marianne huffs a breath that crackles through the speaker. "As if I could forget. Let me see the creature."

Rose taps the screen, still holding the device vertical. The camera lenses wink at me.

"Oh, it's a female. That's interesting."

Rose steps closer. "Is she a succubus?"

"I don't believe so. Her eyes, though the colour is unnatural, aren't solid. Does she have fangs?"

"No fangs."

"Not a succubus then. Like their male counterpart, they feed on blood and sex. They're even rarer than an incubus."

Rose plants a hand on her wide hip. "Even though she's not a succubus, will her spell on him be broken if we kill her?"

"Don't you fucking dare, Rose," Jace snaps.

"Is that him?"

Rose nods. "It's Jace."

"Ah. That's a shame. He's not had an easy couple of years, has he? I can understand the fascination. She's as human-looking and pretty as a succubus. I wonder if all the females of her clan are like this."

Everyone stares at me. I shift in the seat, the metal back bruising my spine. My wings have been pulled between the slats and fastened with more metal.

"Just let her go," Jace says. "She's not violent or aggressive. She's nothing like the males."

"Out of interest, what happened with that incubus—the second one?" Rose says, ignoring him.

Marianne heaves a sigh. "As much as it pains me to say it, he's still alive. He drew Reiley away from her calling, but she made me promise not to hunt him as long as he behaved himself. I believe they're holidaying in the Caribbean if her Twitter page is anything to go by."

"You can do the same with Seraphina. I'll promise anything you want."

Jace sounds strained. I wish I could see him.

"Reiley wasn't trained from a young age, was she?" Rose says.

"No, she slipped through the cracks. It's probably why she was so easily tempted."

"*Would you fucking listen to me!*" Jace yells.

I jump. No one else does.

"Thanks for your input, Marianne."

"You're welcome. Let me know if you need the assistance of my Diviners."

"I will. I'm hopeful we'll have the location of her breeding clan by noon."

Why noon? What happens at noon?

"Rose..." Jace snarls.

Rose jabs her phone and tucks it in her pocket. Ellie smirks at me.

It's not like Jace's smirk. That causes a pleasant little throb down low. Wicked in a good way. Ellie's smirk is not good wicked. Ellie's smirk promises more wing shredding.

"Why don't we try civilised first and avoid agitating Jace any further?" Rose smiles almost gently. "Tell me where your breeding clan is."

I open my mouth. Close it. "I don't… I don't know where it is. I ran away at night. Flew for two hours. It's south. Somewhere."

"You must know more than that. Give me details, demon."

"Um… it's in a wooded valley. With a loch."

"Brilliant," Ellie scoffs. "That narrows it down to a billion places."

"She was cloistered, Rose," Jace says, struggling for patience. "She never left except when she ran. She doesn't know the details."

That's not strictly true. I know *a* detail—a nearby village. Jace knows I know. But he's not telling.

He's such an honourable male.

"What will you do to them?" I whisper.

"What we always do," Rose says.

I shake my head. "They're not all bad. The younglings don't feed on human deaths. The adults… they do terrible things, but let me find them. Let me tell them we can survive on small sips of beatha—of life energy. If they stop killing, will you leave us alone? And let Jace go. It's not his fault. You're right—I spelled him. It's an ability of mine like the, um, like the teleporting."

"You're a terrible liar, for a demon," Rose says.

I make a face. "Okay, so I don't know what a spell is, but the rest is true."

"Nice try, princess," Jace mumbles. He sounds tired.

"Stop calling it 'princess,'" Ellie spits. "You're giving me the boak."

"If it makes you feel any better, it stands for princess of darkness," I say drily.

Jace chuckles, and Ellie wrinkles her nose.

Rose scrubs her hands through her hair. "Is that the last you have to say on the matter, demon? Nothing more specific?"

I shake my head again. She nods, her gaze rising over my shoulder. Oliver appears at my elbow, crouching beside my chair. I flinch, and the cuffs at my wrists rattle on metal. He tugs on my sleeve to expose my forearm.

"What are you doing, Rose?" Jace says.

I watch, fascinated, as Oliver produces a black pencil. The tip dents my skin. He draws a graceful line.

"*Rose?*"

"I'm okay, Jace," I say quickly. "He's just drawing something on my arm. It doesn't hurt."

"Rose, don't do this. *Please.* She's told you everything."

I frown at Oliver. His tongue pokes between his teeth as he concentrates. Unease curls in my stomach.

Jace is too upset for this to be nothing. It may not hurt now, but I'm afraid it will in a minute.

"Don't worry, Jace." Ellie's eyes sparkle, riveted on me. "We're not going to damage your precious, bat-winged doll. Not physically. Unless she's stronger than she looks."

Cruelty twists her broad face. She really enjoyed shredding my wings.

"Rose, Ellie—please. She's a demon, but she's fucking innocent." Metal clangs, as if Jace is shaking the door cut into the arch of bars. "Just fucking talk to her."

"Keep yourself calm, Jace," Rose says in an annoyingly

patient tone. "It's not good for your health to get riled up."

Flesh slams on metal. *"Fuck!"*

I jerk my arm. Oliver's precise loop smears on my skin. He tuts as if I'm a misbehaving youngling. Fond yet firm. It's scarier than if he'd shouted at me.

"Hold her still," he says.

"Oliver, you keep doodling on her and I will shove that pencil in your fucking eye."

Jace and Harmony have a lot in common. They get all gruff and sweary when they're protecting me. That's normal from Harmony. But I never expected it from Jace. It makes my throat tight. My eyes blur. I sniff.

"Christ, is it going to cry again? We haven't even started."

Ellie leans over the crouching Oliver and uses two hands to pin my arm, her weight crushing me against the seat. Oliver cleans the smudge of black with a moist wipe. Goosebumps chase across my skin. The pencil tickles.

"You're hurting my arm," I whisper to Ellie.

She bares her teeth. "Shut up."

Oliver sketches something that looks like the game *Tic-Tac-Toe*, with an elaborate flourish in the centre. He pauses and lifts his head, meeting my gaze. His eyes are as blue as Jace's shirt, minus the blood I got all over it. Still watching me, he adds a tiny asterisk off to the side.

My arm itches. The itch becomes a burn, then a sharp, scraping sensation like claws on flesh. I gasp, though I was anticipating it.

"Goddammit, Rose," Jace moans.

I picture him to distract myself from the pain—forehead pressed to the bars of his cage, his eyes squeezed shut, knuckles white, hair tousled. His long-sleeved top stretched across his shoulders and clinging to the curve of his spine. I'm used to seeing naked male torsos, but a clothed Jace is more intriguing. The suggestion of muscles, the planes of his body—

I swallow a groan, yanked from pleasing images to a sizzle of agony.

I have to stay quiet. I don't want to worry Jace.

The pain worsens. My wide eyes dart to my arm, convinced my flesh has been flayed from the bone. Oliver and Ellie drink in my reactions from inches away. I shriek, unable to help myself. Ellie smirks and steps back, the loss of her crushing weight no reprieve from the agony in my arm. Oliver winces, but stays put. Jace yells.

I can't understand the words. I try to tell Oliver to stop, but all I can do is scream.

My wrists fight against the cuffs, the bite of the metal nothing compared to the hot, slicing pain. My back bows, and my legs kick against more restraints. My breath locks in my chest, but my screams echo in my ears. My vision goes white.

I can't stand it. I *can't*. It's a hundred Diviner knives tearing my skin, my wings, my soul. They peel the skull from my brain and sink their talons in. My heart is all I can hear and taste.

I think I'm dying.

18

A harsh ammonia smell, like the cow pens if they've not been cleaned for a while, catapults me from soothing blackness to nightmare grey. I gasp, and an acrid taste floods my mouth. My whole body aches, as if each individual bone has been stretched too far in its socket.

"Where is your breeding clan?" Rose says.

Her shape wavers through the tears in my eyes.

"Don't..." I croak. "Don't do that again. Please."

"She's had enough, Rose. That's enough." Jace's normally soft and husky voice is ragged, but then, he's been screaming too.

"*Where*, demon?"

I shake my head. "I don't know."

She nods at Oliver. A black smudge on my skin shows where he's rubbed out the asterisk. He gives me a sympathetic smile and touches pencil to flesh.

"Please, *please* don't," I whisper.

Rose nods again at his inquiring glance. "Don't let her faint this time."

"Rose, *for fuck's sake*." Jace's voice breaks.

Oliver paints another star on my skin. I whimper at the burn, my mind shrivelling at the horror to come. I thrash

125

silently in the chair, but the screams claw their way out. I bow almost backwards, my head flopped upside-down over the seat rest, my hair trailing to the stone.

The chair must be bolted to the floor, I muse vaguely, as it hasn't tipped over.

My breaths are fire. There's a rushing, ringing in my ears. My vision fogs. The awful pain fades at the touch of a moist wipe on my forearm. My chin hits my chest, my panting loud in the echoing cell. I shiver in my bonds, unable to stop, though it hurts my wrists. A bead of garnet rolls down the back of my hand and drips from my middle finger.

Cold. I'm so cold.

"Would you look at that—a demon can turn blue."

"Ellie, you bitch, you fucking bitch," Jace mutters over and over again.

"The sooner you answer my question, the sooner this ends," Rose says reasonably. "And the quicker Jace calms down. This isn't good for his condition."

"I don't know," I wheeze. "I don't *know*."

Oliver readies his pencil. I thrash away from him, but no matter how hard I wriggle, he can draw his stupid asterisk.

I whimper, "No. No-no-no."

He ignores me. The awful process starts again. And again. I lose track of how many times. I pretty much lose track of everything except Jace. He shouts until his voice goes hoarse. He rattles the bars. He pleads with Rose.

The cuffs saw my wrists, the back of one hand sticky with blood, the other more protected by my untouched sleeve. My ankles throb. My body throbs. A headache drums on the back of my forehead, my eyes pulsing black and red with each beat. I'm slumped in the chair, too exhausted to sit upright, though the position hurts my neck and lets the blood gather in the front of my skull to pound-pound-pound along with my heart.

An alarm trills. Ellie grunts and fishes a mobile out of her pocket from where she's sitting on the floor, leaning on the bars. She waves it at me.

"Time for Jace to take his pills."

Is it morning already? The light in the cave hasn't changed. It feels like I've been here for ten years. I doubt I'll last til noon.

"If you're a good little demon and tell us what we want to know, maybe I'll give them to him." From her other pocket, she pulls a brown bottle. The capsules rattle inside.

Rose frowns at her, still standing in front of me although hours must have passed. Oliver seems to be napping at my side, but then erasing and re-drawing a star doesn't take much concentration. I sip a little of his energy to ease my pain and chase the tiredness back.

His doesn't have the electric zing of Jace's beatha, only an uncomfortable prickling, like swallowing a cactus.

The shudders continue despite the energy boost. It doesn't heal mental injuries.

They tortured me. They're *torturing* me. And they call us monsters.

"Hear that, Jace?" Ellie calls. "No tablets for you unless your little she-bitch gives us what we want."

"Eloise, that's not—"

"G-give them to… him." My teeth chatter. "I'll tell you—the one—tiny thing—I know."

Ellie whoops and levers herself to her feet. Rose frowns harder, turning towards the corridor.

"How long has Jace been quiet?"

Ellie cocks an ear. "You having a fit there, good buddy?"

The only sound is the soft slap of flesh on stone.

I buck against the restraints. My newly healed wrist reopens.

"Let me help him," I pant. "Let me go. I have to help him."

I try to rock from side to side, but the chair doesn't budge. Tears spill down my cheeks and stick my hair to my skin.

"Please, *please.* I need to help him."

The door to the cage screeches open and Ellie disappears to the left down the corridor. Another metallic scrape. My shaking rattles my cuffs, drowning anything else from the cell next door.

"Tell me then, demon," Rose says.

It takes me three attempts to say, "What?" since I'm hiccupping.

"This tiny thing you kept from us. Tell me."

"I want to see Jace. Please let me see him."

Ellie reappears, minus her leather jacket. She goes to shut the door.

"What are you *doing?*" I shriek, tasting blood.

Rose rubs her forehead. "Is he still fitting?"

"Yes, but I gave him my jacket as a pillow."

"For god's sake, Eloise, stay with him." She jerks her chin at Oliver. "Go. See if you can get him on the bed."

Ellie and Oliver scuttle into the next cell. I struggle to watch through my tears, jerking against the cuffs despite the sharp flares of pain. My chest squeezes tight, my breathing coming in gasps.

"Tell me now, Seraphina," Rose says gently. "They'll keep him safe."

"You… *you* did this! Let me see him. *Let me see him.*"

"No, *you* did this. You could have told us right at the start and avoided all this unpleasantness. Jace wouldn't have shouted himself into a seizure."

I cry harder. "But you're going to slaughter them all."

"My patience is wearing thin, demon."

"Inverie," I gasp. "There's a nearby village called Inverie. That's all I know. Now can I see him?"

"Mum, it's not stopping," Ellie says from next door.

A worried crease pleats Rose's brow. "How long?"

"About five minutes."

"Get the midazolam from the cabinet. Squirt it into the side of his mouth."

"Jace!" I scream. "Jace! Let me go—I can help him."

What have I done? This is my fault. Jace told me he gets seizures if he's stressed out or doesn't sleep enough. Why didn't I tell them sooner? Maybe they won't even find my clan. It could be miles from the village.

I was worried about my family when I should have been worried about Jace. Like he was for me.

I scream his name until I can't breathe. Rose seems to be standing at the end of a rapidly darkening tunnel. Her mouth moves, but I can't hear the words. All I hear is my heart, thrashing on my ribs. All I can picture is Jace, rigid on the floor, every minute of his prolonged seizure risking more damage to his brain.

What if it's too much for me to heal without a death? Two deaths? What then? *What then?* What—

A metal cylinder appears in my thigh, piercing my stocking just below the hem of my skirt. The red puff on the end quivers. *I* quiver. Raising my head to look at Rose takes several lifetimes.

She lowers the long-barrelled gun. "I think we all need to calm down."

"If he dies, kill me," I croak.

Rose's perplexed expression is the last thing I see before I sail off into oblivion.

19

My eyelids flutter open to the arch of a stone ceiling. My head flops on the seat back, my spine and neck burning. I straighten, and my bones creak. Everything throbs again, and not in a good way.

I really miss the good throbbing.

My heart thumps. "Jace!"

Silence from the next cell. I whip my head around, but I'm alone in my cage of rock—no gently smiling Oliver to abuse me, no sneering Ellie or Rose.

"Jace?" I say, louder.

Nothing.

Oh, no. Oh, please, don't let him be dead. He can't be dead. This is my fault. All my fault. Selfish, stubborn, soul-sucking monster.

A sob bubbles in my chest, but I clamp my teeth on it. I suck in a breath, another, and focus on the corridor outside my cell. I almost baulk at the nausea and dizziness. The evil symbol is stark on my arm, smudged all around where Oliver happily wiped and reapplied his torture star. Anxiety sharpens its claws in my belly and my reality starts to slip. I shake my head, and concentrate.

Jace. I have to get to Jace.

My exhale sighs past my lips. Colours blur. I wobble in the corridor and brace a hand on the damp wall. Metal clanks as the band that pinioned my wings falls to the floor behind the chair in my empty cell. I tug my sleeve over the foul thing on my arm. My stockinged feet whisper on cold stone, the material at my ankles somehow intact despite my thrashing against the cuffs. The corridor ends beyond my cage. To the left, it extends past two barred archways and bends out of sight. Two bulbs connected by a black, looping cable emit a harsh white light.

I hustle to the neighbouring cell. Jace lies on his back on the single bed, his face turned to the wall. Unmoving. I flash inside, avoiding the chair bolted to the floor in the centre.

"Jace?"

My hands flutter over him. His chest rises and falls, though it's shallow. My legs threaten to buckle. Shaking him gets no response. I clamber on top of him, the bed so narrow I struggle to plant a knee on either side of his hips. My skirt rucks up, flashing the lacy elastic of my stockings. It gets worse when I cup his face and place my lips on his, but I don't care.

If I have to flash my underpants to a whole roomful of Diviners, I will, as long as Jace wakes up and calls me princess.

The area of wrongness in his brain seems to be the same size. I breathe my beatha into him, but it sputters and dissipates.

"No," I whisper.

I try again, but I barely have enough to function, never mind heal Jace and teleport us out of here. He has none to spare after his seizure. All I've done is trap myself in his cage with him.

Though there's no place I'd rather be.

I curl into the solid warmth of him and cry on his chest. For some reason, the steady thud of his heart makes me cry harder, my fists gripping his shirt, my wings curved protectively around us.

"I'm sorry," I say, my voice thick. "I'm so sorry."

I make a rather large wet patch on his top. I sniff and wipe my nose on my sleeve. My eyes struggle to stay open. Exhaustion weighs my body.

What will the Diviners say when they discover me in Jace's cell, sprawled on top of him?

"Get the fuck away from him, you little bitch," Ellie snarls.

That seems about right.

She glares at me through the bars. A knife appears in her hand, the blade swirling black. My wings shiver in protest.

"I was trying to help—"

She yanks the barred door open and storms inside, her eyes narrowed. The knife rises for a brutal slash.

"Wait," I yelp.

"I'm going to cut your wings off this time," she says.

I throw out a hand. She sneers at it, as if she thinks I'm trying to ward her off. Instead, I do something I've never done before.

I drink her down as fast as I can.

Her beatha fizzes on my tongue and bubbles through my veins, tasting faintly of cherries. She slams to a halt. Sways. Her eyes roll back and she falls on her face, her knife skittering across the rock. A sigh of pleasure escapes me, and I force myself to stop. I shudder, sickened by the desire to keep drinking until there's nothing left. Until she's an empty vessel on the floor. As it is, only a trace of her beatha remains. She pulls in a breath, and I jam my fist in my mouth to stopper a sob. My stomach churns.

I took *far* too much. I should give some back, though I loathe the thought of touching her. But what if she doesn't recover? I don't want her to die. I still don't want anyone to die.

My body feels too small to contain the energy buzzing under my skin. Everything is intense—colours, sounds, scents. Jace smells good enough to eat. My muscles sizzle with coiled power. It crackles at my fingertips.

I should definitely give some back.

"Eloise?" Rose's voice echoes down the corridor.

Footsteps slap on stone.

I hug Jace tight, shut my eyes, and teleport without a hint of vertigo.

20

We bounce onto the bed in Harmony's spare room. Weak sunlight through the window suggests it's early afternoon, though it feels like it should be the dead of night. My knees settle on a duvet cover the same colour as Jace's eyes, my legs straddling his hips. He lies still and breathes, oblivious to our new location.

The bed takes up most of the space, the sheets a rich brown. A painting hangs on the wall above, showing an African plain with giraffes, lions, and scattered, wide-topped trees. Gazelles dip their noses in a pool. A crocodile ripples through the water towards them.

"Harmony?"

My voice elicits no stampede or shout of surprise. She was supposed to be working today, but I doubt she's in the coffee shop. She's probably haranguing the officers in the police station about an unstable Jace Mulholland, or camped at my house, praying for my return.

She doesn't have an immobile phone like mine, so I can't call and tell her I'm okay. Maybe I should get a mobile. She's been right about everything so far.

Even Jace.

His long-sleeved t-shirt has ruffled up past the waistband

of his combats, exposing a line of smooth skin. It takes a silly amount of willpower not to slip my hands under the material. I lean over him, my rump in the air, and tent my fingers on either side of his temples. I touch my forehead to his, inhaling his exhales. My eyes slip shut.

I ease Ellie's fizzy beatha deep into his brain, deeper to the area of wrongness, the haze tickling my senses. My brow furrows, all my attention directed inside Jace. Energy pours from me. My back cramps. My knees protest despite the soft mattress. The haze flares. I send more beatha, willing natural pathways to reform, chasing the scar tissue away. My heart speeds with the effort. Dizziness rolls through my skull. I grit my teeth, and shove every last scrap of Diviner energy into Jace.

With a groan, I slump onto my side, cuddled into his shoulder, breathing hard into the curve of his neck. The room sways. Somehow, the angle of the sunlight has changed, dipped low. Exhaustion tugs me towards unconsciousness, but I have to be sure. I reach a shaking hand to Jace's face, cupping the softness of his cheek, the sharp bone beneath my fingertips. My eyes are shut. I struggle to focus. His beatha is steady. Strong.

No more haze in his head. Not even a tiny speck.

I sigh and pass out for the hundredth time that day.

* * *

Yelling niggles at my awareness, dragging me from the warm darkness. A voice rumbles under my ear. Husky. The second voice is higher pitched and demanding. I groan in protest. Surely I only closed my eyes for a minute? My body aches for sleep. My limbs twitch, swaddled in material and held tight. I'm cradled against something soft and solid. I inhale— blackberries and cloves.

"Stop sniffing me and open your eyes, princess," Jace says, aggrieved. "You need to call off your friend."

"Show her your knives," I mumble, my eyes firmly closed.

"I'm not threatening your best friend with a knife."

"Let her go, you sick freak," Harmony growls. "I'm one second from dialling the last nine."

I crack open one eye. Harmony stands at the side of the bed, her legs planted, brandishing her phone. The duvet is wrapped around me, only my head peeking out. I'm in Jace's arms, cuddled against his chest where he's leaning on the headboard, my face tucked in his neck. Darkness presses at the window, the overhead light on. I snuggle closer to Jace.

"Sleepy," I mumble.

Harmony's arm droops. "Phin? Are you wearing contacts?"

"Hmm?"

Jace shivers at my breath on his throat.

"Your eyes are… purple?"

Oh, yeah. No glamour. No energy to apply it, either. Darn it.

"Lilac and violet," Jace and I say together, though my voice is a bare whisper.

Harmony frowns. "What is going on?"

"Harmony, you like me, right?"

She frowns harder. "You're my best friend, Phin. I love you."

"You'd like me even if I wasn't what you thought I was?"

"Phin," she sighs, sliding Jace a glare, "*I love you*. But I don't know what the hell you're talking about."

I struggle against the covers. Jace finally relaxes his hold and helps to unwind the duvet. My wings flop out, my muscles weak. I shiver, though the room isn't cold. Harmony's phone hits the carpet.

"What the hell?" Her mouth works. "*What?*"

She walks forward until her knees hit the mattress. I crawl closer. She picks up a wing between her thumb and forefinger, examining the delicate skin. She tugs. I squeak and fall off the bed, bowling us both to the floor.

"They're *real,*" she breathes, blinking at me where I'm tangled in her legs, my wings akimbo.

Jace scowls at Harmony, on his hands and knees above us. "I'm taking her back now."

He scoops me up and retreats to lean on the headboard, my spine cradled against the front of his body. His legs frame mine, my stockinged feet hitting him mid-calf. His arms curl around me, wings and all, and he rests his chin on the top of my head.

I've never felt so safe.

Harmony climbs to her feet. "What *are* you?"

"Demon," I mutter.

"Like Satan and the devil?"

I jerk my head. "Not evil. Mostly."

My teeth are chattering again. Jace hugs me tighter, though I'm finding it hard to take a deep breath.

"But you're still the same Seraphina I've known for six years, just with wings?" Harmony smiles softly. "Your eyes are beautiful, sweetie. You shouldn't have hidden them."

I return her smile, though mine is a little wobbly. "Still the same."

"Your heart is racing, princess," Jace says.

Harmony narrows her eyes at him. "What's wrong with

her?"

The tone implies she wanted to say, "*What have you done?*"

"She needs energy."

"Like a sandwich?"

Jace snorts. "Not quite. Take mine, princess."

I manage another head shake, no less jerky. "You have none to spare."

He tilts his chin at Harmony. "She feeds on energy. You might get woozy if she takes too much, but it doesn't hurt. Will you let her have some of yours?"

Harmony crosses her arms, and her eyes spark a challenge.

"Of course I will," she says. "She's *my* best friend. Who the hell are you?"

"I'm Jace."

"Yeah, I got that. And are you an unstable abuser of women?"

"Obviously not."

"Well, she's not exactly looking great after being in your company, *Jace.* What are those marks on her wrists and ankles?"

"They'll fade in a minute."

They watch me expectantly, though all I can see from this angle is Jace's cheekbones and the fan of his lashes. I sip Harmony's beatha—a zing of coffee and oranges. I gulp more before I can stop myself, and she slumps on the end of the bed.

"Sorry," I gasp. "Tough day."

I shudder and Jace cuddles closer, his hands gripping his biceps with me cradled in between. His heart slams against my spine.

There's so much I need to tell him, but Harmony is perched on the bed, her puzzled gaze flicking between us.

"What happened last night? Who were those people? Not

cops, I take it. Where did you go?"

I have a key to her house, so she doesn't ask how I got here. Still, it's probably too confusing if I tell her I teleported onto the bed. I give her a summarised version of Diviners and demons, and being kidnapped to a cave. I don't mention the torture.

"And he's one of them—a Diviner?" Harmony says, now leaning against the wall. Her eyes track where Jace has wrapped as much of his body around me as he can. "He's kinda clingy for someone who wants to kill you."

"He doesn't want to kill me." I pause and add, "Anymore."

He huffs in my ear, and I shiver. A good shiver.

Harmony's brows hitch upwards. "Who is he to you? *What* is he to you?"

"He's… he's my…"

I glance at Jace. He shrugs, which isn't helpful.

I give Harmony a goofy smile. "He's prince to my princess."

"Fucking hell," Jace sighs.

Harmony relaxes for the first time since I woke up in Jace's arms. Her eyes sparkle. A grin tugs at her mouth.

"Are you and he…?"

"Why does everyone assume we've done it already?" he mutters.

"Done what?" I say.

Harmony laughs. "Oh, Phin, you are *so* cute."

"Can you leave us alone?" Jace growls.

Harmony arches an amused brow. "You seem to be forgetting whose house this is."

"Sorry," Jace mumbles. "But can you leave us alone? Please."

"Sweetie? You okay with that?"

I nod against Jace's chest.

Harmony's humour dissolves to her protective lioness face. "Just so we're clear—I can still throw your arse out. Phin is… Well, I was going to say she's not like other women, but she's not like other *humans*. She's sweet and fragile and innocent. *Completely* innocent."

"I know how innocent she is," Jace says in his husky, dangerous voice.

Harmony and I both shiver.

"Right, well…" Harmony clears her throat. "Holler if you need anything."

Then she shuts the door and leaves us alone.

21

"I just need to hold you for a minute, okay?" Jace says.

He buries his face in my hair, his breath hot on my neck. I manage a nod.

He's shaking.

My fingertips skim down his arm to play with his silver bracelet, the plate flashing under the light. The metal clinks softly. Dried blood wrinkles the skin on the back of my hand. More dried blood circles my wrists, but there are no wounds beneath. I wiggle my toes. Jace has taken his boots off at some point, his socks as black as his combats. My other hand idly fiddles with a button on one of his many pockets.

"I did a bad thing to Ellie," I whisper.

"I'm sure she deserved it."

"She really seems to dislike you."

A huff of air tickles my ear. "Rose has treated me like the son she never had since I joined the group. Ellie hates it. Rose is harder on her."

I slide the bracelet up and down his wrist, stroking his skin, no longer careful not to touch him. He shifts, settling me flush to the front of his body. The thud of his heart beats in time to mine.

"I took Ellie's beatha." I swallow. "Almost all of it."

142

Jace stills against my back. "Will she recover?"

"I hope so. She… she might be unconscious for a few days. She threatened to cut my wings off."

My wings shiver, tucked between us. Jace ducks his head, his mouth grazing the sensitive spot below my ear.

"I had a seizure, didn't I?" he says.

I nod, a lump in my throat. "A bad one. They wouldn't let me help you. I should've helped you. I'm sorry."

My breath hitches. Water plops onto his shiny bracelet. He tilts my chin.

"Hey, princess—Seraphina—don't cry. It's not your fault."

His bronze eyes are gentle. I cry harder. He catches my tears on his thumb.

"I should've told them the name of the stupid village at the start," I sob.

"Rose still would have marked you to see if you were telling the truth. I'll never forgive her."

"It was Oliver and his awful pencil."

"A pencil that I am definitely going to shove in his eye."

I smile through my tears. "I like it more when you call me princess."

"I can do that, princess," Jace chuckles.

I sniff and return to fiddling with his bracelet. Words bubble in my throat, but nerves flutter in my belly.

What if he isn't happy with what I've done? I stole Ellie's beatha and forced it on him while he was unconscious. He wasn't in danger, though the seizure had exhausted him. According to the article I read, people can live normal lives with epilepsy.

Though, as a Diviner, his life isn't exactly normal.

I clear my throat. And again. I tap the bracelet.

"You don't have to wear this anymore," I say softly. "Except for the diazepam bit."

His heart kicks against my spine. "What are you telling me, princess?"

"You don't… need your medication, either."

Firm hands clamp my hips, hoist me upwards, and spin me around. I yelp and find myself facing Jace, straddling his legs, my fingers gripping his shoulders, wings flared. His eyes search mine, filled with a surge of emotions that tightens my chest. Hope, tenderness. Awe.

"You healed me?" he says in his soft, husky voice. "*All* of me?"

I place a fingertip to the centre of his forehead and brush a strand of hair away. His gaze is too intense for me to hold.

"No more epilepsy," I say, wobbling on the last word.

He makes a desperate noise low in his throat, and his mouth collides with mine. My whole body melts in his lap on a little whimper of my own.

Was it only last night he kissed me for the first time?

I've missed the taste of him. The glide of his lips. The slide of his tongue stirring my heart into a canter. He kisses me breathless. Hard and hot and deliciously merciless.

He drags me against him until something else hard and hot presses on the thin material of my underpants, my skirt rucked up between us. He swallows my gasp. Slim, strong fingers stroke from my waist to my thighs, tickling me through the material and hesitating on the hem.

Jace groans. "Fucking hell, princess, what are you wearing?"

I'm not sure I can speak. My head is a little woozy at the feel of his body against mine, the sight of his flushed cheeks and heavy-lidded eyes. I remember his weight on top of me.

The wonderful friction.

"Harmony says guys like them," I manage.

He growls. "Harmony is right."

His thumbs brush the lace edge of my stockings and trace to the inner curve of my thighs. My heart swells into my throat. An ache starts deep in my stomach.

"God, I need to touch you," Jace says. "Can I touch you, princess?"

I blink. Frown. Blink some more.

"But… you are touching me?"

He smirks. "A little higher."

His thumbs knead my thighs.

My pulse quivers. "When you say touch…?"

"I'm not taking your virginity where your friend can hear." Jace's eyes darken, his voice dropping to that husky purr. "Though I *will* take it. And soon."

My breath rushes out. I gulp another.

He's not shaking anymore. It's all me.

"Goddamn," he sighs. "You really are cute."

His lips are heaven. In this place, there's no Diviners, no torture, no death. Only his burning kisses and a growing throb that wants more. More Jace. More touching. *More.*

"Stand up, princess."

I wobble to my feet, unsteady on the soft mattress. He tips his head to look at me standing over him, a foot planted on either side of his legs. The material of my skirt stretches at my hips. My wings stroke the air for balance.

"Do you trust me?" he says.

The flex of his fingers is unbearably distracting. They brand my thighs and turn my muscles liquid.

I nod, my mouth dry. My hair slithers forward, and I peek

through it.

What is he going to—

His hands inch higher under my skirt. My heart rate climbs with them. His gaze pins me and all my air stutters in my chest, unable to escape. He sweeps a thumb along silk-clad flesh no male's hands have ever touched. My knees buckle. He catches me before I land heavily in his lap. My hands fist in his top, my eyelids fluttering.

He grins. "Liked that, did you?"

He cajoles me back up. My legs quiver. My skirt is past my waist, exposing my underwear. Jace raises his molten and hungry eyes to my face.

"Nice pants, princess. It's almost a shame to take them off."

"Take them *off?*" I pant. "Jace, I can't. I'm going to fall…"

He smooths my skirt back over my hips, his hands sliding underneath.

"Fuck," he purrs, "you're too perfect."

Fingers curl around my waistband, brushing my stomach and clenching my muscles. My breaths are harsh and loud, shaking on each exhale. Jace teases my underwear off and slides them down my trembling legs. I can barely stand from one foot to the other for him to pull them free. His hands retrace their path. Slim fingers cup where thigh meets buttock.

"Jace…" I whimper.

"Sorry. You're just so fucking soft."

He lets me collapse to my knees. The skirt covers me, but my legs are spread around his, leaving me open and vulnerable. Nothing between me and his questing hands. I struggle to breathe past my heartbeat. My pulse has dropped to throb where he touched.

"Try not to scream, princess," he says.

His thumb swirls on secret flesh. A jolt rocks my whole body. My eyes widen. Jace groans and clasps the nape of my neck, dragging my mouth to his. The kiss is heady and insistent. His tongue strokes mine the same way his fingers stroke between my legs. The delicious pressure starts to build, everything tight and aching.

"God, you're wet," Jace says, his voice a tortured rasp.

"Is that good?" I moan.

He smirks. "You tell me."

His finger glides in the slit at my apex. I make a strangled noise in my throat. Jace bites his lip, his eyes wild. He circles my opening, then dips inside. It's almost too much. His finger stretching me. My muscles clamping at the intrusion. His thumb finds that spot where he started and rubs, sending a rush of tingles outwards, chasing the slight pain away. His finger curls inside me, stroking over and over. My head falls back, my eyes squeezed shut. The movement stretches my stomach and heat flares between my legs. Jace works his hand faster. His lips brand my throat, my pulse hammering under the press of his mouth.

"Jace." I've never heard my voice so frantic. His name is a plea. I say it again. And again and again.

"You're so beautiful, princess," he whispers.

I think I shout his name. Pleasure rushes from his finger inside me to the tip of my toes and the top of my head. Stars explode on my closed lids. My body bucks and squirms in his arms, beyond my control. The orgasm leaves me limp and breathless, panting into his neck.

"Fuck," Jace growls. "You make it hard not to go further."

He drags me against him, so I'm straddling his lap. His erection presses on my swollen flesh, thick and straining at the material of his combats. My muscles tighten at the contact. My hips grind into him. The sound he makes sends a delicious thrill through me.

"Christ, princess, don't tempt me. Just give me a minute." He shudders, breathing fast. "Your friend definitely heard that."

I give him a noise of assent since I can't speak yet. His lips curve against my temple. He strokes my hair, my back, and his arms pull me close. My pulse settles. All the throbbing settles. It seems to be Jace's turn for shaking again.

"Thank you," he whispers.

22

"I guess you're not so bad after all, Jace Mulholland," Harmony says.

She's sitting at her kitchen table with a twinkle in her eye, smirking at us over the rim of her cup. Jace huffs, but a hint of colour flares on his cheekbones.

I've pulled my underwear back on. Afterwards, Jace licked his fingers and it sent a spike of heat to where he'd touched me. I may even have swooned a little. Then he pushed up my sleeve and before I could recoil at the mark on my forearm, he scrubbed it away, placing a soft kiss on my smudged skin.

Harmony grins at me. "Was that your first?"

"My first?"

"Orgasm."

"Can we *not* talk about this?" Jace says.

We linger in the doorway. Harmony's kitchen is cosy and white, a little worn, but every surface gleams. A cute chequered cloth covers her table.

I peek at Jace, and whisper, "Second."

Harmony whoops. "And how many has he had?"

"None of your damn business," Jace says through his teeth.

"He hasn't had any."

Jace pinches his nose. "Stop answering her, princess."

Harmony presses her lips together as if she's trying not to laugh. Her gaze lingers on my wings. There's no revulsion in her face, only wonder.

"Now I know why you picked that tattoo."

Jace's head whips round to me, his eyes sharp. "You have a tattoo?"

"You mean you haven't seen her naked?" Harmony innocently slurps her tea.

"Where?" Jace's hot gaze rakes me from head to toe, and he swallows a groan. "Wait, no—don't tell me."

"You'd like to discover it yourself, huh?" Harmony says, her mouth twitching. At Jace's sigh, she takes pity on him. "Do you want tea? It's getting late, but I have peppermint or chamomile."

"We were hoping to use your shower," I say.

She muffles a squeal. "Together?"

My mouth works, but nothing comes out. My turn to blush.

Harmony laughs. "Sorry, Phin. I'm just teasing. Why don't you show Jace where it is? You and I need to have a little talk."

"Oh, Christ," Jace mutters.

I lead him to the bathroom at the top of the stairs. It's small, with a glass cubicle and no bath. A woven mat of orange and black hides scuffed linoleum. A reed diffuser smelling of lavender sits on top of the toilet. I bend to get a towel from the cabinet under the sink. When I straighten, Jace stands at my back, the heat of him soaking into my shoulder blades. His arms wrap around my middle and his lips graze my cheek.

"All you have to do is ask nicely," he whispers.

I gulp. He makes a noise low in his throat and spins me around, one hand in my hair, the other at the small of my back, pulling my hips against him. The kiss awakens all the good throbbing. My hands slide up his firm chest to the pulse in his throat, my fingers sweeping through the hair at the nape of his neck. He shivers.

"You need to go now, princess," he growls.

I nod, and scurry away on wobbly legs. I glance back and meet his bright, predatory eyes as the door shuts. I lean against the wall, breathing hard. Water hisses on, muted through the closed door. I stifle a bleat of disappointment.

If I were a braver female, I'd still be in there. Part of me wanted to stay. The thought of a naked Jace sends my heart racing. I've not even seen his bare torso, unlike every demon male I've ever encountered. What does he look like out of his clothes, his body hard and ready for mating?

Somehow, the image of him isn't terrifying. Scary in a good way.

I calm my bounding pulse and force my feet towards the kitchen, despite the temptation of pressing my ear to the door to listen to the splash of water.

"You big coward," Harmony greets me with a grin. "At least he seems to be a gentleman. No pressuring you into sex."

"He's an honourable male."

Her grin widens. "And he's the one? The hottie who gets to deflower you?"

I wonder how Jace would feel, being referred to as a hottie. Though it's accurate.

"Is deflowering another word for—"

"Taking your virginity? Yes."

I clear my throat. Glance behind me. Shuffle my feet.

"Then, yes. Soon. Maybe. I'm working up to it."

Harmony squeals properly this time and rushes around the table. She pauses in front of me, her hands on my shoulders.

"Is the real reason for the no-hug policy because you were hiding your wings?" At my nod, she gives me a gentle smile and pulls me into her arms. "In that case, expect a lot of hugs from now on."

I bury my face in the soft wool of her jumper. She smells of wildflowers and meadow grass. I hold her tight to make up for the years lost. The years I could've been hugging my best friend if I'd not doubted her.

"Hey, Phin, don't cry." She eases me away, her thumbs brushing my tears, like Jace did.

"I wish I'd told you sooner," I sniffle. "I was scared."

"I understand, sweetie. I still can't quite believe it myself."

She tilts my chin to examine my face, as if she'll find new secrets. I flick my wings at her, and she laughs.

"Jace better know how lucky he is." Her gaze lifts over my shoulder and her brown eyes widen. "Holy Christ on a bike."

I spin around. Jace is framed in the doorway, wet hair flopping into his eyes and sticking to his cheekbones. His combats sit low on his hips, his feet bare. The rest of him is carved muscle from his broad shoulders to his slim waist, his skin perfect and smooth and anything but boring. My fingertips tingle.

His gaze flits between me and Harmony before settling on Harmony. He raises a brow, and she manages to close her mouth.

"Do you have a t-shirt I can borrow? Mine got blood on it."

"Right. Sure. Of course. Let me check."

She sidles past him and out the doorway, mouthing, "*You lucky bitch,*" over his shoulder. Jace turns around and she ducks, scuttling away like I do under that intense bronze stare.

I find myself a step closer to him. Underneath what must be

Harmony's flowery shower gel, he still smells like blackberries and cloves.

"You took your bracelet off," I say softly.

He rubs his bare wrist. His hand dips into his pocket and emerges holding a spill of silver.

"I was going to chuck it, but… I couldn't bring myself to toss it in the bin."

"Can I have it?" The words slip out, whispered and eager.

He pins me with his gaze. Something flashes across his face, too fast for me to read.

"You want my medical bracelet?"

I nod a little too rapidly. A slow smile tugs at his mouth and swoops through my stomach. He closes the distance between us and takes my hand. His proximity always causes a spurt of adrenaline and nerves, but it's even worse when he's topless. My eyes keep dropping to his naked torso. The sleek curves of muscle, his skin dewy and glowing from the shower.

"My face is up here, princess," he purrs.

He fastens the bracelet around my wrist. The gentle stroke of his fingers is almost as distracting as the planes and ridges in front of my nose. I lower my hand instead of touching him. The bracelet slips off and hits the floor.

Jace smirks. "Needs some adjustment. Your friend got a toolbox anywhere?"

I find a small pair of pliers in the toolbox under the sink. With quick, sure movements, Jace removes several links from the chain, discarding them on the table. The bracelet fastens perfectly around my wrist. I shake it, and the engraved plaque shines under the lights. I grin at Jace. He blinks at me.

"Aww, did you just give her jewellery?" Harmony says. "Now I know it's for real."

She hands Jace a charcoal hoodie, and he zips it closed. His body is no less fascinating under the material, especially where it hugs his shoulders and biceps. I recognise the hoodie as belonging to an ex-boyfriend of Harmony's, which explains why it fits.

I go for a quick shower, nervous about leaving Jace and Harmony alone in case they start arguing. A thrill courses up my spine at the thought of Jace in the cubicle before me, slim hands working the shower gel across slick skin. Those skilled fingers… Shaking my head, my pulse back to a rabbit hop, I dress in a pale-blue cotton nightie, my clothes kept in the spare bedroom since I sleep over regularly. Harmony has never once asked me about the slits in the back of the tops.

Jace and Harmony are at the table. Neither of them looks angry, though Harmony has a considering expression. Jace gives her his calm, implacable face.

I bite my lip to stop myself from asking what they were talking about, and slide into the chair next to Jace. Harmony makes us all peppermint tea and reclaims her seat opposite us.

She blows on the hot liquid. "So, sweetie, I take it what you told me about the cult you grew up in is a sanitised, safe-for-humans version?" At my nod, she says, "Give me the truth."

I tell her all of it—the awful stuff Jace has already heard, but also the good parts. The community, being treated like a princess—Jace smirks at that. His arm rests on the back of my chair. Every now and again, a finger brushes my wing in a tiny, tickling caress. My stomach clenches each time. I press my thighs together instead of squirming in the chair.

"When did you two meet, then? Was it after I made you go talk to him? You seemed a tad reluctant."

Jace slides me an amused look.

He was so angry. Cold and unforgiving. Who knew that cruel Diviner could become this protective male? His touch so different to our clash on Infirmary Bridge.

"*You stabbed her in the back?!*" Harmony screeches half-way through my story. "You motherfucker."

Jace shifts in his seat. "In my defence, every other demon I'd met was a monster."

"Look at her! How can you think she was a monster? She'd never hurt anyone."

"I know that now," Jace says, his eyes warming my belly more than the tea.

His quiet conviction brings a lump to my throat. I gulp minty liquid to hide it.

I have hurt someone—Avzameth. I killed him in defence of Jace. In defence of myself.

By the time I've told Harmony everything—interrupted by her furious outbursts at the exploits of the other Diviners—my mouth is dry and scratchy from talking.

"So, what's the plan now?" Harmony frowns at Jace. "I take it your Diviner pals aren't going to leave her alone anytime soon?"

He rolls his empty mug between his palms. "Not likely. But searching for her clan will keep them occupied."

I swallow hard. My heart slams against my ribs.

"I have to go back," I wheeze. "I have to find them. Warn them. I can't... I can't let them be slaughtered."

Jace nods, though his expression gives me nothing.

"I figured," he says. "And I'm coming with you."

I gape at him. "You can't! They'll treat you like your friends treated me. Maybe worse. They'll..."

I shiver at the memory of Father Benjamin, pinned to the

slab beneath Avzameth's clawed hand. What if it were Jace? Struggling on the marble, eyes wide. The punch of a knife. His blood splattering bright and red.

"Breathe, princess."

Jace places a hand on mine where it's clenched on the table, my knuckles white. Harmony watches me, a wrinkle of concern furrowing her brow. I suck in a gulp of air. Another.

"I can take care of myself," he says.

"You're a great warrior, Jace, but even you can't fight a whole clan."

"Then let's hope they listen."

"Your people didn't listen," I whisper. "Why would mine?"

He shrugs one beautiful shoulder. "It's worth the risk. Showing them how you've lived without killing is worth the risk. If they all turn vegan, the Diviners won't have justification to quarrel with them. The change won't happen overnight—the hatred is ingrained—but it should change."

"And you'd be all right with that—a normal life? No more fighting? You said you can't just stop being a Diviner."

His mouth ticks. "No doubt a few will refuse to be anything but monsters."

I shudder, and he squeezes my hand. Harmony regards our interchange with interested eyes.

"You think Rose and Ellie will accept you back?" I say.

"I can be *very* persuasive," Jace growls, and I shudder for a different reason.

Harmony, failing to mask a shudder of her own, clears our cups into the sink. "I'm heading to bed. I didn't exactly sleep last night, imagining my best friend in the clutches of the sick and twisted Jace Mulholland."

"Who says I'm not sick and twisted?"

That husky and dangerous voice, still so full of menace. It speeds my heart and pools heat between my legs. A delicious burst of excitement and fear.

"I could sleep," I squeak.

Before I can argue—as if I would—Harmony steers me into her bedroom. I catch Jace's eye as the door closes and his gaze is no less piercing and hungry than when I left him in the bathroom. He slips inside the spare room and shuts the door. My breathing eases a fraction.

I've never slept with a male. In the literal sense. It's also a euphemism for mating since humans love their innuendo.

I climb into bed beside Harmony after another hug and a, "Goodnight, sweetie." I curl on my side and listen to her breathing in the darkness. A car passes outside, its headlights sweeping the curtains and chasing shadows across the ceiling. I roll onto my back. I'm exhausted, my eyes gritty. My muscles ache bone-deep despite the energy I got from Harmony. The memory of the torture lingers like a stain.

I need... I need something. I'm missing... something.

I turn onto my other side. Breathe for two minutes. Slump on my back. My wings tangle in the sheets. I jiggle the tension out of my legs.

"Phin, for the love of god," Harmony chides. "Go next door, if that's what you want."

"That's not—"

"You don't want to slither in bed with Jace? Feel that hard body against yours? Shout his name in the dark?"

"Um..."

Harmony chuckles. "Go. You both went through a lot today. That's why he was so clingy earlier. He can comfort you in ways I can't. Just be sure it's what *you* want."

Cheeks blazing, I swing my bare legs from the warm pocket of the duvet. Harmony's grin shows white.

"Use protection," she trills.

I totter into the hall on quaking legs.

What exactly do I need protection from? Definitely not Jace.

My heart thunders in the stillness of the house. I tip-toe to the closed door and hold my breath. No sound from inside. I twist the handle. The door swings silently to reveal a slice of black. Nerves flutter in my belly. Bronze eyes flash in the dark.

Why am I here? What should I tell him? I'm not sure I can explain myself. Not sure what I want except to be near him.

Jace throws the covers back.

"Come here, princess," he says.

23

I've never been in a car before. It's a few years since I thought of them as a wheeled metal conveyance, ignorant to the terminology of the human world I'd thrust myself into. I've been on a bus a few times, mostly when Harmony wanted to go to the shopping centre or the cinema in Eastfield, which is bigger than the one at Eden Court.

Jace's car is bright blue, low slung, and mean-looking. He drives it with the same confidence and intensity that he tackles everything else. When he accelerates, the vibration of the engine purrs in my belly and tugs at my chest.

He said he could teach me, but the levers and dials and the touch-screen menu in the centre of the dashboard—a new word for me—are too confusing. I got excited at all the buttons and managed to blast the air conditioning and change the language on the radio to something that resembles Diviner torture symbols. Jace told me to sit on my hands after that, though his tone was amused. I'm content to peek at him under my lashes as he zooms onto the main motorway—second new word of the day—heading south from Inverness.

He's taking me to his home. Briefly.

His slim fingers grip the shaft—the *gear stick*—between us, and he slides it forward. His legs tense and relax as he presses the pedals lined at his feet. His other hand is curled lightly around the steering wheel, which also contains a multitude of buttons and blares really loud when you lean on it by accident.

I got a smirk for that one.

His hair is in his eyes, though he doesn't seem to notice. He's chewing on the inside of his lip. He does that when he's concentrating. He's wearing his black combats and the charcoal hoodie. The zip is a little loose and has slipped down to show the lines of his collarbones and a glimpse of smooth skin.

We didn't do anything after I climbed into his bed last night. He tucked me into his side, my head on his bare chest, my legs tangled with his. The steady thud of his heart lulled me immediately to sleep. When I awoke in the early hours from a nightmare of grey stone and pain, gasping and afraid, he stroked my hair and soothed me back to slumber, and pleasant dreams.

Dreams of him.

I'm more aware of his hands. Those skilled fingers. He hasn't touched me like that since. The hollow ache in the pit of my stomach says I want him to. Not that I can ask—

"You're staring at me again, princess," Jace drawls.

I duck my head and put my hands in my lap, fiddling with the woven ties at the end of my belt. I'm wearing jeans and a wool sweater. A skirt and tights aren't suitable for where we're going. A bag of my stuff is also tucked in the boot, collected from my house by Jace after strict instructions that I wasn't to leave Harmony's and follow him in case the Diviners were there.

The thought of him packing my underwear sends a hot, squirmy feeling through my belly.

"Are you sure?" I say.

His brow cocks. "Am I sure you were staring? Or are you asking me what you've asked five times already?"

"You're going to be the monster, not me. What if… what if they hurt you and I can't stop them? What if they hurt me, too?" I whisper the last.

I worried about him every second he was away picking up my clothes and getting his car from where it was parked near the Revolution nightclub. So much has happened since then, it feels like a year ago.

"They won't hurt you."

"But no one's ever been this disobedient before."

"They'll probably want you back. But they're not keeping you."

I shiver and avoid his gaze, frowning out the window at the fields and trees slipping past.

It's a lovely autumn day—blue sky, a sparkle of frost in the sun, the leaves a tapestry of gold and orange and bronze. My wings are glamoured and tucked between me and the seat. I left my eyes lilac and violet, the cars around us whooshing by too quickly to see any detail. And if they do, maybe the humans inside will think I'm wearing contacts.

My focus drifts to Jace.

I want to touch him. But I can't voice that, either. The request gets stuck in my throat somewhere and mobbed by the cloud of moths in my stomach. Or butterflies. Harmony says they're butterflies.

I *really* want to touch him. From the ridges and valleys of his knuckles to the hollow of his throat where his pulse beats. His cheekbone. The line of his jaw. I want to curl my fingers around his hips and draw his firm, strong body against mine.

Feel just how hard—

"Unless you want me to pull the car over, I'd stop looking at me like that, princess," he growls.

"Like what?"

"Like you want to eat me."

Heat unfurls from my chest to my belly. His tone implies he's not talking about me feasting on his beatha, as electrifying as it is, though I'm not entirely sure what he does mean. A kiss, maybe? He tends to devour my mouth as if he can't get enough. His tongue stroking deep. His lips—

"*Princess*," he groans.

I snap my eyes forward to the double-lane motorway out the windscreen. "Sorry."

"Don't be sorry. It's fucking hot. I just… don't want to go too fast."

I glance at the needle behind the wheel, the one showing the speed of our vehicle. "How fast are we going?"

Jace chuckles. "Not the car—you and me."

My gaze zips to his. "How fast are *we* going?"

"Given I first kissed you a day ago and you've never done this before, probably too fast. Also not fast enough. It's excruciating."

He grins at the end, as if this pleases him. I find it a little difficult to breathe. Giddiness blooms in my heart.

We fall silent. A yellow speed camera arches over the road.

Are we going too fast for that? The car is zooming along, way faster than the buses that lumber to Eastfield.

A screen of willows presses close to the right-hand side of the carriageway, fields stretching on the left to spruce plantation and hills. Jace taps the screen on the dashboard and bass fills the vehicle, the vocalist's voice a deep, husky croon.

"I love this song," I say, bouncing in the seat.

Jace's eyebrow hikes upwards. "You like heavy metal? What am I saying—of course you do. You're a demon."

"Do *you* like heavy metal?"

His lips twitch. He peeks at me out the corner of his eye.

"Yes," he says.

We listen in silence, both of us smiling.

Jace is the first male I can relax around. When did that change? I'm comfortable in his presence yet his proximity still buzzes through me. The anxiety is no longer fearful. It's exciting. Anticipatory. Good nerves.

I should touch him. No, I can't.

Do it. *Do it,* you coward.

Holding my breath, I place my hand on top of his where he grips the gear stick. I feel him start, his head jerking to face me, but I avoid his gaze, staring at our hands instead. Mine are so much smaller. Jace flexes his fingers and threads them between mine from below. His tender smile stirs the butterflies into a mad flutter.

Darn it, I'm looking at him.

I focus out the window, but don't move my hand from his. Five minutes pass. Jace squeezes my fingers and slips his hand free, nudging a lever sticking from the steering wheel. A green arrow starts to flash. He slows into a separate lane and turns right, the road surrounded by towering green spruce. He turns right again onto a gravel track. Stones ping on the underside of the car. After a minute, he parks in a space at the side, the way ahead blocked by a rusted metal gate, though the path continues on and bends out of sight.

"We'll walk from here," he says.

"Do you think they're watching your house?"

The car doors clunk shut in the quiet. The wind sighs through the branches and smells of pine. Trees creak and sway above us.

"Maybe," Jace says. "Rose might be preoccupied if Ellie is still unconscious. Or she's prioritising your clan above finding us."

He takes my hand, and my heart skips a beat. We step into the forest, the undergrowth springy beneath my shoes—heather and blaeberry. Reminds me of home.

"What if they find them first?" I say softly.

"They won't. It'll take them a few days to mobilise. And Rose won't leave until Ellie recovers. For a hunt this big, she'll want to lead."

"I'm not sure I want to find them, either," I mumble. "Is that bad?"

Jace tugs on my hand, and I look at him. "It's not bad. You lost a friend there. Saw horrific stuff. You realised you wanted something different to what they forced on you. But I know you still care about them, princess. It's okay to care."

"Even when they're human-killing monsters?"

His mouth quirks. "Even then. But I'm hoping we can change that part."

"Me, too," I whisper.

We crunch through the trees, angling away from the gravel road. Jace eases me to a stop at an elder bush, the bark deeply grooved. A pine has fallen next to it, the trunk furred with moss.

"Wait here. I'm going to scope it out."

He stalks towards an area where the wood thins, something flashing through the trees. Before I can worry too much, he reappears and guides me to a white, pebble-dashed bungalow off the gravel track, the roof grey, sloping tile. He takes a key from his pocket, still holding my hand, and unlocks the back door. I trail him through a narrow but neat kitchen into a square hallway containing the front door and an entrance into a living room with a wood-burning stove and a large TV. A short corridor leads to a large bedroom and an en-suite. A glass of water sits on his nightstand next to a framed photo of a beaming couple. The male has Jace's eyes.

"My parents," Jace says, and I jump. "They died when I was young."

"Mine, too."

His finger tilts my chin. "I'm sorry."

"Relationships are different in the clan. Even if the sires are alive, they aren't close to their young. We were raised by our teachers and elders—the infertile adults. Our mothers were more likely to die during birth. Not that the females know that."

"We can tell them that truth, too."

I nod. Jace's gaze lingers on the picture of his parents.

"When did you meet Rose?" I say softly.

"She found me in foster care when I was eleven." His mouth ticks into a sardonic smile. "I scared off a few potential adopters talking about wavery monsters. I don't know what would have happened to me if Rose hadn't taken me in. Trained me. She owns this house, too. Or the Diviners do."

I squeeze his arm. "I'm sorry."

"What for?"

"For pitting you against them."

He shrugs one shoulder. "Things haven't been the same since my brain injury. And when someone comes along and shatters your whole worldview, well… you have to pay attention."

I hide a smile as Jace pulls a rucksack from a cupboard and starts tossing clothes in. He disappears into the en-suite. I perch on the edge of his bed, the sheets a rich burgundy with a subtle, silver pattern. I run my hands over them.

Jace sleeps here. The covers wrapped around his body. Vulnerable in the dark. The sheets smell of him.

Does he dream about me?

"Are you sniffing my pillow, princess?" he says in his soft, husky voice.

I yelp and twist around, somehow sprawled on his bed. He crawls onto the mattress, his slim, strong body arching over me. A jolt of heat pulses to my toes. Jace pins my hands above my head and holds them tight, our fingers entwined. He nuzzles my hair, then trails his nose from behind my ear and along my jaw, sending shivers outwards. My breath locks in my chest. My lips tingle, but he doesn't kiss me. He snuffles at my neck and I squirm, a strangled noise in my throat. He rests his forehead on my collarbone, his hot breaths puffing between my breasts.

"Goddamn, you look good in my bed. But we can't stay here." He raises his head, his eyes sparking. "I want to take my time. Get you trembling and aching and so fucking wet, you can't help but beg me for it. I want to watch you unravel."

"Jace…" I whimper, my skin flushed. I'm already trembling, aching. Wet.

He groans. "Fuck, princess, what are you doing to me?"

He swallows my next whimper, drinking me down, his mouth punishing and glorious on mine. His tongue thrusts between my lips, and I open for him. His pleased growl vibrates low in my belly. I try to rub against him, but he holds his weight off me and I can't get any friction. I whine in his mouth.

"Christ," he pants, shoving himself away. "You're so innocent yet eager. It drives me insane."

I blink at him. My lips feel swollen. My whole body feels swollen.

His wicked expression softens. He draws me to my feet and hugs me to his chest, his cheek on the top of my head. His heart thrums in my ear. His stiffness presses against my stomach, but he just holds me, quietly, for a few minutes until his heart rate slows.

"Come on," he says. "It's not safe."

He slings his rucksack on and I follow him in a daze, my mind still reeling from the overwhelming sensations he stirs in me—lust, heat, yearning. Nervous excitement. I'm barely aware of the grey linoleum beneath my feet, distracted by my unruly pulse.

The back door swings open. Every muscle in Jace's body tenses.

"Oh, good," Oliver says, "you're not dead."

My arm burns with remembered pain. A frightened mewl slips from my mouth before I can clamp my teeth on it. Jace glances over his shoulder, his eyes narrowed and glittering bronze.

Then he moves as fast as a demon male.

His fist cracks into Oliver's jaw. Oliver spins around and collides with a female behind him—the woman who guarded the bathroom door at Revolution and watched, bored, while Ellie shredded my wings. She tumbles to the grass, Oliver limp and unmoving on top of her.

"Your eyeball has a date with the sharp end of a pencil, you fucker," Jace growls through his teeth.

The woman shoves at Oliver, trapped under his weight, her eyes wide and darting to Jace. Jace grabs my hand, steering me around the struggling couple. Our footsteps pound on the grass.

"You can't run from us forever, Jace," the woman yells. "You have to face what you're doing eventually."

"I know *exactly* what I'm doing," Jace yells back, not slowing.

"Like fuck you do," comes the furious reply.

24

"Have you lost your virginity yet?" says the voice on the phone.

"Harmony!" I yelp. "Why is that always the first question you ask me?"

My eyes dart around the rustic kitchen, although I'm alone. Jace is sprawled on the couch in the living room, his heels on the seat arm, flicking through a book on Scottish folklore. I'm curled on the cushions in the bay window, the blinds drawn against the night. I tuck my knees to my chest and squeeze my phone tight to my ear.

I finally relented and bought a mobile on the two-hour journey to Kinloch Hourn. It has no fancy settings or touch screen, but it's small, silver, and flips open. I like it. I like it even more that Jace gave me his number, though his phone is switched off and separated from its battery in case the Diviners can track it.

There are no roads to Inverie. That's why Father Benjamin said it was the remotest village in Scotland. Reaching it takes a thirty-minute, pedestrian-only ferry from Mallaig or a two-day hike over the hills from Kinloch Hourn. Jace hired a cottage on the edge of a pine forest overlooking Loch Beag.

Like Ellie said, there are a billion places with mountains and lochs and trees.

"Well?" Harmony says, and I can hear the smile in her voice. "Have you?"

"My answer is the same as yesterday and the day before that." My voice climbs with anxiety. "Also, why is it called *losing* your virginity? It's not something that can be misplaced. Shouldn't it be giving your virginity? Or taking it?"

Harmony cackles. Silence from the living room. Hadn't I heard the idle flip of pages before?

"Jace?" I cock my head. "Are you listening?"

"Definitely not listening to you talk about your soon-to-be-lost virginity," comes the slightly strained reply.

Soon-to-be-taken, more like.

I gulp and duck my head, though no one can see.

"Has he at least given you another orgasm? Or five? I know you guys spend the days slogging through the hills, but that's no excuse for neglect."

We've slept in the same bed the past few nights. Sleeping in the same bed as Jace is wonderful. Cuddled against his firm body, his soft breaths in my ear. But his hands don't stray to my secret places. Every morning, I find I've climbed on top of him, my face in his neck, my wings tenting the sheets and the stiff length of him pressed to my hip.

My sigh whooshes into the speaker. "No."

"Seraphina van Ize, are you pouting?"

"No," I pout.

"You should ask him."

"I can't ask him!"

"Better yet," she says as if I haven't spoken, "remove all your clothes and stand in front of him. God, I'd love to see his face. It's sexy as hell when a guy can't control himself. And he's already sexy as hell. He'll devour you in the best way. *Damn,*

I'm so jealous."

It's a little harder to breathe with my heart flapping against my ribs.

I can't imagine being nude in front of Jace. Exposed. Vulnerable. The thought of him naked sends my pulse racing and a flush across my skin.

"I'm not doing that," I whisper.

"Coward," Harmony says fondly. "Fine, tell me about your day. Are you still unable to teleport to your clan?"

"I don't know what's wrong. I can picture every part of the compound as if I were there yesterday, but no matter how hard I concentrate, nothing happens."

"Could they have blocked you somehow?"

"I've never heard of such an ability. Maybe it's a mental block." I pluck at the knee of my leggings. "I'm nervous about finding them. Dreading it, almost."

"Of course you are, sweetie. But they're your family and you're trying to help them. Jace will keep you safe."

I glance at the kitchen door. "He will. But… what if I can't keep *him* safe?"

"The way he watches you, he's not going to let anything happen. To either of you."

He is an honourable male. Protective. His presence calms the spikes of panic that threaten to impale me at the thought of finding my clan. How they'll react to him. What if they hurt him? I'd rather they hurt me. He's risked his relationship with the only family he has. For me and mine. I hope Ellie and Rose will forgive him.

"Is he still grumbling about the lack of teleporting?"

I laugh. "Yes, and he hates teleporting, so you can imagine how difficult it's been the last few days."

"I hate trudging through the wind and rain more," Jace calls from the living room.

A smile teases my mouth. "He's not very outdoorsy, for a Diviner. It's kind of cute."

"I am *not* cute," he says, affronted.

Harmony chuckles. "Why do boys get insulted by being called cute? He so is. If you want to soothe his ego, tell him he's hot, too."

"Harmony agrees you're cute," I say.

"Christ's sake," he mutters.

We giggle for a minute over the phone. The rustle of exaggerated page flicking comes from the living room. Warmth blooms in my chest.

I thought I was happy. I had the coffee shop. A real friendship, despite the touching limitations. A future without pain. But I never expected this—my best friend staying my best friend, aware of what I am, and a Diviner standing against his own kin. A Diviner who wants more. Who wants *me*.

Joy fizzes in my veins.

"What's your plan for tomorrow?" Harmony says, her voice high and bright from laughing.

I picture her lying on her bed, her braid tossed across her pillow, wearing one of the silky nighties she loves to sleep in.

"We're hiking to Inverie. I offered to fly to scope things out, but Jace worries about me being spotted. He wants to stay together."

"Inverie—that's where the other Diviners are probably based, right? Is it dangerous?"

"We hope we can avoid them. They won't be pleased after Jace punched Oliver in the face."

"That tool deserved it," Harmony growls. "If I ever meet

him, *I'll* punch him."

We hang up a couple of minutes later. I drop the phone on the cushion and slide Jace's bracelet around my wrist to stroke the carved letters.

I wish it said his name. Is it strange to want his name on me?

Goosebumps creep up my bare arms to the hem of my pink t-shirt, a unicorn prancing on my chest. Jace props his shoulder against the door frame, watching me with the same expression Harmony gets when I've done something adorable. My stomach flutters.

"Let's go to bed," he says.

The flutters become a thousand buzzing wings. They multiply after brushing my teeth and climbing under the covers. I roll on my side and stare at the antique wooden furniture and the small window set in thick stone, the blind lowered. The mattress dips. The light clicks off. Awareness tingles on my skin. Jace spoons against my back, but, unlike the other nights, he nuzzles my throat, trailing his nose up and nibbling my ear. My breath catches.

"I was trying to be good," he murmurs.

His hot breath fans across my cheek. His hand splays on my belly, pulling me closer. His body is hard yet soft, and fascinating. Terrifyingly unknown. Gentle kisses trail from my cheekbone to my jaw. A deep pulse throbs under the scalding heat of his palm. I squirm, unable to hold still, my thighs clenched together. Anything to quell the ache. I flop onto my back, wings squashed, my bones liquid beneath his burning kisses. His mouth finds me in the dark. His tongue glides against mine and a jolt kicks to my heart, gut, and the crest of my thighs. His leg slides across my hips, his hand buried in my hair and guiding my head, offering no escape from the plunder of his mouth. His weight makes me dizzy. His lips make me dizzy. I curl my fingers around his nape and tug on the ends of his hair. With a shiver, he breaks the kiss and rests his forehead on mine.

"Go to sleep, princess," he pants.

25

Relentless rain pours from a sky the colour of bruised plums. The forest offers little shelter, the orange-hued trunks widely spaced over a carpet of soft needles and heather. Water lashes between the branches, the wind chasing pockets of mist. The air smells of wet pine and loam. I duck my head against a squall that rattles my hood. My hair sticks to my cheeks, damp strands flopping free no matter how many times I tuck them into my jacket.

Jace stopped at a camping shop on the way to Kinloch Hourn, kitting us out in proper hiking clothes and boots, as well as finding me a mobile phone. The waterproofs match my eyes. I felt bad cutting slits in the back and immediately ruining their effectiveness.

Cold fingers of wind slither up my spine. I shiver, my fleecy jumper and sweat-wicking top both damp, though that feature is wasted on me. Dirt streaks my trousers around clumps of moss on my knees. Blisters throb on my heels despite the dressings Jace applied this morning, his slim fingers cradling my legs and tickling my ankles.

There are few humans out here, though I feed from the hikers we pass on the trails. Jace told me to take beatha from him whenever I needed, but I'm resisting the temptation. My

175

blisters are not a mortal wound. Time to suck it up and heal like a human.

Jace isn't faring any better. A fern frond is plastered to his shoulder from when he slipped down a hill. His trousers are black and muddy where he landed on his rump. General gloop smears the lovely sea-green material of his jacket around the sodden lump of his backpack.

Huffing, I shove my hood clear and scrape my hair off my face with rain-wrinkled fingers. My wings arch to shield my head from the downpour, glamoured though we haven't seen a hint of another person.

No one else is mad enough to trek in this. Just us and the other Diviners. Somewhere.

Jace curses and flails, his leg tangled in a clump of brambles. He kicks at the offending plant, freeing himself. I bite my lip at his aggrieved expression.

He cocks a brow at me, his eyes flashing. "Something funny, princess?"

"You're just"—I clear my throat—"lacking your usual grace."

"You have a leaf stuck to your forehead."

I scrub my face, realising too late that my fingers are filthy from gripping onto trunks to keep my balance. And from the multiple times I've slipped on *my* rump.

Jace smirks. "Much better."

He swipes a thumb above my eyebrow. His cheeks are slick and shiny with water, his hair clumped in wet spikes beneath his hood. He has droplets of rain in his lashes and beaded on his lips.

Even soaked and miserable, he's a beautiful male.

His thumb skates down the side of my face to my jaw. Strong fingers tilt my chin. He bends his head and warms me with a kiss, his mouth slippery on mine. He tastes of rain and Jace and electricity. My hands clutch at his shoulders as my tongue meets his—just as slippery, just as electric. My knees quake. Jace grips my hips and hoists me aloft without breaking contact, slinging my legs around his waist. He presses me against a tree and I forget the rain, the cold. Forget I'm tired and hungry and sore.

My wings flare on rough bark and catch on the lichen. Jace strokes across fragile skin, exploring the arch of delicate bones and the valleys between. My glamour dissolves. He swallows my gasp, his mouth and touch drawing tingles to the surface. I clutch him tighter, squirming at the clench of my muscles down low, the ache in the pit of my stomach. My hips grind on his hard body, chasing the wonderful friction that ratchets my heartbeat into my mouth.

It doesn't help that I lay awake for hours after his scorching kiss last night, hollow and yearning.

"Fuck me, princess," Jace groans, dropping his forehead to mine. "Does touching your wings make you horny?"

"Is horny like lust?" At his nod, I murmur, "Then, yes."

His fingers flex on my wings. A delicious shudder surges up my spine. My hips thrust against Jace without any instruction from me.

A growl rumbles in his chest. "That's it. I can't fucking take anymore."

My boots thud on the ground. Before my mind can process the sudden position change, my legs are scrambling to match Jace's stride, my hand wrapped in his as he ploughs through the trees, tugging me along.

"Jace," I yelp. "I can teleport—"

"Nope. Need to walk or I'll claim you like a fucking animal."

My breath and words evaporate. I'm glad Jace is intent on our path since my mouth is flapping like a door in the wind. My gaze drops to the churned mud. Water beads in the moss and drips from the bracken. Rain sheets through the open canopy, plastering my hair to my head and gathering in my hood.

It's cold and wet. Even demons don't mate in the rain, though we do rut outside. Like animals.

I picture Jace stretched above me, his weight splaying my thighs, his hips pumping between. His arms braced on the ground, muscles slick and trembling. His bronze eyes dark and hungry and fixed on me. Only me.

I want to be his Chosen.

I want to be his.

My breath wheezes out, shaken by my pulse.

"You're not helping, princess," Jace says through his teeth.

I open my mouth to apologise. A brutal grip fists in my hair and yanks my head back, tearing my hand from Jace's and threatening to dislocate my neck bones. I scream louder than my scalp, though it's not by much. My vision spins with the sky and thrashing pine branches. Voices shout. Rainwater fills my mouth. A muscled arm slams me into a tree and pins my chest, mashing my breasts into my ribs.

"I knew you were a liar," Ellie snarls in my face, "even before you tried to kill me."

She raises her black, swirling blade.

"Ellie, no!" Jace yells.

The knife hangs inches from my eye, the eddies of black on the blade sending a swoop of nausea to my stomach. Rain plinks on the silver beneath the pollution of a Diviner's touch. Ellie's fingers tighten on the handle, her knuckles white and stippled with dirt. Chill water dribbles under my collar and down my spine.

Ellie's arm punches out, the blade pointing at Jace. "One more step and, I swear to god, I'll slit her open."

Jace halts, his hands empty and held out, almost patting the air. Panic brightens his eyes to gold.

"Do we really have to do this shit again, Ellie?" He swallows, and his gaze darts to the side. "*Rose?*"

I struggle to breathe against Ellie's weight, all of it concentrated on her arm across my chest. She smells like toffee apples and wet leaves. The knife returns to hover at my throat, out of my sight, tucked under my chin. I stand very still.

Strange that something able to burn on contact doesn't feel hot.

Rose steps from behind Ellie, her thumbs hooked in the pockets of a jacket patterned with green and brown leaves. Ellie is wearing the same, both of them blending into the forest unlike our teal and lilac coats. I survey the gaps between the trees, but there's no sign of Oliver or the others.

"She's my daughter, Jace," Rose says, a thread of anger warming the coolly patient voice. "She tried to kill my daughter."

"I didn't," I whisper.

My focus flicks from Ellie's sneer to Rose, her face shaded by a wide hood and the gloom of the stormy sky, then back to Ellie. Her lip curls higher, baring her teeth. She has the same green irises as her mother. Like spring leaves.

I'm sure she would appreciate the compliment even less than Marrichar.

"The fact you were unsuccessful is not a point in your favour, demon," Rose says.

"She means she didn't try to kill her." Jace shuffles forward an inch, but stops at Ellie's warning growl. "She didn't want to kill you, Ellie."

Ellie snorts and leans harder on me. My ribs creak.

"You were going to hurt me," I wheeze. "I just wanted to stop you."

My heart thumps against her forearm. She searches my face, stocky but still taller, her figure hunched over me.

"How did you do it? How did you suck my energy away with nothing when your males need death to feed?" She grinds her elbow into my chest. "Try it again, little she-bitch, and I'll give you a real intimate tour of your own guts."

"I… I don't…"

I glance at Jace. His face is pale, his lips pressed together and slightly blue.

Ellie doesn't even look at him when she snarls, "One step. *One more fucking step,* Jace. I'm not kidding."

"Answer the question, demon," Rose says, watching Jace

with something like pity.

My fingertips flex against gritty bark. I keep my wings spread, instinctively wanting to tuck them tight to my sides.

"It's how I've fed since my sixteenth year. How I can live without killing anyone. I draw on small sips of beatha—life energy." I drop my eyes, but force myself to meet Ellie's gaze. "You're the first person I've actively drained. But I didn't try to kill you."

Rose starts to pace, disappearing behind the bulk of Ellie before reappearing on the other side. She rubs her mouth, her expression grim. Jace tracks her progress without moving.

"I told you all this, Rose," he says with a lick of impatience. "I told you she didn't kill anyone."

"Can your males do this?" Rose shakes her head. "No—they would drain us before we could touch them. Is drinking small amounts a female ability or unique to you?"

Jace twitches, probably struggling with the urge to throw up his hands or curse at being ignored again.

"I don't know," I say.

Ellie scoffs. "You don't know fucking much, do you?"

"I hope it's something we all can do," I say to Rose.

I can ignore people, too.

She cocks her head. "Why?"

My gaze trails from Ellie's smothering frame to Jace rigid with tension, ending on Rose. She crosses her arms, a finger tapping her elbow.

"Or this will never end," I say softly.

"Oh, this will end." Ellie's smile is terrifying up close. "This will end real soon."

"Get off her, Ellie," Jace growls.

Ellie's brows shoot into her hairline. "Are you high? She

could drain us all in a blink."

"She. Doesn't. Kill. People."

There was Avzameth, but I guess he's not people. Not to a Diviner.

"Jace," Rose says, back to calm and patient, "I know this is difficult, but we'll get you the help you need. Once she's gone, I have no doubt you'll think clearly again."

Jace's teeth clack together. "You know what, Rose? Fuck you."

Rose gapes at him. "What?"

"Fuck. *You*. She's the only one who's helped me, the only one who bloody *listens* to me, unlike you two with your condescending bullshit and your 'poor, sick little Jace' crap."

"Letting you get your dick wet doesn't count as helping," Ellie says.

Jace glares at her with furious eyes, his whole body wired tight. Ellie makes an, "Ah-ah-ah," noise and leans her fist on my collarbone, the knife a whisper away from sizzling my flesh.

"I don't have epilepsy anymore." Jace pronounces each word carefully. "Seraphina used your beatha to heal me."

"Fuck's sake, Jace. Just because she's had your cock in her mouth, doesn't mean you should believe everything she says."

"Eloise," Rose sighs.

Jace jerks his gaze to Rose since I'm pretty sure he's two heartbeats from charging Ellie and throttling her.

"I've not taken a pill in five days. Remember what happened when I missed one dose? *One*. Not even a day."

Ellie flicks the ends of my damp hair, and I miss Rose's response. Moisture flecks her curled lip.

"I bet you like having his cock in your mouth, don't you?"

she says.

"In… in my mouth?" My cheeks flush. "Humans do that?"

My eyes zip to Jace. I tell myself not to look. My gaze drops lower. To his slim hips and the mysterious juncture of his thighs.

What would that be like?

Jace groans. "Stop staring at me, princess."

I whip my gaze back to meet the revolted twist of Ellie's features. Pain sears a hot line across my throat. I yelp and thrust onto my tip-toes, attempting to climb the tree with my spine. Anything to get away from the awful scald of the blade. I wait for my blood to patter on my boots. For dizziness and blackness and Jace screaming my name.

Twenty-two years on this earth and I've experienced so little. I ran from the clan to a new life, but I hid in a bubble of routine. I followed Harmony. I didn't do anything for myself. Nothing exciting. Nothing risky. Nothing that made me feel alive.

Until Jace tried to kill me.

Sadness and loss catch at my chest. My breath hitches.

"Ellie." Jace's voice is low, husky, and dangerous. Filled with menace. Scarier than a shout. "Look at me, Ellie."

My eyes are squeezed shut. They pop open. Ellie and I turn our heads in unison. My neck throbs, but the blade is no longer pressed to my skin. Jace's eyes are the only colour left in his face, narrowed and blazing through the wet cage of his hair. He clenches his hands into fists. Clench and release. Clench and release. A shudder trembles across his shoulders.

"If you hurt her again," he says in the same quiet, deadly tone, "I will kill you."

Ellie rolls her eyes. "Sure, good buddy."

He flicks his wrist. A knife appears in his hand. Rose's gasp is nearly lost in the shushing of the rain. Jace claims a step, and Ellie jumps.

"I'll slit her throat. I'll do it, Jace."

Another step. A baring of teeth. A growl vibrates in his chest.

"If she dies, you die two seconds after. *I'm* not fucking kidding."

Ellie twists to look over her shoulder. "Step in when you want, Mum. He's gone full psycho."

We all stare at Rose. Instead of fury or shock, astonishment sweeps across her face.

"Oh, Jace, please tell me you haven't," she says.

Jace frowns. "Haven't what?"

Rose scrubs her cheeks. Crimson hair sticks to her skin like streaks of blood. The knife drifts from my throat. I slowly raise my hand, wincing at each rustle of my jacket.

"You soft-hearted idiot." Rose heaves a sigh. "You've fallen in love with her."

Jace blinks. Blinks again. His gaze collides with mine. An electric jolt, like a mouthful of his energy, sizzles down my spine and fizzes in my belly. Ellie flaps her lips, but no sound comes out, for once. My heart swells and thuds frantically against my ribs.

Demon males don't love. But humans do.

I place my palm on Ellie's chest. She startles. Starts to turn. I blast her backwards and she sails into Rose. They tumble into the heather in a whoosh of breath and a thrash of limbs. Sodden bracken churns under their boots. I launch myself at Jace, wrap my arms around his beautiful, shivering body, and teleport us to the cottage.

27

"Motherfucking Christ," are the first words out of Jace's mouth when our muddy boots thud on the bedroom carpet of the cottage. He staggers and the backs of his knees hit the bed. He flops onto the mattress, an arm flung over his eyes. His chest rises and falls with ragged breaths, as if we ran here.

Weak light filters from the small window set in thick stone. Rain strikes the glass. The room is warm, a door leading to the en-suite on my right. Water drips from my jacket to dampen the floor.

"Jace?"

He doesn't move. Uncertainty curls in my stomach. My fidgeting grinds more dirt into the carpet. Flakes of vegetation pepper the floor. My fingers hurt from the cold.

He crossed a line today. Pulled a knife on Ellie. When Rose first cornered us, she said there was hope for him yet if he didn't confront his own people with a weapon. Does this mean he's too far gone? Is it remorse that has him stretched out on the bed as if he's suffered a blow?

"Jace?" My voice wobbles. "Are you all right?"

"Shit," he says.

He rolls to his feet, leaving a mucky print on the bed covers. Icy fingers cup my chin and gently tilt my head. I wince at the pull of burned flesh.

"Are *you* okay, princess?"

I nod, forgetting, and wince again. A quick burst of energy and intense concentration heals the wound. Jace's hand drops to his side, the loss of his touch cooling me more than my damp clothes. I hold his gaze, though his eyes are guarded.

"I'm sorry you had to do that." It takes all my willpower not to stare at my shoes. "I never wanted to drive a wedge between you and your people. Threatening Ellie must have been difficult."

"Threatening Ellie was the easy part. She's practically my sister."

"Humans often threaten to kill their sisters?"

His mouth tilts. "When they're as irritating as Ellie? Definitely."

"Do you think they'll forgive you? Or is it too late?"

"You trying to get rid of me, princess?"

I search his face, but his expression gives me nothing.

"I like having you here," I whisper to my boots, "but it's okay if Rose was wrong. I'm not expecting… I mean, demons don't even…"

"Demons don't fall in love?" Jace says in his soft, husky voice.

I peek at him, a strand of wet hair flopping across my forehead.

"Demon mating is simple," I say. "Functional. No confusing emotions."

"You want to see what human mating is like, princess?" he purrs.

I suck in a breath, choke, and splutter it back out. All my blood rushes from my head and leaves me woozy. Jace grins, and that doesn't help.

"You're cute when you're flustered." His voice deepens. "Now get in the shower."

I bite my lip and scuttle into the en-suite, my accelerating heart rate assuming he will follow. He smirks through the gap in the doorway.

"You still haven't asked nicely," he says, and shuts the door, leaving me alone.

My reflection stares at me from the mirrored cabinet above the sink, cheeks pink and eyes sparkling. Each inhale catches in the back of my throat.

I need to call Harmony. Quiz her on the exact mechanics. Ask how much it will hurt. Deirdre said it would hurt, but that was with Avzameth and Avzameth was a brute. Jace is tall and lean and lovely. Harmony is my best friend. She wouldn't be so eager for me to give up my virginity if it would hurt.

Maybe human mating is gentle.

I sit on the toilet seat in a crinkle of waterproofs and put my head between my legs, huffing the scent of mud and wet grass. My heart eventually stops flapping. I strip and dive into the shower cubicle, flinching at the needles of water on my marbled skin. Dirt and leaves swirl down the plughole on bubbles of coconut shower gel. The warmth eases into my chilled bones. I tip my head, eyes shut under the pounding spray.

Jace is going to see me naked. I'm going to see *him* naked. Unless humans don't get naked, either. I should've questioned Harmony—researched—instead of shying away from anything sex-related. She would talk about her favourite shows on the television where characters mated, but Maggie didn't have one and, like the mobile phone, the device seemed too noisy and overstimulating to bother with.

I scrub myself dry harder than necessary, flapping my wings to air them out and splattering water across the mirror. The towel wraps around me twice from armpit to calf. Taking a deep breath, I crack the door and peek into the bedroom. Empty. My heart skips.

Did I expect Jace to ambush me? Hurl me on the bed? I liked being pressed against the tree. Kissed senseless. There may have been force, but he's nothing like Avzameth.

I yank on a pair of soft, grey leggings, hopping from foot to foot. My wings tangle in a backless, powder-blue top. Being dressed calms me. Drying my hair to a waterfall of black calms me.

Still no Jace. Has he changed his mind? Do I want him to change his mind?

I pad through the dark and narrow hallway. Jace's car in the driveway is a smudge of blue through the rain-streaked glass bordering the front door. The kitchen is large and airy, bright compared to the rest of the cottage with its French doors onto the veranda and the bay window where I make my daily call to Harmony.

What will I tell her tonight when she asks the inevitable question?

Jace glances up from his seat at the rustic table in the centre of the flagstone floor. My pulse jumps. He nudges a mug of hot chocolate topped with whipped cream towards me. I collapse more than sit into the chair opposite.

His hair is wet—wetter than before—and sticks up in all directions, as if he's been running his hands through it. He must have used the shower in the separate bathroom. A clean, black top hugs his shoulders, the sleeves pushed up to show muscled forearms. My eyes trail higher to the column of his throat and the line of his jaw.

"You're staring at me again," he says.

I drop my gaze and fiddle with my bracelet. His bracelet. I gulp the hot chocolate, burning my tongue. The liquid—sweet and rich and delicious—heats my insides.

"Is this part of human mating?" I slurp another mouthful.

"No, this is because we haven't eaten anything since lunch and it's a miserable day. You'll know when we get to the mating part."

I dig a fingernail into the table. My pulse leaps from a modest thrum to a thundering gallop.

"Look at me, princess," Jace says.

I hunch my shoulders and trace a knot in the wood with my fingertip.

"Seraphina, look at me."

"Stare at me; stop staring at me," I huff. "Make up your mind."

A chuckle drags my gaze to his. His expressions sends a burst of warmth to my chest.

"We don't have to do anything you don't want to," he says, his face turning serious. "We don't even have to do anything right now, if you're not ready."

"I want to." The words slip out faster than I intended. A little breathless. "But I'm scared."

Jace's smile softens. "You want to talk about it?"

I trace the knot, round and around.

"Will it hurt?"

He sips his cocoa. Licks cream from his top lip.

"It might, at first, but it shouldn't be bad. You could bleed a little, but no screaming, I promise."

"What about good screaming?"

Jace's eyes spark like a flame captured in copper.

"I can try for good screaming," he says, and my stomach gets all wobbly. He stretches his hand out, palm-up, on the table. "Take my hand and we'll go into the bedroom. Or don't and we'll stay, finish our hot chocolate, maybe curl up in front of the fire. Later, you can tell Harmony that I haven't availed you of your virginity despite my best efforts."

I stare at his smooth palm. Those slim, strong fingers.

"Your choice, princess," he says.

I take his hand.

The closer we get to the bedroom, the more my heart kicks. Jace's hand is warm and steady in mine. My knees wobble with each step. It's like when I first took him to my house— the bursts of adrenaline at his proximity. The tension. His exhilarating intensity.

Though he wouldn't have held my hand back then.

Is he nervous? Excited? Maybe I should feel his pulse to see if it's racing.

He squeezes my fingers. "Remember to breathe, princess."

I draw a shaky lungful. He rewards me with a smile over his shoulder, then we're in the bedroom and I forget what breathing is. My stomach churns. If I could sweat, my palms would be dripping.

Jace steers me to the centre of the room. I stare at his feet. His bare feet. As slim and lovely as the rest of him.

"You sure you're ready?" he says. "Your eyes are really wide."

I try to speak, but the words get tangled. I nod instead. I'm having some trouble coordinating the need to swallow and breathe. Gentle hands cup my face.

"We can stop any time. *Any* time. You just tell me, okay?"

"Okay," I whisper.

A thumb brushes my cheek and tickles across my lips. His

gaze captures mine, patient yet dark with a hunger that sends a tingle to the base of my spine.

"We'll take it slow." He steps backwards. "So slow, I'm going to stand here and not move until you tell me to, no matter what you do. Touch me, undress me. You're in charge."

"*I'm* in charge?" I splutter.

Why does that make it harder to breathe?

"You're in charge," he says.

He holds his hands at his sides, shoulders loose. His long legs, encased in black combats, are slightly spread. His top hugs his flat belly, his chest. Wet hair frames his cheekbones.

He's offering himself to me. Demon females are the offering. The Chosen.

He's always given me a choice.

"I can touch you wherever I want?" I say, as if he might change his mind.

"Wherever you want, princess."

"And *do* anything I want?"

He clears his throat. "Within reason."

Finally, a crack in his unruffled exterior. It soothes the mad flutter in my stomach.

I claim the step he took, and lift his hand. He stays perfectly still, though the chill of his scrutiny raises the hairs on the nape of my neck. I kiss his knuckles, his palm, his fingertips, marvelling at the softness of his skin and the roughness of callouses. His eyes are hot—molten bronze—but the rest of him is calm.

Maybe I want *him* to unravel, just a little.

I release his hand and he lowers it to his side. I grip the hem of his shirt. Inch it higher. Hip bones and the dip of his navel. Pebbled muscle. The splay of his ribs, his skin sliding silkily as he breathes. He moves only enough to let me pull the top over his head and arms. It drifts to the floor. This close, his sweet scent is heady, his bared torso smooth, uncharted territory. I peek at him from under my lashes. My breath chases goosebumps across his chest, and his nipples pucker to tiny buds. I place both hands on solid muscle. His heart slams against my palm. My eyes fly to his.

His mouth twitches. "I get nervous, too."

Emboldened, I splay my fingers, bending closer. The ghost of my breath caresses his skin and mine.

"You're safe with me," I say, and kiss one pert, perfect nipple.

He makes a noise in his throat. A shudder runs beneath my hands.

"Fuck," he sighs.

I flick my tongue across the bud and suck it into my mouth.

"Jesus fuck," Jace groans.

His hands clench, but he doesn't grab me or push me away. He tips his head back, his lashes fluttering shut.

"That feels good?" I say.

"Oh, princess, you have no idea." He chews on his lip. "No one's done this to me before."

Satisfaction buzzes through my veins. I want to explore every part of him. Every hollow and peak and plane. I want to touch him like no one else has, tease more sounds and shudders from his strong, male body. The power is intoxicating.

Why don't demons mate like this?

I lave his other nipple until he's wet from my mouth. Then I let my hands wander from the bunch of his abdomen to the line of his collarbones and the column of his throat. He shivers when I scrape my nails on the nape of his neck and stroke the delicate curve of his ears. Slipping around him, I knead the slabs of his shoulder blades and glide a finger down the channel of his spine. He has scars on his back—the mark of claws. I kiss each one, and he shivers again. I hesitate, my fingers light on his hips.

He did say I could touch him anywhere. Do what I wanted.

My hands palm his taut rump. Squeeze.

"Are you grabbing my arse, princess?"

There's a tremor in his husky voice. That loss of control sends an ache to the juncture of my thighs. I press myself to the warmth of his back and cuddle into him, my cheek cushioned between his shoulder blades. My wings stir the air. My hands grip his stomach, his chest. He's so smooth. So solid. His heart thuds against my palm.

My nerves have vanished. I'm fascinated. Bewitched. Completely safe with him.

My fingertips graze the waistband of his combats. A swirl of desire leaves me breathless, almost dizzy. I pop the button, and his heart skips under my ear.

"You're not supposed to be good at this," he grinds out.

"Good at what?"

"Torturing me."

I slide the zipper of his combats down, the metal teeth scraping as they part.

"Is that what I'm doing?" I breathe against his spine.

A sigh gusts from him. "God, yes."

"Do you want me to stop?"

"Hell, no."

I remain pressed to his back, questing with only the touch of my hands. There's another layer of material beneath his combats. Something elasticated. I slip underneath to the core of him. To heat and velvet muscle. His guttural noise makes my stomach quiver. His heart rate triples, though my fingers are still. He's lean and long. Ready to mate.

"You're shaking, Jace."

"I know."

His voice. So husky. So desperate. My inscrutable Diviner stripped raw.

I push the rest of his clothes down his legs. He's so wonderfully proportioned—wide shoulders, the slope of his back, the swell of his buttocks, the dip of his flanks. I circle him slowly, my heart bouncing between my gut and my throat. I'm biting my lip.

His head is bowed, his breathing ragged. He lifts his gaze, and all my air locks in my chest.

He's beautiful. Every part of him is beautiful, not scary.

And he's definitely not shy.

"Move, Jace," I say and my voice is hoarse. "I need you to move."

29

Jace moves before the last word has fallen from my lips. His mouth, his body, collides with mine and I topple onto the bed beneath a naked Diviner. He swallows my gasp, kissing me without mercy. Unrestrained. Ravenous. His tongue finds mine, and electricity sizzles to my toes as if I've taken a gulp of his beatha. His hands skate up my sides, tangle in my hair, press my hands to the mattress, fingers entwined and gripping frantically. The weight of him between my thighs makes me giddy, grinding the already damp material of my leggings against my core. A hollow ache blooms in the pit of my stomach.

"Christ," Jace pants, easing away and resting his forehead on mine. "Give me a minute."

This close, his pupils are dilated and dark, surrounded by a circlet of gold-flecked bronze. A tremor transfers through our bound hands, a little from us both, but his breathing slows. His lips graze mine—teasing, seeking. A stroke of his tongue to coax me open. The tender kisses melt me into a single, swollen pulse. Tension curls in my belly, demanding release. A whine slips from my throat.

"You need something, princess?" Jace smirks between devastating glides of his mouth.

"Jace…"

His lips steal my words, not that I can articulate anything except his name.

"Jace…"

The second is imploring. Desperate.

"You need me?" he says.

I nod too fast, sobbing against his mouth. "Yes. I need you."

"So innocent yet so fucking eager," he growls.

A fervent kiss ignites rather than soothes. My skin sings. Jace shoves up onto his knees, pushing my top high to bare my midriff. His fingers hesitate on the flesh above my hip.

"There's your tattoo," he whispers.

A thumb traces the heart in the centre, the halo above, and the bat wings curled protectively. Two forked tails entwine from the bottom, like the tails of the dragons on my favourite mug. I squirm at the light touch, my thighs caging Jace where he kneels, naked and unperturbed.

I'm clothed yet totally exposed.

My top ruffles beneath my breasts as Jace lifts it further. The material catches on my wings and refuses to slide off.

"How attached are you to this top?" He gives it an experimental tug.

"Not attached—"

With a rip, he tears the material and tosses it in a flutter of powder blue, revealing my upper body to his darkening gaze. My nipples pucker, my skin awash with goosebumps under the intensity of his stare. I grip the sheets to keep from covering myself, but my cheeks blaze and betray me.

I'm definitely the shy one.

Strong fingers curl in the waistband of my leggings, scorching the sensitive flesh of my lower stomach. Jace's focus drifts from the pulse jumping in my abdomen, slower past my breasts rising and falling with my rapid breaths, to my face where I'm almost certain my eyes are wider than when we started. Heat wars with cold, leaving me hot and shivering.

"You still want to go further?" he says, his voice rough.

I manage a single nod, up and down.

"Going to need you to articulate it this time, princess."

"*Yes,*" I hiss a little wildly, and he grins.

While I'm still recovering, he shuffles backwards and pulls my leggings with him. I squeeze my thighs together, but gentle hands tease them apart.

And Jace becomes the only male to look upon my soft and secret places.

Flames erupt beneath my skin—flames of anxiety, of longing, of affection. Anticipation and impatience.

Should I tell him I'm honoured? Because I am. The scripted words crowd my mouth and dissolve to nothing under Jace's awe-struck gaze. His eyes meet mine.

"Christ, princess," he says. "You slay me."

He's the demon slayer. I'm just a barista, sprawled on my back, legs akimbo, my wings tangled in my hair, the tips fluttering as quickly as my pulse.

Jace leans his lithe body over me, forearms framing my head, and kisses me until my heart thuds faster than before, though it seems impossible. His thighs nudge mine wider and only then can I feel the fine quiver running through him. His lips buss my cheek and suckle my earlobe, trailing down my throat to the mound of my breast. His hot mouth closes over my nipple after a second's pause. I gasp as a storm of heat boils through my gut to the slick cleft between my legs.

"Feels good, doesn't it?"

"Jace," I pant. "Jace…"

He nuzzles my belly, my tattoo, and circles his nose around a hipbone. His hair flops across his forehead and tickles in his wake.

"Remember what humans like to do with their mouths?" he says.

I frown. Understanding draws another gasp from me.

"You can't!" I squeak.

His wicked smirk tells me he can. And he's about to.

Hot breath ghosts through the dark down at my apex. My thighs tense, wanting to slam shut and hide.

But I've been hiding my whole life.

Jace pins me with his gaze. He tilts his chin and places a gentle kiss on the peak of flesh between my legs. Every muscle jolts rigid. Heat and tingles flare outwards like a detonation. My eyes roll, my spine bowed. When Jace withdraws, I go limp, throbbing and dazed and aching for more. He cocks a brow.

"Do that again," I plead.

He grins and lowers his head. My breath rushes south with all of my blood. Jace kisses the core of my body as if he's kissing my mouth—nibbling, sucking, licking through delicate folds to swirl around my wet peak. Garbled noises flop from my lips. Nonsense entreaties. My stomach clenches, everything tight and heavy. Jace dips his tongue inside me. I think I shout his name, but I'm lost to the glorious burn of release and uncontrollable squirming. My lashes flutter, offering glimpses of the room, Jace on his knees, his lips glistening and full.

"And that's good screaming," he says, his smile tender.

While I lie completely boneless, he opens the drawer of the

bedside cabinet. Something crinkles. A pink and silver square appears in his fingers. He tears it open and places a disc of material over the flushed head of his sex. He smooths it down his erection, masking his tight and shining flesh. I smell a hint of rubber, like the pencil erasers we used back in the classroom.

"What is that?" I whisper, my mouth dry from the sight of him.

All that hard and straining length has to go somewhere.

"A condom," he says. "It stops you getting pregnant. If I could even get you pregnant."

"Humans get to choose if they want to fall pregnant?"

"Humans get to choose a lot of things."

I manage to shove up on one, quivering elbow. My fingers reach for him, but he catches my wrist.

"I'm hanging on by a thread here, princess," he husks. "Touch me and it'll all be over."

I realise I've been staring at his organ since he sent me reeling from the press of his mouth. My gaze lifts. Sweat dews his skin, his hair sticking to his forehead. His eyes are tormented. Drowning. His body twitches to the thud of his pulse.

I recall snippets of conversation. Ellie's mockery.

Jace hasn't mated since his epilepsy. For two years. Demon males can mate almost daily, depending on the fertility cycles of their Chosen, though females mate once a month.

How lonely Jace must have been.

I lower myself back to the bed.

"If it gets too much, tell me to stop," he says, utterly sincere despite the need hardening his body and trembling in each word.

Emotions tangle in my throat.

Two years without the touch of a female, yet he would stop, deny himself what he must ache for, if I ask.

He leans over and kisses me, distracting me from the sting of tears. I taste myself on his lips—metal and musk.

What does he taste like? Electric, like his mouth?

He trails said mouth along my cheekbone. Ragged breaths tickle my ear. The head of his sex parts the lips of my cleft, but goes no further. I gnaw on my lip. My harsh breaths join his. I stare at the ceiling, and my heart slams against my ribs. Effort shudders through Jace. I can practically hear his pulse, never mind mine.

"Princess," he says in my ear, deep and low, "Rose wasn't wrong."

My forehead crinkles, though I'm one thrust away from deflowerment.

Rose wasn't wrong? Rose... *wasn't* wrong.

My breath catches.

But that means...

Jace Mulholland, rebel Diviner and very much *not* a deranged abuser of women, whispers, "I fucking love you, princess," and sinks his body into mine.

There's pain—sharp. A tearing. Panic bubbles in my chest, bidding me to shove and claw at the weight on top of me. Images of Avzameth and screams and blood slice at my mind. I tense, scorching hot, the word on my lips. Jace sheaths himself fully, settled in the cradle of my thighs, and gives a tiny whimper of pure ecstasy. The noise captivates me, and I forget what I was going to say.

Jace loves me. I'm a monster—a demon—but he *loves* me. And this is how humans show their love.

Our hearts thunder together, as if struggling to reach each other through flesh and bone. Jace stays perfectly still. The sharp pain fades to a burning stretch. An aching fullness. I suck in a breath that wobbles all the way to my chest. Jace props himself up on trembling arms, not moving where his groin is pressed to mine. His eyes are feral and bright, on the cusp of madness.

He licks his lips. Clears his throat. "You okay?"

"Yes, but…" Another wobbling breath. "You're so *big*."

He bows his head, but I glimpse a flash of relief on his face, and something else. Triumph. Elation. Wonder. He lifts his chin and kisses me on the lips, as soft and tender as he kissed between my legs. A ghost of remembered pleasure chases the last of the pain, replacing it with another ache. An ache for him to move.

"That's right, princess," he purrs. "Keep telling me how big I am."

His hips flex. The stroke of his flesh, where no one has ever touched, draws a gasp from my throat.

"I feel you so deep," I babble. "It's… amazing."

Jace looks like he's been zapped between the eyes with electricity. His mouth claims mine in a frantic kiss. My arms wrap around him, palms cupping his shoulder blades, desperate to be closer, though he's the closest anyone has ever been. He surges between my thighs. My hips match him, meet him, and he moans on the apex of each thrust. The sound of him unravelling pools heat between my legs, helped by the glorious friction of all that hardness gliding in and out. I tense muscles I never knew I had, and Jace curses—pleads—every word spilling into my mouth to expand in my stomach, and throb and tighten, threatening to burst.

And I do. I come apart in a rush of exquisite heat and tension. Jace plunges once more. And again, hard, head tossed back, every muscle strained and singing. He shouts my name—Seraphina. Shouts it like an answered prayer. Then he collapses on top of me, his lovely body shivering and slick and spent. Ragged breaths puff across my scalp. His heartbeat shakes his frame, only a little faster than mine. I kiss the curve of his shoulder. My fingers dip into the channel of his spine and play there.

"Did I hurt you?" he mumbles into the covers.

"It hurt at first, but… I need to thank Harmony."

Jace snorts a laugh. "What for?"

"She always said she'd set me up and I'd be thanking her for the rest of my life. I really, *really* need to thank her."

Jace shoves onto his elbows, and grins. The movement, not so careful this time, reminds us that he's still buried inside me. His grin turns to a shudder, his eyes fluttering shut. I writhe at his reaction, little aftershocks of pleasure zinging out from where we're joined.

"Jesus Christ, stop that," he says, but not like he's angry. More like I'm torturing him in the best way. He heaves a breath. Another. "She didn't exactly set us up."

"She forced me to talk to you, after the bridge. I would've avoided you otherwise." I stretch my arm and brush a strand of hair back from his face. It swings forward again into dazed and sated bronze eyes. "Maybe things would've gone different with Avzameth. Maybe you would've used me against him."

Jace captures my hand and kisses my knuckles. "Then I should thank her, too."

He slips from my body slow and gentle, but I still wince. There's a streak of garnet on the condom.

"Bleeding a little your first time is normal," he says before I can panic. "How you feeling?"

"Sore. *Good* sore." I yawn. "And tired."

Smiling, Jace slides the condom free and ties a knot in the end, dropping it off the side of the bed. He flops on his front, curls his hand around my hip and tucks me into his side. His breaths fan across my cheek. I shut my eyes and doze, savouring the ache between my legs, the scent of Jace on my skin.

Rain patters against the window, the sound comforting in the warmth of the bedroom. The afternoon trickles away.

I peek at Jace, expecting him to be asleep. The one eye not smothered in the pillow is watching me, as if memorising my face.

"Jace?" At his lazy, "Hmm?" I smirk and say, "You're staring at me."

His mouth twitches. "Can you blame me, princess?"

His fingers trace circles on my flank. An innocent caress, if we weren't both naked. The touch awakens a clench of need deep in my gut. I wriggle, and press my thighs together, a languid throb starting between them. Jace's fingers pause. His head comes up.

"Are you horny again?" he says, incredulous. "I thought you were sore."

"I don't have to *stay* sore."

He blinks at me. A slow, hungry grin stretches his lips.

"I knew you were going to be trouble," he growls.

He rolls onto his back and pulls me on top of him.

I'm straddling a male. A male who smells of sex and cloves and wickedly sweet delights.

"Take what you need from me, princess," Jace says. His voice deepens. "Then take what you need from me."

My wings flare. "You want to mate like this? With me on top?"

A minute passes, his focus on my spread wings before it swoops over my shoulder to follow the hair falling to my breasts.

"Christ, yes," he finally says. "I've dreamed about it."

Jace has dreamed about me?

I squirm on his thighs. He's stiff and ready, lying straight and proud on his flat belly. He holds out another of the square foil packets, though he has to wave it in front of my nose until I notice.

"Put this on first."

Shakily, I tear the wrapper like he did. The condom is a slippery circle of tight elastic with a rounded tip. I balance it lightly on the crown of his penis. He gives me a fond smile and stills my fumbling fingers, flipping the condom over and pinching the rounded end. His hand guides mine, rolling the material downwards over scorching flesh and velvet muscle. He captures my fingers before I can take his shaft in an experimental fist.

"The first time hasn't quite dulled the ache as much as I thought, princess," he says.

"The ache?"

"The ache to come immediately all over your beautiful skin."

The need is a kick in the gut. A flare of heat in my cheeks and between my legs. Jace encourages me higher onto my knees, spread above him—wings, thighs.

"Heal yourself, princess." He cocks his head, his hair sliding on the pillow. "Could you actually heal yourself right back to being a virgin?"

My eyes widen. "I don't know. Maybe?"

"Yeah, let's not do that. Just the soreness. Nothing else."

I sip his beatha and his energy sizzles to my core, leaving goosebumps in its wake. My eyes flutter shut, my head dropping back on a sigh, a reminder of when I first tasted him in my kitchen—the heady rush. Like being drunk. My heart tremors in the flow of it, both memory and reality.

Strong fingers grip my waist. Jace slides between my legs while the electric tingle of him is still on my tongue. The feel of his beatha inside me, his body inside me, is almost too intense. Too perfect. It pulls an animalistic sound from my mouth.

"You're going to make me embarrass myself, princess," Jace

hisses through his teeth.

His hands direct my hips, rocking me against him, gliding me along that hard length. The angle is deep, deeper than before, and it's fantastic. I don't realise I've taken command until Jace curses, "Sweet-fucking-Jesus."

His head is tossed back on the pillow, the cords in his throat straining. Black lashes flutter over half-moons of bronze. He's biting his lip. Not just the inside, like he does when he's concentrating, but full-on teeth in plump flesh. He's stretched out beneath me. At my mercy. His skin flushed and glowing. Frantic hips buck to meet mine.

No demon female has ever seen a male like this. Demon females do not go on top. And they definitely do *not* mate twice in one day.

My muscles quiver with delicious effort. Jace's fingers tighten on my hips, grinding me against him. Drilling deep.

The whine in my throat spills into startled words. "Jace! I'm going to—"

"Me, too," he groans, "in about two fucking seconds."

With another thrust, I am undone. Our cries fill the rain-darkened bedroom. Jace twitches inside where our bodies are joined, and I clench around him. The swell of pleasure leaves me weak. Dizzily euphoric. I slump on top of a hot and panting Jace, my face buried in his neck.

I kiss the happy throb of his pulse, and whisper, "I fucking love you, too."

I'm already grinning when Harmony answers her phone with a fond, "Hey, sweetie, you're calling late tonight."

She gets sweary when I tell her about our latest run-in with Rose and Ellie, but calms after a couple of assurances that Jace and I are both unhurt. I squash my wings further against the headboard, my knees tucked to my chest, Jace sprawled beside me. My wet hair flops over my shoulders, dampening the cotton of my pyjama top.

"You didn't ask me the question," I say when Harmony finally stops grumbling about narrow-minded, arsehole Diviners who deserve a swift punch in the throat.

"Question? What quest—"

She sucks in a breath so hard, I'm surprised she doesn't swallow her phone. Her air whooshes into the speaker in a rush of words.

"Haveyoulostyourvirginityyet?"

"Lost," I say, grinning wider. "Taken. Poof—gone."

"Seraphina van Ize, you beautiful little hussy!" she squeals. "Give me all the details."

"No details," Jace mutters, his face buried in the pillow.

My eyes trace from the lovely dip of his bare back to where the sheet covers his equally lovely rump.

He staggered to the bed after our shower and has been semi-comatose ever since.

The satisfaction of tiring him out—Jace, a skilled warrior and a Diviner with more-than-human stamina—blooms warmth in my chest. I've been smiling for the last ten minutes. Can't seem to stop.

"He was amazing," I whisper into the phone.

Jace grunts. "Fine. Some details are okay."

His head tilts, a half-smile curving from the pillow. One smug and sleepy eye watches me through the spill of his damp hair.

I wait for Harmony's happy noises to abate.

"He was perfect. And gentle. We did it twice."

"*Twice!*" Harmony shrieks.

"Then I put him in my mouth in the shower. He really liked that."

"Christ, princess." Jace ducks his face into the pillow once more.

"You gave him a blowjob?" Harmony says, her awed voice now high enough to shatter crystal.

"Is that what it's called? Was I supposed to blow on it?"

At Harmony's cackle, I direct the question to Jace. His shoulders hunch towards his ears.

"Hang up now, princess," he groans.

Even if I didn't blow on it, the result speaks for itself.

The thought had been tumbling around in my brain ever since Ellie accused me of liking his cock in my mouth. I've always been a curious soul.

After we mated for the second time, I slid out of bed and sashayed to the en-suite, buck naked and unabashed, a new and exciting confidence simmering under my skin. I paused on the threshold, glancing over my shoulder at Jace still panting on the bed.

"This is me asking you nicely," I said.

Under his shocked gaze, I stepped into the bathroom. He scrabbled to join me and my shyness returned in the intimacy of the shower, his body so close and wreathed in steam. But watching him wash himself—such a private, secret act—bolstered my courage. Or maybe it was the sight of his long, lean muscles caressed by bubbles and water. I dropped to my knees to explore the one place I hadn't properly touched with my hands or my mouth. His stunned expression and the catch in his throat sent a spear of tenderness through my chest.

I fumbled at first. Choked and gagged a few times since all that hard and straining length still had to go somewhere. Jace struggled to focus with his usual intensity, his eyes dazed and half-lidded, his lean frame sagged against the tile. I knew I was getting the hang of it when his soft and patient guidance turned to a frantic, "Jesus god, princess, yes—*keepdoingthat.*"

My arousal danced with his, spurred by the quiver of his thighs beneath my palms, the desperate grip of his hands in my hair, his husky cry when I swirled my tongue around his firm head and the slit at his crown. My perfect warrior unravelled from the glide of my mouth. The power was intoxicating. He managed a breathless, "I'm gonna come," a second before hot liquid spurted into my mouth.

He tasted as sweet as his scent.

"I hope he knows he's one lucky bastard," Harmony giggles in my ear, dispelling my memory of the shower, but not the desire sparking in my stomach.

"He knows," Jace mumbles into the pillow.

My grin flares again. "He says he knows. You should see

him—he's all tuckered out. It's so cute."

His head comes up. "It's not cute. And I'm not tired—I'm basking after thoroughly fucking my girlfriend."

"Aww, he called you his girlfriend," Harmony says, "that *is* cute."

"Christ's sake," Jace huffs.

He goes to throw himself face down, but halts mid-motion, his gaze narrowing on me and heating my already flushed skin. It's like he can read my mind, every lustful thought.

"Or maybe I need to be a little more thorough," he growls in his dangerously sexy voice. "Say goodbye to Harmony, princess."

He shoves onto his hands and knees. The sheet slides low to bare the smooth line of his flank and the delectable curve of his rump. Anticipation swoops in my belly.

I gulp. "I think we're going to mate again."

"*Again?*" Harmony hoots. "Damn, sweetie, he's a keeper. Ask him if he has a brother."

Jace wraps his fingers around my ankles. "Hang up the phone."

"He's an only child," I tell Harmony, and she makes a disappointed sound.

Jace tugs and I'm suddenly underneath him, pinned by his weight. His erection nestles at the apex of my thighs. My yelp of surprise dissolves to a moan when he flexes his hips, teasing his crown across my opening.

"Hang *up,* princess," he purrs into my throat.

I stutter a farewell to a laughing Harmony. My phone tumbles from tingling fingers. Jace spreads my thighs and proves for the third—or fourth—time why he will always be better than any demon male.

32

My breath fogs white and drifts towards the unmarred sky. The sun, barely cresting the hills, sparkles on frost and the loch we've been circling for the past hour. Pinewoods cover both sides of the wide valley. Crossbills twitter from the needled branches, unperturbed by the cold. I pick my way through the hummocks of heather, soothed by the gentle lap of water from the shore and the earthy scent of peat. Jace follows a step behind, tense and alert, his eyes scanning the landscape. Every now and then, the prickle of his gaze brushes goosebumps down my nape before his vigilance returns to the peaks and troughs.

No more getting ambushed by Rose and Ellie, or any of the other Diviners.

My boots crunch on the pebbles surrounding the loch, the water deep and dark. A fish jumps with a glimpse of silver, and a splash.

We collapsed into sleep last night, naked and exhausted, my muscles singing and spent from Jace's attention. His stamina puts a demon male's to shame, not to mention his focus on my pleasure before he chases his own. Though he's never far behind.

I woke up completely on top of him this morning, as I do

212

every morning. Except this time, instead of easing away and getting out of bed, his hands cupped my rump and pressed me harder against his erection, his heart speeding under my ear. His hips flexed and the crown of his penis slid inside me. One inch. Two. He cursed and stopped moving, strain showing in the pale column of his neck and the line of his jaw, shadowed and scratchy with stubble.

"I really want to fuck you bare, princess," he said through gritted teeth, "but I don't think either of us is ready for pregnancy."

He claimed another inch despite his words, a pained yet pleading noise slipping from his throat. I clenched around him at the sight of his shattering control.

He hissed out a breath. "Christ. We can't do this. We may never be able to do this. Hormonal birth control might not work on you." Another tortured hiss. "Okay, we have to stop. Let me get a condom."

His hands slid from my rump to ease me away.

"Wait," I said.

His fingers paused on my hips. His pulse thudded in the hollow between his collarbones and in the organ so temptingly sheathed inside me. His eyes were dilated, wild.

I loved seeing him like that—half-crazed with arousal, desperate for me. Vulnerable and exposed.

My Diviner is as insatiable as I am, now that I know mating feels wonderful. When it's done right.

"I'm at the least fertile part of my cycle," I said. "Keeping track is a habit."

We were taught from a young age to chart our ovulation cycle in the clan. When your only purpose is to breed, knowing your most fertile window is essential.

Jace shook his head. "Still too risky."

I tilted my pelvis, driving him deeper. My head fell back on a sigh at the pleasant ache and stretch. Tension vibrated through his hands on my waist.

"Jesus fuck, princess, what are you doing?"

"I'm terrified of getting pregnant, Jace. Do you think I'd continue if I thought it was a possibility?" I rolled my hips again. "But I want nothing between us. I want to feel you spill yourself inside me. I want all of you inside me."

Jace seated me fully on his length, and we both groaned.

"You have me, princess," he said. "You have every part of me."

Another splash and ripple tug me from pleasant thoughts of Jace's mating prowess. Though it must be said that the aftermath of sex without a condom was a lot stickier than I expected. But no less fun.

The pinewoods and heather recede to reveal a cliff stippled with grass and glossy ferns, a large stone visible at the top where the trees continue on a gentler slope to a plateau. Jace bumps into my back, shunting me forward a couple of steps before his hands grasp my upper arms to steady me. Only then do I realise I've stopped.

"What is it?" he says, his voice low and dangerous.

I point a shaky finger towards the cliff.

"Something you recognise?"

"I think... I think it's my favourite viewpoint. I'd come here to watch the sunset. I brought Father Benjamin here." I look out over the water, but nothing else seems familiar... from this angle at least. "If I'm right, the clan is just in those woods."

A shiver transfers from me to Jace. His fingers give a squeeze of reassurance.

"Come on," he says gently. "Time to go introduce me to your family."

He crunches across the pebbled shore to the base of the cliff, and I scrabble in his wake.

"Jace," I say breathlessly, "are you sure—"

"Yes, princess, I'm sure."

Stubborn, honourable male.

I'm so glad he's here.

I crane my neck, the edge of the cliff now framed against the sky. Nothing happens when I focus and centre myself. No streaking colours. No hint of vertigo. My pulse skips.

I shake my head in disbelief. "This is it. It's really it. I can't teleport."

Jace's mouth ticks up. "Home, sweet home."

"I could fly up. Scope it out. I won't be able to carry you, though."

"Let's just do this the human way, princess. We stick together."

The steepness of the climb and the slamming of my heart in my ears and throat distract me from worrying about my imminent reunion and how the clan will react to Jace. How I can hope to keep him safe, especially if I still can't teleport to within the clan's boundaries. My hiking boots struggle to find purchase on the rocks, thin mud, and slippery moss. I dig my hands into the muck for leverage and haul myself upwards using the orange-tinted trunks of the pine trees. My air saws in and out of my chest, sucking strands of hair into my mouth, then sticking them to my cheeks when I puff out, the cold forgotten. Jace fares little better. I follow his floundering steps and muttered curses with a smile.

It takes an hour to crest the top of the cliff. We reach it

panting, dishevelled, and filthy. I plant my hands on my knees and focus on breathing, my wings flexing as if that will help. Jace paces in a tight circle, his chest heaving. I watch his boots pass in and out of my eye line.

"I'm glad we've reached the demon horde part of this adventure," he says between breaths. "I'm done with these hills."

I straighten, and scrub the hair from my face. A worn stone hulks near the edge of the cliff, the view stretching over the placid loch to the horizon of mountaintops and trees.

I remember sitting here with Father Benjamin when he gave me his rosary and told me about the devil. He described a demon and called it monstrous.

Then we slaughtered him.

"I'm not sure I'm ready for the horde," I say quietly.

"I won't let them hurt you, princess."

My turn to pace. "You're a great warrior, Jace, but if things go wrong, we're outnumbered."

He captures my wrist and eases me to a stop. "Then let's see what our options are. Can you teleport yet?"

Colours blur. A swoop of dizziness. I blink at Jace from the edge of the trees, his hand still held out and fingers curled where he gripped my arm. He crosses the plateau of stone in five long strides.

"What about to the base of the cliff?"

I concentrate, but nothing happens.

"Okay, so whatever wards they're using keep you from teleporting across the clan boundary, but not from moving freely either inside or outside. If we get into trouble, you can take us to the edge of the territory, then we cross it and you teleport us to the cottage. We're not trapped here."

I nod, my eyes on the ground. He tilts my chin until I meet his bronze gaze.

"We don't have to do this today. Not if you're scared."

"Don't you ever get scared?"

He gives me a tender smile. "Course I get scared."

"Are you scared now?"

"Nervous maybe. Mostly curious."

"I'm less scared with you here," I say shyly.

He kisses me; a quick press of lips. "I love you, too, princess."

I take a deep breath. "Let's do this. Now. Today. The longer we wait, the more likely the Diviners—the other Diviners—will find them. If they've not already."

"They've not." Jace's smile turns grim. "There would be smoke. And no birdsong."

A jay shrieks from the trees to punctuate his words. We enter the shade of the pine forest, our boots hushed on the carpet of needles. Jace keeps a hand in his jacket pocket, gripping at least one knife. No doubt he has three or more stashed somewhere on his long, lean frame.

We follow the trail worn by footprints and scattered with pine cones. Ferns brush our legs. The jay cackles and darts between the branches in a streak of mauve, its rump flashing white. Anticipation rushes through my blood, a tiny thread of excitement swirling around the fear and anxiety.

It's been so long since I've seen my family. Excluding Avzameth. I plan to talk to Teacher first. Éabha. Gather the other females to spread the word of horrific births, beatha, and the advancing Diviners. If I can get their support, it'll give me a stronger position when we approach the elders to negotiate fundamental changes to our way of life.

I just hope they don't yet know we're here.

A figure steps from behind a trunk to block the narrow path. I swallow a gasp. Silver wings and hair—longer now, almost to his lower back—spines on his shoulders. Jace tenses, his arm ready to sweep me behind him. The figure hisses, no doubt at the icy prickle of Jace's attention. Topaz eyes, dark with betrayal, fix on me.

"Seraphina," Felecior says, "what have you done?"

<h1 style="text-align:center">33</h1>

I grip Jace's arm, the sleeve of his jacket gritty with mud, his muscles rigid beneath. His other hand stays in his pocket, no sight of his Diviner blade yet, though his posture is tense and ready to fight. Felecior bares his teeth at him, eyes blazing with hate and fury, wings arched, legs bent to spring.

"Felecior, wait," I say, my voice as shaky as when we first spoke in the amphitheatre. When he nearly selected me as his Chosen before Avzameth shouldered him out of the way.

Would things have been different if I had been Felecior's Chosen? Less fear of the mating ceremony, perhaps, but I would still have watched Deirdre die. I would still have discovered the lies. Witnessed Father Benjamin's slaughter.

"We're not here to hurt anyone," I say a little steadier. "We just need you to listen."

"Release her now, Diviner, and I shall grant you a quick death," Felecior snarls, ignoring me.

It doesn't bode well.

"She's here of her own free will," Jace says, his voice calm but full of the husky menace I heard on the bridge when he tried to kill me. "And she will leave of her own free will. With me. All you have to do is listen."

"All you have to do is *die*," Felecior spits.

He leaps at Jace, dropping his shoulder to aim his spines for Jace's chest. I dodge around Jace's protective arm and plant myself in front of him, my wings flared, hands raised. Felecior flaps frantically and skids to a halt, his clawed feet scouring deep furrows in the soil and moss. He dances backwards a few steps.

Not touching a female—beyond the mating ceremony, of course—is too ingrained for him to breach that sacred decree.

A tightness in my gut eases. He won't hurt me. My clan won't hurt me. I'm too precious, even if it's only for my function as a breeder, and healer.

Jace, on the other hand—they would love to hurt.

"Jesus Christ, princess, are you trying to give me a heart attack?" he mutters, his fingers curling in the back of my jacket.

Felecior glares over my head at Jace. "What have you done to her? Whatever pain you inflicted to force her betrayal shall be carved on your flesh a thousandfold."

"Great," Jace sighs. "He listens as well as Rose and Ellie."

"Step away from him, Seraphina. He will not dare to hurt you further unless he wants an agonising death."

"Felecior, he hasn't hurt me. He's not going to—"

"You have three seconds to release her, Diviner, before I call the rest of our warriors and we tear you limb from limb."

"Shut *up*, Felecior, and *listen!*" I yell.

Felecior's eyes widen and finally rest on me. The echo of my shout fades among the pine trees. Jace snorts quietly, probably at Felecior's dumbfounded expression, but otherwise stays silent. I swallow my pulse and gather my thoughts.

I now understand Jace's increasing frustration whenever he tried to get through to Rose and Ellie. I pray we're more successful with my family.

"We're not here to hurt anyone," I say, patient and slow. "We're here to help you. And to warn you. There are other Diviners searching for the clan. They know it's located near Inverie—"

Felecior's hot gaze snaps to Jace. He flexes his claws. "Did you torture her for this information, you human scum? I will rip—"

"*Felecior…*" I growl.

He shuts his mouth, but his chest rumbles his displeasure. His wings flick in annoyance before settling against his back.

"Jace is helping me." I ignore Felecior's scoff. "We need to talk to the elders. Not just about the Diviners, but about things that could save all of us. Change everything. We have to work together."

"Congratulations, Diviner," Felecior says, once more ignoring me in favour of glowering at Jace, "you've found a new and distasteful way to attack us. You will suffer until your last breath for brainwashing one of our females."

"The only brainwashing is the lies the elders tell to keep the females docile and get them to do whatever they're told without question," I say hotly.

"Yet you always asked questions," a male says from behind Felecior. "It's lovely to have you returned to us unharmed, Seraphina."

Two elders approach through the trees, dressed in loose cotton, their feet bare. The two elders who witnessed Deirdre's horrific death—Zev and Kalyan. Their elliptical pupils flick from me to Jace. Their faces are craggier, the humps on their shoulders distorting the line of their clothes.

Jace's hand tightens on the back of my jacket. "She's not

staying. This is a courtesy call."

"As if we'd let you leave with one of our treasured females," Zev says. The elder who'd sired Deirdre and watched her die. Did he treasure her then?

"As if we'd let you leave at all, *Diviner*," Felecior sneers.

"You will listen to us *and* you will let us leave because we're trying to help you," I say, my voice rising.

"Seraphina, stop this foolishness," Kalyan barks. "You had your rebellion when you ran away, but now it's time to do your duty."

A calculated gleam lights Zev's eye. "Perhaps we can overlook your behaviour and consider the Diviner a gift. His beatha will sustain the clan for months."

"Like hell it will," Jace bristles.

Felecior licks his teeth and scans Jace from head to toe, though much of his body is hidden by mine. "With Avzameth presumed fallen, the honour of cutting out your heart falls to me."

The males watch Jace with hungry eyes. My stomach swoops into my mucky hiking boots.

"Princess," he whispers, "there are demons behind us."

My heart joins my stomach in my shoes.

He must feel the heat of their gaze on his back. We're surrounded, all of them intent on slaughtering Jace and drinking his energy. Just like Father Benjamin.

Except I'm not the naive and terrified Seraphina of six years ago.

I pivot into Jace, his hand still fisted in my jacket. My arms wrap around him, my head on his chest. His heart beats once, twice, against my ear, rapid and strong.

Amidst the yells of my brethren, I teleport us away.

34

I transport to a clearing on the opposite side of the clan territory, beyond the rugged peak of a hill. Pines tower over us, filling the space with gloom and shadow. Yellowed stems bow under the weight of dew, the rest of the vegetation brown and withered.

I loved to come here in the summer and lie in the grass, breathing the scent of wildflowers and contemplating the perfect blue circle of sky. It's a little like the amphitheatre, but without the dread and killing.

Jace staggers a step, though he's getting better each time we teleport. Less disorientated.

"That went about as well as expected," he says. He rubs his eyes, then grasps my shoulders and searches my face. "You okay?"

My mouth twitches. "Part of me was hoping it would be different. That I could gloat at how rational and forgiving demons are compared to you Diviners."

"Looks like you and I are the only rational and forgiving ones," he chuckles.

He pulls me into a hug. I unzip his jacket and snuggle into the warmth and sweet, fruity scent of him. The thud of his heart soothes the anxiety churning in my belly.

"How far away are we?" His voice rumbles under my ear.

"A thirty-minute walk or ten-minute flight. Do you think they know we're still here?"

"I suspect they have wards either tied to you, Diviners, or anything non-demon. Maybe all three."

"Do you want to leave?"

His arms squeeze me against him. "Shouldn't I be asking you that?"

"You're the one they're threatening with bodily harm." I ease back enough to look up into his face. "Maybe we should let them cool down a bit."

"I'll do whatever you want, princess."

I trace a pattern on his chest with my fingertip. "What if they never listen, no matter how many times we try?"

"Then we did our best, but there was nothing else we could have done." He captures my finger and kisses it, his smile sad. "Some people don't want to be saved."

I swallow the burn of tears, and nod. "Can we try once more today? Maybe it'll go better if I get Teacher's attention, like we planned."

"Sure. It's only fair I get to be the focus of all the hate this time." He raises a sardonic brow, and I manage a laugh. "How many demons in your clan can fly?"

"Only Felecior. Unless another male has joined us from a different clan while I've been absent."

"Take us to the roof of the highest building. I can handle Fleecy."

"Did I tell you your fight with Avzameth was the most impressive battle I've ever seen?"

Jace smirks. "No, princess, I don't believe you did."

His lips find mine for a frantic kiss. I grip his top, and his heart beats hard against my fingers.

"Brace yourself," I whisper into his mouth.

He makes a noise low in his throat. "It never helps."

I teleport to the roof of the birthing-cum-death hospital.

"Fuck," Jace sighs, blinking fast, but managing not to stagger, his arms still wrapped around me. "How many have you got left in the tank?"

"Once without taking some of your beatha, and I don't want to risk that while we're surrounded."

"As much as it pains me to admit it, your teleportation is more valuable than my fighting skills in this situation. Drink some now before they realise we're here."

We hunker next to the curved ventilation duct I crawled through to witness Deirdre's awful death. Frost sparkles on the roof, slowly melting in the sun.

If only I could have saved her.

Jace touches his cold lips to mine. I sip his energy, addicted to the electric chill of it. The icy zap arrows straight to my heart. I pull back and study his perfect face. Warm, bronze eyes. Sharp cheekbones. A streak of mud in his hair.

His mouth tics up. "What're you thinking, princess?"

"I'd rather be back in the cottage." I give him my own wicked smile. "Underneath you."

It seems relinquishing my virginity has gifted me some confidence.

"Fucking hell. I didn't need the incentive, but now we definitely have to hurry this along." He tugs me upright, spins me around, and slaps me on the rump. "Get to it."

A wash of nerves smothers my giggle as I stagger to the edge of the flat, wooden roof. Tall pines circle the compound and cast shadows across the grass. None of my brethren scamper in the spaces between buildings. Everyone but the males and elders would have been ferried to the bunker as soon as a threat was detected. But unlike the times we practised before, this is not a drill.

I cup my hands around my mouth. "Once we reach maturity, we have to feed on the life force of humans. That's why the Diviners hate us. Because we kill people to survive. And the elders keep this from us. The elders keep a lot of things from us."

My voice echoes before it's swallowed by the trees. Jace's comforting presence warms my back.

Can Éabha hear me from the classroom? She knows about beatha—she was there for Father Benjamin and there will have been others since she reached maturity. But does she know the rest?

"The Diviners will keep hunting us unless we can live without slaughter. They're already on their way."

"Let them come."

Zev steps around the dining hall, followed by Kalyan and the female who was indifferent to Deirdre's distress.

Inda. I'd wanted her name, too.

I feel Jace tense beside me, though we're safely above them. For now.

"We don't need to kill people," I say.

"Yes, we do, Seraphina," Zev says gently. "There are many aspects you do not understand."

I resist the urge to stamp my foot at his patronising tone. "We *don't*. I haven't murdered anyone and I'm still here."

A glance passes between the huddled elders. Hope sparks in my chest.

Maybe I can get through to them. I'm living proof that we

can all go vegetarian.

"Incoming," Jace mutters.

A silver streak heralds the arrival of Felecior. His claws tap on wood as he lands out of reach on the opposite side of the roof. He flicks his wings, then settles them against his back. Jace positions himself in front of me, but I peek around his shoulder.

"You are not the smartest, are you, Diviner?" Felecior says. "You should have run when you had the chance."

"I'm here for Seraphina. She still thinks she can talk some sense into you idiots."

Felecior bristles, but calms quickly and turns sad, topaz eyes to me.

"I failed you, Seraphina. For that, I am sorry."

I frown at him. "Failed me?"

"I should have fought for you. You should have been my Chosen, not Avzameth's, then none of this would have happened. You left us because you were afraid."

"I *was* afraid, but that's not the only reason. If I'd stayed, I'd probably be dead by now."

Felecior cocks his head. "Why would you be dead? We would protect you with our lives. *I* would protect you." He spares Jace a dismissive glance. "This puny Diviner will not keep you safe. He's using you for his own ends."

Jace's turn to bristle. I place a hand on his arm and ease out from behind him.

"Most females die in childbirth, Felecior. That's why I'd be dead if I'd stayed."

"I do not understand."

"Females travelling to other clans is the lie the elders tell us after they've died giving birth. They don't leave. They never leave."

Felecior shakes his head. "The only lies are the ones this Diviner has fed you to turn you against us. Come, Seraphina. I will do now what I should have done then—I choose you."

"She's taken," Jace growls.

Felecior's lip curls, flashing pointed canines. "She is my Chosen. You are nothing."

Jace steps towards the male, his fists clenched. The fact he's not threatening my stubborn kin with a knife makes me love him even more.

"I don't choose you, Felecior." I raise my chin. "I choose Jace."

Felecior blinks. "But… you don't choose. You do not need to be scared. I won't hurt you like Avzameth. Our mating will be gentle. Enjoyable for us both."

"You won't touch her," Jace snarls, "because she's *mine*."

"You have no claim, human. You will regret the day you sullied her."

"*Sullied!*" I gasp. "Fuck right off, Felecior."

Felecior gapes at me. Jace snickers, pausing his advance towards the dumbfounded demon.

It may be the first time I've ever cursed. It feels good.

Harmony would be proud.

"Maybe I have sullied you a little, princess," Jace says, the smirk clear in his voice, though I can't see his face.

Felecior closes his mouth and straightens to his full height. "I have many regrets with you, Seraphina, but removing the stain of his influence will not be one of them."

A leathery flap is my only warning. A dark shape barrels into Jace from behind. The unfamiliar male pins Jace's arms to his chest and scoops him into the sky. I manage a startled bleat of his name before they disappear over the side of the hospital.

35

I leap from the roof of the hospital. Any further bleats of Jace's name are lodged beneath the clog of fear in my throat. Felecior flaps in pursuit, though he doesn't touch me. The unfamiliar male swoops over the grass towards the amphitheatre. His wings are a mix of dirty-white feathers and bald, pink skin. A yellow horn spirals from the top of his skull.

Jace kicks in his grip, but gravity is working against him and his arms are pinned. The demon's head snaps back. Jace drops. His feet hit the slope of the amphitheatre. The thud is louder than the frantic swell of my heart. He tumbles into a graceful roll, straightening to his full height on the lowest grassy level before the space becomes unyielding marble. He pivots smoothly, a knife in each hand, face tilted up. Blackness creeps along the blades.

The unfamiliar male clutches his nose. Garnet blood drips between his fingers, stirred by the wind from his wings. It stipples his bare torso.

"*Diviner*," he spits.

I dive for Jace. A silver streak buffets me off course and collides with my Diviner. They slam onto the floor of the amphitheatre and their tangled bodies squeak across the marble, carving a furrow in the frost and narrowly missing the slab where Deirdre was sullied and Father Benjamin was sacrificed. Limbs and wings flail. The bleeding male stoops to assist.

I zoom into his path. His heavy body rams between my shoulder blades and punches the air from my lungs. A yowl indicates he may have led with his bloodied nose. Claws scrabble at my jacket. I plummet towards glittering marble, too winded and low to correct my flight. I shut my eyes, as if that will make it hurt less.

A grunt and a scuffle. I crash into warm and solid muscle. The scent of blackberries and cloves. Jace staggers three steps before he steadies himself, my body draped diagonally across his chest. Safe in his arms.

"Watch it," he barks in his deadly voice. "If either of you cretins hurt her, I'll make you *wish* you were ash."

He places me carefully on my feet. Material rustles, my jacket shredded from panicking claws.

"We are not the ones who will hurt her," Felecior hisses. "Who *have* hurt her."

Gentle fingers pat me down. "You okay, princess?"

"Are *you?*"

His jacket is ripped along the arms and chest. There's no hint of blood, but I see smooth flashes of skin when he moves.

He smirks. "Fleecy is a spiky arsehole."

Felecior, probably more irritated at being ignored than the name-calling, growls, "Quit using her as a shield. Embrace your fate, coward."

"And back behind me you go." Jace sweeps me around, putting his body between me and the two demons, but not before I glimpse Felecior's tilted head and puzzled frown.

Jace's knives appear in his hands like magic. He claims a

step. I peek past his lean frame. The other male is a snarl of bloody teeth hunched beside Felecior.

"The only coward here is you for refusing to listen," Jace drawls, perfectly calm. "But I'm more than happy to cut you up until you do."

Zev, Kalyan, and Inda appear at the lip of the amphitheatre, silhouetted against the sunlight. Jace's shoulders stiffen, but he keeps his focus on the closest demons.

"You have nothing to say that is worth my attention," Felecior spits.

"Not me, you twat."

Felecior blinks.

Jace sighs. "Would you just fucking listen to Seraphina?"

"Enough of this," grunts the other male.

He launches at Jace. I gasp, which doesn't help anybody. Jace dodges easily and slashes at the demon as he sails past. The male's momentum barrels him into me and I find myself flat on my back, squashed under a hot bulk smelling of salt and fish. I wrinkle my nose. The weight disappears. Jace and Felecior glower at each other over my prone form, each of them with a hand curled around the bicep of the other male. Blood daubs the front of my jacket.

Jace's eyes widen. "Princess—"

"Not mine," I say quickly.

He shoves the groaning demon into Felecior and reaches for me. I grab his firm forearm.

"Felecior," Zev shouts from the top of the amphitheatre, "detain Seraphina. Clearly, she is a danger to herself. We will deal with the Diviner."

The elders march down the slope towards our huddle.

Jace bares his teeth. "Don't you fucking dare, Fleecy."

The groaning demon, no longer groaning or limp, grabs Jace's ankle. Jace's gaze zips to mine.

"Fuck," he says.

The demon leaps skywards, dragging Jace upside down. His palms slap the marble to keep his face from greeting it. My grip on his arm yanks me to my feet before my fingers slip on the slickness of his jacket. My grasping hands grab at air as Jace is whisked higher. I bunch my legs to follow.

My turn to catch him.

"Forgive me, Seraphina," Felecior whispers.

Strong arms wrap around my torso and pin me to a broad chest. My feet leave the ground. I wriggle and thrash, but it does nothing except tangle my hair over my face.

"Felecior, no, please." My voice breaks. "Don't let them hurt him."

The other demon flaps hard against Jace's weight. Jace's jacket bunches around his shoulders, flashing his flat stomach. A knife clatters to the stone of the amphitheatre. The elders reach the floor, their faces upturned to watch the spectacle.

"Do not worry," Felecior says gently. "Once it is over, you will feel like yourself again. Whatever Diviner ward he's manipulated you with will be broken."

Demons and Diviners—they all sound the bloody same. Spells, wards, whatever. As if Jace and I don't know our own minds. Our own hearts.

"You really are a twat," I say through my teeth. I buck in his hold and heel-kick him in the shin. "Now—*let me go.*"

Felecior flinches, but doesn't relent. I claw at his thighs. Bursts of energy from my palms stagger him, but he refuses to release me.

And Jace gets higher and higher.

His arms dangle past his head. I worry he's fainted, but he pistons himself upright, folding in half and lunging for the demon. The male lets go.

I scream. Jace screams. For a horrible, eternal second, he falls.

The winged demon twists and latches on to a flailing limb, halting Jace's descent with a bone-jarring jerk. He holds him aloft by the arm, swooping around the amphitheatre.

Felecior shivers against me. "Already, his fear tastes so sweet."

It's not his fear Felecior is tasting, it's his beatha. Does that mean he can feed without death to release it? Have they just never tried? Slaughter and cruelty are ingrained in the clan.

Though there is also fear. Jace has been here before. Carried into the sky by a monster and dropped on his head. He's reliving a nightmare that I can only watch.

My own fear is bitter on my tongue.

"Please, Felecior," I sob. "I love him. Don't let him die."

Felecior's sigh ruffles my hair. "This is for the best, Seraphina. He may be pretty, but he is a Diviner. You are confusing love for lust."

Heat bubbles in my chest and evaporates the tears on my cheeks. I slam both heels into Felecior's shins and keep kicking. He sits hard on his rump, but wraps his legs over mine, immobilising me against the cold marble. I struggle and fight until my breath rattles in my chest and my vision sparkles white.

I force myself to stop. Suck in deep and even gulps of air. Rage and panic won't help Jace. I need to be like him—calm and icy in the face of danger.

I close my eyes and teleport to the side, free of Felecior's gentle restraint. Zev drags his gaze from the aerial torture of my beloved.

"Seraphina, *behave*," he snaps, as if I'm an errant child.

I stick my tongue out and jump into the sky, arrowing for where Jace alternates between clawing at his tormentor and scrabbling at his clothes, no doubt attempting to pull another knife from wherever he's stashed them on his body. The demon drops him or flips him every time Jace's hand gets close to a weapon. My heart follows suit.

Jace's pale face is my own torture. Blood streaks from his lip where he's bitten it.

I reach for him.

A muscled form wraps around me and tugs me away, cocooning me in silver wings. I grit my teeth and teleport again. But Felecior is too fast. Frustrated tears burn my cheeks as I'm whisked back to the edge of the marble floor. Exhaustion has me sagging in his arms.

I can't risk teleporting again. Not yet. I have two teleports left in me and that may not be enough. I need to escape Felecior's suffocating embrace and transport Jace to the edge of clan territory, where we can flee the wards and return to the safety of the cottage to lick our wounds.

This reunion has been as awful as I feared.

The winged demon turns sharply and dives for the centre of the amphitheatre. Jace's heels hit the raised slab and the male lets go, tossing him onto his back. The elders crowd in, grabbing him before he can roll off or lash out. Chains rattle, binding my warrior to the sacrificial stone by wrist and ankle. He pulls against the restraints.

"Motherfuckers," he growls, though his voice is cracked and raw.

Zev pulls a knife from his tunic. The wicked blade glints brighter than the frost in the sunlight. Kalyan and Inda are too close, their fingers clutching Jace.

If I teleport into occupied space, I could give us all a horrific and painful end.

Felecior's grip tightens. Zev raises the knife.

"Know this, Diviner," he says, a cruel smile twisting his lips. "Your death will be neither quick nor painless. I will slice you until you are slick and screaming and we have drunk our fill. Starting with your face."

Kalyan and Inda ease back to give Zev some stabbing room. The scene bleeds and swirls. I miscalculate, teleporting a fraction too high. My body slams onto Jace, and his breath huffs out.

"Cutting it fine there, princess," he wheezes.

I flash us away before Zev can do more than yelp.

36

My hiking boots hit the bedroom carpet. I shove Jace to arm's length perhaps a little too wildly. He flops onto the bed, no doubt depleted from his ordeal and the beatha I took for the extra trip to get us here once we'd stumbled beyond the wards. I scrabble on top of him and perch on his hips. My shaking fingers pet his sweat-dampened hair and bloodied mouth. Weariness shadows his lovely eyes.

I tug at his jacket. "Where are you hurt?"

Ripped material rips further. I drag the ruined and rustling garment from his torso, jerking him in my haste.

"Princess..." he grunts.

Light scratches streak his forearms. No blood. I bunch the hem of his t-shirt in my fist and yank it to his chin. Blotches of red mar his perfect chest and stomach. They'll darken to bruises in a few hours. My free hand skates between them, palpating warm flesh over hard bone. Intact bones. No broken ribs. I knead his belly. Jace wriggles beneath me.

"Christ, I'm not hurt," he grumbles. I press harder on a mark, and he winces. "Okay, I'm not *that* hurt."

But how will I know unless I touch every part of him?

I shimmy off his lap and flip him over so that he's sprawled across the end of the bed, legs dangling off the edge.

237

"What the hell—"

I slot myself between his thighs and lean on the curve of his rump, which silences his protest. My hands glide up his smooth back, pushing his t-shirt higher. More areas of bruising. His shoulder blades rise and fall under my palms. A little fast—faster than before?—but he obviously has no trouble breathing. I massage the dip of his spine to check for discomfort or swelling.

"If you're interested in this position, I wouldn't say no, princess."

My hands still at the husky purr in his voice. He turns his head to peer over his shoulder. The eye I can see is all dilated pupil and molten bronze. My heart thuds in a panic.

Does he have a head injury?

He flexes his hips and only then do I realise my crotch is pressed hard against his rump. I blink at him.

"Does your penis bend this far?"

He snorts into the bedsheets. "Not quite. We'd have to get a toy for you to use."

"A toy? How would that work?"

"I'll show you some videos."

He stretches on the bed, the arch of his spine distracting my gaze and begging me to stroke it. The swell of his buttocks grinds against me. My cheeks flush, and I retreat a step. He flips on the mattress, herding me back between his legs and trapping me there, his hands on my hips.

"But first, I need to check *you* for injuries." He lifts his eyes to mine. "With my mouth."

Deft fingers remove my top layers. Scorching lips chase goosebumps across my stomach. My breast surrenders to the brand of his tongue and the playful nip of teeth. The heat of him banishes the last of the chill from his treatment at the hands of my clan.

He put himself in harm's way to try to save them. He deserves anything he wants. Anything I can give him.

I card my fingers through his hair. He raises his face from nuzzling my chest.

"I love you, Jace," I whisper.

He makes a noise low in his throat. "I love you, too, princess."

His mouth crushes mine before I can process that he's on his feet. The force drives me backwards, though the kiss is unrelenting. A demand of lips and teeth. The dip of his tongue. I climb up his body and wrap my legs around his waist, kissing him with the same frantic hunger. His hands squeeze my rump, dragging me over his erection.

I crave him inside me as much as I crave the zing of his beatha in my veins.

He lowers my feet to the ground and drops to his knees. He watches me as he unzips my trousers and strips me bare. Tender hands widen my stance.

"Does it hurt here, princess?" he says.

His hot breath brushes the apex of my thighs where my pulse throbs under his attention.

"Jace," I moan.

"Mmm… that sounded like a yes. I'll need to kiss it better."

His lips close around my little nub of flesh. He suckles, and the wash of tingles drains the strength from my legs. His mouth curves.

"Lean against the wall." The rumble of his words flares a burst of pleasure straight to my gut. "I'm going to make you come, then fuck you against it."

Garbled noises fall from my mouth. The wicked light grows

in Jace's eyes. I sag into the wall, digging my fingers into the paper to anchor myself. My thighs quiver under his hands, but I manage to spread them further.

"God, you're so fucking perfect," he sighs.

I sob his name. It's all I can say when he returns to his suckling, when his fingertips delve into my cleft, curling and stroking and drawing more desperate sounds from me. A finger slides deep, circling and stretching me. A second. The glorious ache swells and pulses as he expertly drives me towards ecstasy. He glides his fingers in and out and flicks his tongue against my clitoris. I groan and tremble at each slick touch, balanced on the maddening edge.

"Come for me, princess," Jace growls.

I fall apart at his command. My cry echoes in the room. I writhe against the wall while his wicked, merciless mouth somehow extends the blaze of pleasure and tension and heat. My cry becomes a scream of his name.

Definitely good screaming.

He kisses me on the mouth this time, the press of his body the only thing holding me upright. I taste myself on his lips, but can't open my eyes. My muscles are liquid. Languid. Jace lifts me up, his hands cradling the backs of my thighs while his lithe form slots between, strong and warm and mine.

"You with me, princess?" he says.

My eyelids continue to flutter, but I mumble, "Yes. More, please."

He chuckles. "No longer innocent, but still so fucking eager."

He slides easily inside me in a slow, delicious thrust. He moves no further and I can't help a whimper even though I'm half-blind and flushed from climax. A groan catches in his throat. He rests his forehead against mine.

"Shit, princess. You're going to make me lose it like I'm fourteen."

"Is that good?"

"If you don't mind me coming in under five seconds. But give me ten minutes and I'll be raring to go again."

I follow his huff of breath to the softness of his lips. He lets me lick inside his mouth and his tongue teases mine. I clench around where he's buried deep, eliciting another tortured sound. I flex my hips a tiny bit, dazzled by the power I have over his body. Captivated by my warrior and the vulnerability only I get to see. He rewards me with a shiver and an, "Oh, fuck. You asked for it, princess."

He pulls out, then plunges inside me. My laugh becomes a constant moan of his name. He ruts not like an animal, or his fourteen-year-old self, but with finesse. With a skill that has my nerves singing. A thrum of tension gathers at the base of my spine. Everything is wet and tight, electrified by the thrust of his hips. He pants in my ear, a soft whine escaping each time he buries himself to the hilt.

My body spasms, utterly undone. I scream his name louder than when he devoured me with his mouth. His shout joins mine, his head tossed back, the cords of his neck taut. My orgasm roars in an unending wave at his loss of control and the feel of him pulsing inside me, the jerk of his hips wringing every last drop from us both.

We collapse in a heap at the base of the wall, my wings akimbo, my hair tangled everywhere. He holds me close, his skin slick and his muscles spent. It takes at least five minutes for us to catch our breath. I cuddle into Jace, lulled by his slowing heartbeat.

"Felecior thinks you're pretty," I murmur to his collarbone.

Jace twitches. "I'm not sure what you want me to do with that information."

I shrug one shoulder. "Just thought it was interesting."

"Well, I guess Fleecy's not too bad. For a demon. And, uh, a man. He's a bit of an arsehole, though." Jace's lips curve against my temple. "Don't get any ideas, princess."

"You're the only male for me, my prince."

"Christ's sake. I've obviously not tired you out enough."

He hoists me up and tosses me, laughing, onto the bed.

Things with my clan do not improve for Jace. Their sole focus is hurting him. They post males on the boundary to wait for our crossing. On every attempt, we have seconds to ourselves before they descend on us, no matter what direction we approach, and we try several. Most are impassable, the rest a muddy or thorn-strewn scramble. I beseech them on the urgency of our message, the threat of the hunting Diviners who could discover their location at any moment. They ignore me in favour of attacking Jace.

I have never teleported so much in my life. Jace hardly bats an eye at it now.

On our fifth attempt, I thought evening might catch them unawares and mellowed, but they chased us through the darkened woods and still refused to listen. Frustrated, I teleport us to the entrance of the birthing hospital.

Maybe they will still their tongues and bloodthirsty claws if I can prove what I'm saying.

Rain drums on the wood and paints bronze streaks through the beams of security lights. The demon on the roof hoots a warning.

I barge through the door, Jace on my heels. Automatic lights ping on, illuminating a long corridor and five archways into rooms. Water drips from us onto grey linoleum. The air holds a hint of smoke and the salty tang of demon blood.

"I'd stay right there, if you know what's good for you," Jace growls.

I whirl from my survey of the hospital. The demon from the roof stands in the doorway. Rain curls around his broad frame and splashes from his horns. His twitching tail smears dampness across the floor.

He is another unfamiliar male. There are many.

"The others are on their way," he says, smirking at Jace. "You have achieved nothing except to trap yourself at our mercy. I can be patient until I'm allowed to squeeze the breath from you."

His muscular tail corkscrews on the linoleum, like a python wrapping around its prey in the wildlife programmes Harmony and I watch.

Jace's fingers tighten on his knife. "Keep moving, princess."

I scuttle down the corridor, glancing through each archway into birthing suites like the one where I witnessed Deirdre's death—breathing apparatus, a table with straps, and a metal sink for washing the blood from their hands. Jace follows a couple of paces behind, stalking backwards to keep the demon in his sights, though the male stays in the doorway, watching our progress with malevolent red eyes a few shades lighter than his skin. He blows Jace a kiss before we turn the far corner of the corridor.

Jace shudders. "I'm trying not to hate your kin, princess, but they're making it difficult."

"Don't worry," I huff. "I'm starting to hate them a little, too."

The corridor continues along the rear of the building much like the first—five archways leading to inner rooms. No windows. We hustle to the next corner. The route dead-ends past four archways and a single door with a shiny padlock.

Jace cocks a brow. "Well, that's not suspicious at all."

He tugs on the lock, but it remains fastened. His knife disappears into his jacket, the material repaired with waterproof tape so it hangs crinkled and slightly askew. The same as mine. He slams his shoulder into the door. The wood around the jamb cracks and splinters on the second hit, the door swinging open to tumble him into a long, narrow room spanning the entire width of the building. He rolls his shoulder, his gaze tracking along the floor-to-ceiling shelves. I find myself beside him without any memory of moving my feet.

Simple clay pots line each shelf, stacked at least three deep. My heart twists at the neatly printed label on one near the middle. I stagger towards it.

"Uh, princess, sorry to interrupt, but…"

Zev and Kalyan step into the room. The bolt relinquishes its grip on the shattered door and clanks to the ground. Felecior and the male from the roof crowd in behind the elders. Jace plants himself between us with a knife in each hand. I thrust a trembling finger at the pot named 'Deirdre.'

"You told us she left to travel to another clan when she wanted to stay and mother her young herself," I hiss, swallowing around the tears in my throat. "She was your *child*, and you let her die."

"That is a different Deir—"

"Stop *lying!*" My shriek silences Zev and bounces around the room of dead females. "I saw you. You did nothing while the youngling clawed itself from her belly. You watched her die and then you *lied to us.* You lie about so many things."

Instead of sneering at my tone, Zev's expressions turns patient and pitying. "Seraphina, you are a curious and gentle creature; of course you do not understand."

"Then help me understand," I say through my teeth.

Zev flicks a glance at the younger males blocking the door. Felecior tilts his head, but the other male has eyes only for Jace.

Kalyan clears his throat. "Zev, it's not wise—"

"Because all that matters is the survival of the young no matter what," I snarl. "Isn't that right?"

Kalyan levels a frown at me. "You are too meddlesome for your own good, Seraphina. Perhaps now is the time to finally keep your own counsel."

What a polite way to tell me to shut up.

I open my mouth, but a quiet, sorrowful sound zips everyone's attention to Felecior. He cradles an urn in his hands, his claws scraping the clay despite his care. His thumbs obscure the label.

He raises accusatory, topaz eyes. "You said she left after our young was stillborn. That she never wanted to see me again because she was ashamed. I searched for her, but there was no trace."

The pain in his voice stabs into my chest. He felt her loss, whoever the female was. He probably thought *he'd* failed *her*.

I raise a brow at my elders in perfect imitation of Jace. "Are you going to tell Felecior he's a curious and gentle creature, too?"

Kalyan's frown transfers to Zev, but his face soon smooths, and he sighs. The other male shifts in the doorway, his focus no longer on Jace, but flitting between the hunched Felecior and the elders. Jace maintains his defensive stance, his warrior blades swirling black.

"We could not tell you your Chosen had died giving birth," Zev says to Felecior. "We could not tell any of you lest it distract you from your duties. We're not just talking about the survival of the young. *Our* survival depends on it."

Felecior straightens, cuddling the pot to his chest. "I don't understand."

"What would you do if you knew seven out of ten females die during birth?"

"Seven out of ten!" I gasp.

Felecior's eyes widen. "I… I would refuse to mate with… a female."

He looks at Jace when he says the last, though I'm not sure it's deliberate. His cheeks flare a pretty pink before he musters his expression into a scowl and drags his attention back to Zev. He hugs the urn tighter.

"Christ's sake," Jace mutters, though his cheeks seem a little pink, too.

A giggle tries to bubble up my throat, inappropriate given the subject matter.

"Exactly," Zev says, reminding me of the dark acts that brought us all here. "And if enough males refused to mate, we would have fewer warriors. We are barely surviving as it is. If our population were to drop even an increment, we would be no match for the Diviners."

Zev aims a sneer at Jace who rewards him with a smirk for his trouble.

"Maybe if you stopped slaughtering humans for your energy, like Seraphina has been saying—and doing—all along, we wouldn't have to fight," Jace says.

"As if you could comprehend anything of which we speak,

Diviner," Zev says.

Kalyan bristles and the male behind him returns to glaring at Jace.

Felecior tilts his head. "But Seraphina wasn't lying when she said most females die in childbirth."

"I'm the only one here who tells the truth," I say softly.

Jace clears his throat.

"And Jace," I continue. "Jace is an honourable, truthful male."

Instead of glowering, Felecior looks at Jace with a considering, "Hmm…"

"We cannot feed on small amounts of beatha," Zev barks.

My stomach drops to my sodden hiking boots. "Is it only the females who can? Have you tried?"

Demon males will not let themselves wither and die to placate the Diviners. Even if they did, it would still lead to the eventual extinction of my race. Which means this war will never end. I will always be hated by Jace's kin. And they will hate him for loving me.

"You may paint us as monsters, Seraphina, but we have tried to save our females from the horror of childbirth," Zev says. "We experimented with small amounts. No deaths. It did not seem to limit the females, but the males grew weaker. They could never consume a large amount without death's release, like the females. It was also riskier to let so many leave the clan in search of food. Although it achieved our goal of easier births, the effect on future generations was unacceptable."

My turn to join in the frowning. "Unacceptable how?"

Felecior slips the urn of his dead Chosen onto its shelf, his intent fully on the elder. Kalyan crosses his arms and glares at the floor, seemingly displeased with Zev's final spilling of the truth. The other demon looks confused.

"Males were born with fewer demon characteristics." Zev curls his lip. "And there were more incubi among them."

The other demon settles on disgusted rather than confused, his face twisting almost comically. Even Felecior shudders.

"Wait a minute," I say slowly, my fingertips tingling. "You're telling me that you *can* feed off of sips of beatha—you *can* live without killing humans—and you *can* stop females from dying an excruciating death, but you won't because of some prejudice you have against incubus demons? *Are you fucking kidding?*"

"Seraphina," Zev snaps, "you will watch your language when you address your elders."

I wish I had talons so I could turn Zev's stupid stubborn face to ribbons. I spin to Felecior, my hands clenched into fists.

"You can't possibly agree with this. Your Chosen would still be alive. You wouldn't have to fight and inevitably die in battle with the Diviners. You wouldn't have to kill people."

Felecior shuffles his feet, glancing at Zev and Kalyan.

"Having our population flooded with incubi is too high a price to pay," Kalyan says before Felecior can open his mouth.

Felecior side-steps to face the elders, bringing him closer to Jace and our end of the room. Jace eases back, but doesn't raise a weapon against the male.

"That *is* a high price," Felecior says, then raises his chin, "but one I'd be willing to pay to protect our females."

Okay, so he focused on the female-protecting part and not the no-human-killing part, but it's something. Maybe everything.

"That is not your decision to make, not until you are an elder." Zev rubs at his temple. "This discussion is a waste of time when these matters have already been decided before you were born. Our only business left is to rid ourselves of the Diviner and return Seraphina to where she belongs—on her back beneath a *demon* male."

Another sneer aims at a bristling Jace. I wrap my fingers around his forearm. His fury vibrates the muscles beneath my touch.

I keep my voice calm, though it's a struggle. "And what about the Diviners hunting you? Unless you change your feeding habits to *protect us all,* they will never stop hunting us."

Zev graces me with his sneer, mirrored by Kalyan. "As I said before—let them come. Thanks to your escapades, we are already on alert and have many warriors drafted in to assist. We will defend ourselves against their scourge as we have always done."

"You are the scourge," I say hotly, and now it's Jace's hand holding *me* back. "There's a peaceful way for us to live yet you'd rather doom us all because you're racist."

Kalyan scoffs, but Zev slices a hand through the air.

"Enough, Seraphina. You are in sore need of relearning your place." Zev clicks his fingers. "Felecior, detain the Diviner. I will deal with our errant female."

Errant female? *Errant female!* I don't care about my lack of claws. I'm going to scratch his face anyway.

Felecior slides in front of me, blocking my view of the elders and the other male in the doorway, especially when he spreads his silver wings.

"No, I don't believe I will," he drawls.

Ignoring the stuttered disbelief of his elders, Felecior cranes his neck to look over his shoulder. His gentle focus lands on me.

"Go, Seraphina," he says, and lifts his gaze to Jace. "Keep her safe."

Jace nods. "Always, Fleecy."

Felecior rolls his eyes, but watches as I wrap my arms around Jace. His wings flick, and a thud signals a heavy body hitting the floor.

"Thank you," I whisper, and teleport away.

38

"Fleecy's going to be pissed," Jace says, though his smirk indicates he's not cut up about it. "This isn't exactly keeping you safe."

We creep through the silent pines. A sift of snow sprinkles down from the heavy, grey sky, the light closer to twilight than noon.

My boot crunches in a frosted puddle. "I have to try one more time with our original plan. If Éabha and the younger females don't listen, even after Felecior's reaction yesterday, then demons and Diviners deserve each other."

Jace's snort forms a white cloud in the still air. He prowls beside me, his eyes always moving, his fingers poised above a sheathed knife at his hip.

No one greeted us when we crossed the warded boundary. Perhaps they assumed we'd give up. Part of me wants to. Every attempt increases the danger for Jace. I want to whisk him back to the cottage where I can keep *him* safe.

And I miss Inverness. I miss Harmony.

My kin have one last chance to let me save them from themselves.

"Are you sure this teacher will listen any better than the rest?" Jace says, ducking under a low branch. Frozen droplets scatter to the ground.

"No, but she is an intelligent, caring female. She is young for a teacher. Was young. I'm hoping she'll be more open-minded than the elders. And I was her favourite pupil."

Jace grins. "Course you were, princess."

The chill disguises my blush. We reach the edge of the forest. I circle around until I can see the empty playground stretching between the classrooms. The windows reflect the clouds, concealing anyone inside. I creep across the snow-stippled grass while darting glances at the surrounding buildings and trees. Claw marks from grappling males scar the mud. Everything is unnaturally quiet, like when the clan hid at the arrival of Father Benjamin.

I pray today's conclusion will be less bloody and horrifying.

I press my shoulder to the wood at the corner of my old classroom. Jace slots in behind me, close enough for my wings to brush his tattered waterproof jacket. His breath warms the nape of my neck. I slide around the building and aim for the stairs to the entrance.

"We're being watched," Jace says at the same time a smug voice purrs, "Well, if it isn't not-so-perfect little Seraphina."

Marrichar clomps onto the top step of the classroom entrance, looking down her snout at me. I've wondered, over the last six years, if she was alive or if she became another casualty of demon pregnancy. She hasn't changed much, though the breadth of her shoulders now rivals any male's, accentuated by her hump. Her soft-grey eyes lift to Jace.

"Everyone gushing over you—everything gifted to you—yet you're the one who betrays us."

I raise my chin. "I'm not betraying you. I'm trying to help, but you're making it impossible."

"How many young have *you* birthed?"

My brow furrows. "What's that got to do—"

"Three," she says, smacking a hand to her muscled chest. "I have birthed three warriors."

"And how much did it hurt? How many times did you almost die?"

Her arrogant expression falters. She shakes herself and sticks her snout in the air.

"The pain was worth it to fulfil my duty."

The door of the classroom building creaks open behind her and Zev slinks from the gloom, joining Marrichar on the stairs.

"If only you had followed in Marrichar's footsteps, Seraphina," he says. "She is a shining example of what a female should be."

Marrichar slides me a triumphant look. Her stubby claws catch on her beige tunic as she smooths it over her wide hips.

I wave at my slim figure. "If I had, I would have died during my first birth, if not my first mating."

I shiver at the thought of Avzameth and his brutal strength. His brutal frame. Jace squeezes my fingers for a brief moment of comfort, earning a sneer from the demons above us.

"But we don't have to endure that pain or risk death," I continue despite their scorn. "How many humans have been killed to sustain you, Marrichar?"

Uncertainty flickers across her face. She glances at Zev, and her expression hardens.

"It is no different to the cattle they slaughter to sustain *their* lives. You were taught this at your first feeding, Seraphina—*we* are the predators at the top of the food chain."

"Excellent response, Marrichar."

"Thank you, Elder," Marrichar preens.

Frustration builds in my chest. And fear. The longer I stand here rehashing the same words, the longer it gives the others to ambush us. I'm surprised we've not yet been surrounded, but I stay close to Jace, just in case.

"Where is Felecior? Maybe you will listen to him if you won't listen to me. He knows the truth of everything, and he wants us to change. To live a better way."

"Felecior is being reminded of his priorities." Zev curls his lip, flashing pointed teeth. "As you will soon be. Marrichar—do it now."

Marrichar grins, her focus switching to Jace. Jace staggers. His breath catches in his throat.

"Princess..." he wheezes.

My heart flips. She's drinking his beatha! Unlike a male, she can drain him to death without laying a claw on him.

I lunge for Jace, but wiry arms grab my waist and swing me away in a tangle of wings and hair.

"Your human tastes delicious," Marrichar says, stomping closer.

Jace drops to one knee. He shakes his head, his eyes dazed. Marrichar licks her lips.

"Stop squirming, Seraphina!" Zev barks into my scalp. "Marrichar, hurry up and finish him. You are taking too long."

Marrichar's glee crumples into a pout at his harsh tone. She raises both hands, as if that will help her to focus as she sucks the life from Jace. I stop wriggling, though my heart does not. I buck in Zev's arms and place my palms on the prickly underside of his jaw. His muscles tense. Jace's groan rips claws of anxiety through my gut.

Energy bursts from my palms. Zev jerks backwards. There's

an awful crack. We slam to the ground, but I scramble upright without pause, kneeing him in his soft parts in my haste. Marrichar's eyes widen as I charge towards her.

"Seraphina, I was only—"

My fist ploughs into her snout. She squeals and lands on her rump. I dive for Jace, who's on his hands and knees, his head hanging low. There's no hint of his usual beatha. No electric sizzle. I fold myself over him, my arms around his hitching chest, and teleport us to the edge of the clan.

A male shouts and starts running towards us. Others answer his call, though the voices are distant. I grab two fistfuls of Jace's jacket and drag him face-first across the boundary, flapping madly to give me extra lift. I trip and scrape my knees on rock.

The pines streak and fade. We slump on our bed in the cottage. Jace's breaths are shallow. Laboured. I flip him and seal my mouth over his cold lips. My air and my energy gust into his lungs. His ribs expand beneath my grasping fingers.

I'll give him everything. He can have all of it, all of me, even if I faint.

I shove my beatha into Jace. Dizziness swirls through my skull. Firm but gentle hands pry me off. I fight to reach him, to give him more. His husky voice finally penetrates my panic.

"Princess… Seraphina—stop. I'm okay. You've given me enough."

He brushes the hair from my face, though it falls all around us with the way I'm hunkered over him. My wings arch protectively, completing our dark cocoon. Jace smiles softly, his bronze eyes open and aware and filled with the spark that is purely him.

"I'm fine, I promise," he whispers, and I realise I'm petting him again.

I collapse on his chest, probably a little too forcefully if his huff of air is any indication.

"I'm sorry," I sob. "My stupid clan can go to hell. I'm done risking you. You must hate me. This is all my fault. I—"

Jace ends my watery babbling by rolling us over and silencing my mouth with his. His tongue quiets me further, licking inside to tease my own and fill me with tingles. Desire replaces the tiredness weighing on my limbs.

Jace kisses the tears from my cheeks. "I don't hate you, princess. I agree your clan are stupid, but if you change your mind tomorrow and want to try again, I'll be right there with you."

This male is too perfect.

I cup his face and draw him into a kiss. The soft tease turns frantic as I suck and lick and nibble, devouring his mouth. I wrap my legs around his waist and tilt my hips to rub myself against him.

"Show me you're okay," I whisper into his mouth.

He props himself on his elbows, looking almost as dazed as when Marrichar was draining his beatha. His lips are swollen from my attention, and that sends a frisson of heat to my core. To where I want him.

He clears his throat. "You're exhausted. Your energy must be depleted after all that."

My honourable warrior—always trying to protect me.

"Show me you're okay," I growl, and drag him into another biting kiss.

I swallow his groan. Material rips as we wrestle the clothes from our bodies. Then it's his hot skin gliding against mine, impaling me in the best way. Claiming me. Showing me that being drained half to death has done nothing to diminish the sexual prowess of my Diviner.

He makes me scream louder than I ever have before.

Instead of collapsing on me, he tugs me to my feet and helps me dress.

"Now *I'm* depleted," he says with a smirk, "so you have to feed me if you want me to show you, again and again, that I'm okay."

He swats me on my rump. I giggle and stumble ahead, but he slings an arm across my shoulders and tugs me into his side.

The door to the en-suite crashes into the wall. Ellie strolls out, a blade in each hand.

"Well, thank god I only have to bleach my ears and brain, and not my eyeballs," she drawls as a horde of Diviners spills in from the hallway.

39

A light flush paints Jace's cheeks. I choose not to ponder on how long Ellie was hiding in the en-suite and what she might have heard. Definitely my screaming. Jace climaxing on a groan of my name.

Nope. Not thinking about it.

Jace cocks an eyebrow at me. I shake my head.

I have no energy to teleport. There's a feast of Diviners surrounding us, but I'm tired of running. Tired of being ignored. They think they have us captured, but this time, they are where *I* want them.

Hopefully.

Ellie jerks her chin at Jace. "Search him."

Oliver and a female Diviner step forward. No sign of Rose yet, but no doubt she'll pop in when it suits her.

Jace bares his teeth at Oliver. "Touch me and I'll break your fucking face, then stab you in the eye."

Oliver blanches. Another female takes his place. Jace stands calmly while they search him, their hands patting his clothes and tracing over his body. I crowd in close, and they glare at me for getting in the way.

"Stop growling, princess," Jace smirks. "Though it's hot."

Ellie scoffs. I mash my lips together, cutting off the rumble in my chest. My cheeks heat. The two Diviners retreat with a fan of knives swirling black.

"How many did you get?" Ellie says.

"Five."

Rose eases through the group filling the hallway door. Her maroon t-shirt brings out the red in her hair and has a slogan that reads 'Please don't feed hallucinogens to the geese.'

"He has at least two more," she says with something like pride. "Search him again."

Jace directs his smirk at her, and her lips twitch. One Diviner pats him down, rougher this time. She makes him remove his boots and steps away with three more knives.

I honestly have no idea where he puts them.

"How did you find us?" he says to Rose.

Ellie wears her customary scowl, and crosses her arms. The rest of the Diviners maintain their battle readiness, blades in hands and their watchful gazes lingering on me when they're not flicking to Jace.

"I'll tell you as soon as you sit on the bed and your demon stands over there." Rose points a finger at the corner of the bedroom, like I'm a youngling she's putting in a time-out.

At least she acknowledged who I belong to, even if I'm not a bloody child.

"Yeah, not happening." Jace takes my hand, twining his fingers between mine.

"You cannot fight all of us, Jace. I simply want to prevent her from teleporting, since she won't go without you."

Jace squeezes my hand and sprawls gracefully on the edge of the bed, leaning back on his palms, his legs slightly spread. The picture of relaxation and sexiness. One of the females roves her gaze over his warrior's frame, and the growly noise vibrates in my chest again. Her eyes catch mine, and widen. My wings are spread, my fingers imitating the claws I—sadly—don't have.

"Corner, demon," Rose says. "Please."

It's reluctant, but at least polite. Jace gives me a tiny nod, so I put myself in the corner, trusting he knows what he's doing.

"Looks like your little bat-winged doll has a possessive streak," Ellie says. "At least she's dropped the innocent act."

Jace sends me a knowing smile tinged with heat. Warmth blooms in my chest and curls to my stomach.

I'm definitely not as innocent as I was when we last encountered Ellie and Rose.

"Are you going to answer my question now that you've separated us?" Jace directs to Rose, ignoring Ellie.

Rose tilts her head. "You have your demon to thank for that."

"Me?" I gasp. "I only told you about Inverie and that's miles over the hills from here."

"Oliver drew a ward on her."

Jace's head snaps to Oliver, who sinks deeper into the mass of Diviners.

"He can't have. I've seen—"

"Yes, we all know you've seen her naked," Ellie sneers. "Gross."

"Thank you, Eloise," Rose says drily. "Oliver marked the nape of her neck under her hair when she was unconscious in the cave. Unfortunately, it's smudged or didn't connect quite right. We struggled to pinpoint your location, but it kept jumping back to here."

A shiver trickles down my spine. I rub at the base of my skull as if I can rid myself of the foul stain of Oliver's pencil. Or permanent marker, I suppose, if it's lasted this long without fading.

"Sit down, Jace," Rose says, her voice a low husk of command.

He ignores her, his bronze eyes only for me and filled with concern.

"You okay, princess?"

I nod and force myself to stop scrubbing at my nape. It's not the torture symbol. There's no pain. I would never have known it was there unless they told me.

Still, my skin prickles with the awareness of its presence.

Jace lowers himself back to the mattress. "So what now? More bullshit about how killing her will save me?"

"Sadly, it's too late for that," Rose sighs, her expression grim, "but we will support you through your grief as best we can."

Jace manages a shout before he's buried beneath a scrum of Diviners. Fists thud on flesh. Voices cry out. But Rose was right.

Jace can't fight them all.

Ellie and another woman pin his wrists to the bed. Three Diviners lie across his torso, two more shackling his legs. He pants and twists beneath their grip, his hair in disarray across his forehead. His eyes spark with fury, but also fear.

"I'm sorry, Jace," Rose says.

"Fuck you and your apologies. Don't you dare touch her."

"I accept the burden of your hatred." Rose draws a knife from the belt at her hip. "I hope it will fade in time when you realise I do this from a place of love. We're your family and we need you."

Rose steps towards me. The remaining Diviners not pinioning Jace to the bed spread out behind her, blocking all exits with their black blades and dogged doctrine. Jace wrenches a hand free. A leg. Oliver peels from the group and throws himself on the Jace-pile, earning a stream of colourfully violent threats from my Diviner.

"Rose, don't." Jace's voice cracks. *"Please."*

"Accept this, and I will make it quick and painless, for his sake," Rose says, her hard green eyes on me as she continues her advance.

"Fuck you, Rose," I say.

She stumbles on her next step, her mouth agape. *"Excuse me?"*

I cross my arms, praying it hides the wild thrashing of my heart against my ribcage. My wings arch and brush the walls.

"I'm done being nice with you or my clan, so you need to shut up and sit down." I manage a small, sardonic smile despite the number of blades pointing at me. "Or lying down may be more accurate, in a second."

Ellie snarls something. Rose continues to goggle. Jace blinks at me from beneath his scrum of humans.

I stick my fists on my hips and embrace what a demon can do. What only a *female* demon can do.

I drink them all down.

40

Beatha pours into me. The cherry fizz of Ellie; something malty and dark from Rose. I taste the other Diviners, but it's too much to hold, and I let the energy swirl free. A citrusy zing, salt, a burn of ozone.

Rose sags against the dresser, then slides down to sit on the carpet. The advancing crowd stutters to their knees. Jace kicks free from his restraining pile of bodies, shoving off the limp and slumping limbs of his brethren. Ellie flops on her back, her eyes half-lidded.

Power overflows my small frame. It spills from my fingers, my mouth, and even my eyes, invisible but disconcerting all the same. I feel strong enough to teleport us all to Australia without a hint of vertigo.

Not that I've ever been there.

The temptation to take everything is strong, like when I drank from Ellie to save myself from a second wing-shredding. The urge to glut and fill the air with their fragile life force, leaving their husks behind on the floor.

But that's not who I am.

Jace picks his way across the room to avoid stepping on groaning Diviners. I sway against the overwhelming sensation of fullness. He steadies a hand on my elbow, but snatches it

264

back.

"Christ, princess, your skin is burning."

I wrap my fingers in his ruined jacket and pull him to my level. He gasps at the press of my lips, moans at the brand of my tongue in his open mouth. I feed him energy while he buries his hands in my hair and pushes me into the corner, his body a hot, hard line against mine. He breaks the kiss, panting, though his fingers are gentle as they cup my face.

"Jesus," he whispers.

His beatha sparks and sizzles and nibbles deliciously along my skin. His erection presses against my stomach. I look up at him and manage a smirk.

"Later," I say.

He chuckles. "I've created a monster."

He slings an arm across my shoulders and we survey the bloodless carnage of the room. There's a lot of blinking and shaking heads. Trembling arms struggle to hold their weight off the carpet. Discarded blades lose the sickening swirl of black. Ellie fights against the softness of the mattress and the weakness of her own body. Rose sits with her hands in her lap, her head lolling on the wooden dresser.

"Why…?" she croaks.

"I can drain you in a heartbeat," I say, my voice quiet and grim, as hers had been right before she was going to stab me. "But I chose not to. I *choose* not to. I imagine it'll always be something you fear. So isn't it better if you stay on my good side and stop trying to murder me?"

"Your girlfriend is a psycho, Jace," Ellie wheezes.

He gives me a fond smile. "Yes, she is."

"Great. Admitting the demon is your girlfriend is the first step to getting you free of the crazy bitch."

"She's not just my girlfriend—she's my everything," Jace says, "so watch your fucking mouth, Ellie."

I match his smile. His finger traces the curve of my lips before he chases it with his. Ellie gags weakly from her position on the bed. We ignore her and refocus on Rose.

"What do you propose, demon?" Rose grunts, attempting to boost herself higher against the dresser.

"First—you call me Seraphina."

Rose bestows a grudging nod. "Fine. Seraphina."

"Then I show you where my clan is."

Jace stiffens beside me. "You don't have to, princess. We can find another way."

"No," I sigh. "Diviners and demons are the bloody same— pig-headed and resistant to broadening their worldview. The only way to change is to join forces. Like we have."

"I am not having sex with your demon," Ellie grumbles, still prone on the bed and frowning at the ceiling.

"That's not what she meant," Jace growls. "And no one touches her but me."

"You would show us willingly?" Rose says softly. The unspoken *after all we've done to you* lingers in the air between us.

"I've tried—" I swallow past the tightness in my throat and gut. "I've tried to sway them, but they won't listen to me. Six years ago, I ran away to save myself. Maybe I needed to—to learn the truth of how to feed. And meet Jace. To see that the biggest thing I feared could also be my biggest strength. But Jace and I aren't enough on our own. If I don't risk losing my clan, then this war will never end, and they'll probably die anyway."

Rose manages to haul herself to her feet using the dresser,

though her thighs shake and she keeps a white-knuckled grip on the edge of the furniture.

"What are the rest of your terms, dem—Seraphina?"

Jace's arm tightens across my shoulders, giving me a squeeze of reassurance.

I'm doing the right thing. The slaughter has gone on long enough—of both demons and humans. It has to stop. Even if my clan hates me for it.

If any of them are left in the aftermath we create.

I tick off the rest of my conditions on my fingers.

"You stop trying to hurt and kill me. You don't punish Jace for anything he's done." I raise my chin. "And when we get to my clan, we do things *my* way."

"This is going to be a fucking disaster," Ellie mutters.

<h1 style="text-align:center">41</h1>

"What are you looking at?" Ellie snaps.

She hunkers next to me in a raspberry thicket. The few remaining leaves are wrinkled and brown on the straight, prickled stems. She's dogged my steps the whole way here despite Jace's huffs of annoyance from his steady presence on my other side.

It took the Diviners two full days to recover from my glutinous beatha sapping. The cottage has been stuffed to the brim with them. I couldn't move from one room to the next without the icy stamp of their attention. But none of them argued with my plan or my terms. They tried to hide their unease, but I caught their subtle glances. Ellie masked her fear beneath an armour of irritation and anger. Rose was as calm and placid as always.

She reminds me of Jace.

"You have pretty eyes," I tell Ellie, and wait for her to push me in the mud like Marrichar.

Maybe I'll punch her in the snout, too.

Her mouth drops open and she almost inhales a spiderweb from her sudden intake of breath. Jace muffles a snort and shifts in his crouch, scanning the undergrowth where the other Diviners are spread in a rough semi-circle, Rose on the far side of the gaping Ellie, and Oliver as distant as he can get from Jace, for his own safety.

It took us a day to trek to the northern boundary of my clan's territory. The Diviners refused to let me teleport them in groups and Jace insisted I reserve my energy, even though I'm buzzing with it.

An orange sunset glows between the pine needles, the air clear and crisp with the promise of frost. The space under the trees is damp and gloomy and smells of soil and dead leaves.

Ellie slams her mouth shut and renews her scowl. "Jace, your demon is hitting on me."

"She's just being friendly."

Ellie squints at me. "Well, quit it. It's freaking me out."

"She's a lost cause, princess. Ellie doesn't do friendly."

"Yes, I do, you arsehole," she says. "But humans and demons are not meant to be friends."

"My best friend is a human. She's called Harmony."

Ellie rolls her pretty green eyes. "We've met. And it doesn't count if she doesn't know what you are."

"She knows now," I say fondly, "and she still loves me."

"Then she's as simple-minded as Jace."

"Fuck you—"

"Focus, please." Rose's simple command silences the bickering. She leans forward to peer around the bulky shoulders of her daughter. "How close are we, Seraphina?"

"Five more steps and they'll know we're here."

Ellie scoffs. "I still can't believe *demons* use wards."

"Yes, the actions of demons have been surprising of late," Rose says, catching my eye.

My cheeks flush beneath her gaze.

I cornered her in the hallway this morning as everyone was

preparing to leave. Shy little Seraphina had a scold or two for the leader of the Highland Diviners. She watched me with increasing astonishment when I told her that Jace regarded her as a mother figure and he didn't deserve to have his feelings ignored or belittled nor his capabilities doubted when he was a superb warrior, epilepsy or no. I got carried away with my impassioned speech until she placed a hand on my arm and said she was glad he had me to protect him, and that she was sorry. I sniffed and countered it wasn't me she needed to apologise to. Then I shed a private tear when she disappeared in search of Jace, who promptly caught up with me in the driveway and kissed me silly in front of all the Diviners.

With the cottage crammed full, we've had few opportunities for mating, especially as Ellie gags as soon as we even touch lips. That left us to desperate and slippery fumbles in the shower, though I did love having Jace's slick skin beneath my palms, watching him while he bit his lip to try and be quiet. My favourite hobby was breaking through his icy control; my reward his moans that tore free, often accompanied by a hushed yet frantic, "Fuck me, princess, don't stop."

"What are you thinking about?" Jace whispers in my ear.

My flush flares brighter, and I clear my throat. "Nothing. Battle tactics."

He smirks and curls a lock of my hair around his finger. His gentle tug sends shivers from my nape to my lower back.

"Sure you were, princess."

"Can we get this show on the road before these two start humping in the foliage?" Ellie hisses. "I knew Jace was a horny fucker, but this is ridiculous."

"Shut up, Ell—"

"Eloise is right," Rose says over Jace. "If you're ready,

Seraphina, lead the way."

I manage a nod, my muscles tensing. Jace's pull on my hair is somehow comforting.

"I'll be right beside you," he says.

My second nod is more confident. I suck in a breath, straighten from my crouch, and stride past the warded boundary. The Diviners follow in a rustle of leaves.

I pray my plan works and my actions haven't just secured the slaughter of my clan.

The silence of the forest settles on my shoulders, weighing each step. We reach the clearing where Jace and I fled from our first encounter with my brethren—a yellow circle of dead grass surrounded by towering pines. A line of grim-faced demons waits to greet us. Zev steps forward, the trousers beneath his simple tunic damp at the knees and shins.

"It is funny that you accused me of dooming us, Seraphina," he says, "when you are the one to bring the Diviners to our door."

Rose and her warriors spread out on either side of me. Blades flash under the deadly swirls of black. Jace's hands remain empty, though his pose indicates he's ready for a fight.

"You refused to listen," I say tightly. "But we're not here for slaughter. We're here for your surrender."

Zev chuckles and tilts his head to something behind him. "You see, Felecior? She is full of lies and betrayal. This it what happens when a female attempts to rise above her station— she ignores her elders and no longer cares what's best for the clan."

Felecior eases around a rotten trunk while I splutter on the hypocrisy of Zev's statement.

"What are you doing, Seraphina?" he says softly. "How could

you bring them here? Don't you know what they'll do to us? To the younglings?"

His eyes narrow and he spears an accusatory stare towards Jace. Jace spreads his hands.

"Sorry, Fleecy, but with me she has free will, meaning she can do whatever the hell she wants."

"And that is what got us here in the first place," Zev sneers. "Seraphina's wilfulness."

"We're not here to kill anyone," I say to Felecior, beseeching him with my eyes. "There's been enough death on both sides. I want this war to end and for us all to live the lives we *choose*, not the lives we're forced to suffer."

I aim the last at Zev. Kalyan stands at his shoulder, glowering at me. No females grace the gathering of demons around them, not even Inda. Angry male gazes scour my frame, then rake across my defensive line of Diviners.

Rose claims a step, putting herself level with me and Jace.

"Seraphina is right," she says, her voice calm even though this is probably the first time she's ever addressed a group of demons directly in conversation. "It took some convincing, but we're not here to fight. I promised Seraphina we would negotiate. If you can agree to stop feeding on human deaths, we can agree we have no further quarrel."

Zev spares a disparaging sneer for the leader of the Diviners. "We *choose* to be formidable warriors. We will not accept weakness to pander to your human frailty."

"And how is never-ending battle for the good of the clan?" I say, my wings bristling.

"It makes us strong. Gives us purpose. Perhaps humanity should be the ones to surrender. They have ruled this world for long enough while we hide in the shadows, slaking our hunger. Raise your young to feed us and we will spare the rest of you."

My scoff joins Rose's.

"Are you insane, Quasimodo?" Ellie spits. "We're not sacrificing children to you."

"I was hoping you'd say that." Zev's smile sends chills to my wingtips. "Kill the Diviners. Every last one. And if Seraphina interferes, she can join them."

Felecior's eyes widen. My yell of protest scares a jay from the branches above, but it does nothing to stop the disaster Ellie predicted.

A wall of baying, snarling demons launches at us.

42

Jace sweeps me behind him. He grunts, using his arm to block the slashing claws of the male who taunted us at the birthing hospital. Jace slams his elbow into the demon's face. And again. Garnet blood splatters on the male's bare chest. An uppercut to his bloody chin bowls him onto his back, his heavy form crushing the grass. Jace spins to me.

"Princess, get—"

A muscular tail loops around Jace's calf, and tugs. Jace sprawls on his front at my feet. The male seems to have used the last of his scattered wits as he does nothing but blink at the darkening sky. Chaos swirls around us—grappling bodies, howls, the smack of flesh on flesh. Jace pushes up onto his palms, his gaze darting behind me.

"Princess!"

Fingers clamp my hair, and yank. I stumble back, but twist in the grip despite the pain, opening my mouth to yell at Ellie for pulling my hair again when we're on the same side. Zev curls his lip and raises a fist.

"You have been nothing but trouble," he says.

I brace myself.

I've never been hit before. Manhandled, stabbed in the back, wings sliced, but never struck.

A hand grabs Zev's wrist. Claws rake across his elliptically pupilled eye. Zev howls, relinquishing his hold on my hair and staggering away to trip on the sprawled male, joining him on the ground. Jace and Felecior regard each other over the downed elder while the sounds of battle clash and roar around them. Blood drips from Felecior's claws. Jace thrusts out a hand. Felecior hesitates, then wraps his garnet-stained talons carefully around it.

"You think you can keep them down?" Jace says.

Felecior grins, flashing fang. "It would be my pleasure."

"I knew I liked you, Fleecy."

The two males release each other. Felecior bows his head to me after checking Zev and the other demon are still on the ground.

"Thank you, Seraphina, for showing me a different way." His topaz eyes slide to Jace. "And you do not need it, but I approve of your choice."

He turns to his charges before I can reply, his cheeks a little pinker. Jace smooths his hands over my tangled hair.

"You okay?"

I manage a nod, stepping close until his chest is all I can see. My fingers pluck at his jacket.

"How many are dead?" I whisper, a lump in my throat.

"Take a look, princess," he says.

I peek past his bicep, trusting that he wouldn't want me to witness the slaughter and bloodshed of my family. I blink at the scene in the clearing. My chest tightens, and my eyes film with tears.

The yowls and roars of my brethren continue, but in protest, not pain. Diviners pin struggling demons to the dirt. Burn marks mar the worst wrigglers, but not a single fleck of ash litters the crushed grass.

They listened to me. They actually *listened* to me.

Maybe we really can change things for the better.

"Mum!" Ellie yelps.

My gaze darts across wrestling bodies to the far side of the clearing. Ellie straddles the back of a hissing demon. The mud around him is furrowed from his claws, exposing the roots of grass and wildflowers. His shoulders are stippled with weeping burns from her knife, but he levers himself up, tearing Ellie's attention from Rose.

Rose sways on her knees.

Jace sucks in a sharp breath. I scan the trees behind Rose. Kalyan leans on an ancient pine trunk, his smile smug. Inda stands next to him, her focus all for Rose.

Rose slumps to the side, her eyes rolled to show only the whites. Jace's gaze collides with mine. Panic dilates his pupils to leave a sliver of bronze. He leaps across the clearing in a blur of movement. I dive in his wake, my frantic wing beats brushing demon and Diviner alike.

Kalyan tackles Jace into the undergrowth. Ellie jumps to her feet. The demon she was pinning returns the favour, sweeping her legs and slamming her to the dirt. I arrow for Inda, my fist clenched.

Rose stops moving.

Inda slashes an arm through the air, the back of her hand catching my cheek and dragging her fingers painfully across my lips. I thud into the tree Kalyan was so casually leaning against, and rebound onto my rump, the salty taste of blood in my mouth. My cheek stings. Inda returns her gaze to the woman slumped at her feet.

Ellie grapples with her demon, seemingly unaware of the

tears streaming down her face. Jace pummels Kalyan, trying to get free of his grasping claws. Felecior is in the air, his talons locked with the other male, Zev nowhere to be seen.

I can't tell if Rose is breathing.

Oliver yells and sprints for Inda. Zev steps into his path from behind a tree and sinks his claws into Oliver's guts. Oliver folds in half and collapses onto the pine needles. I haul myself upright. Kalyan shrieks, a knife buried hilt-deep in his innards. Jace's panicked eyes meet mine again, his face ashen.

There's no time for words. No time to hesitate.

Sickness and sadness swirl in my stomach.

I throw myself at Inda. Her hand clamps around my throat. My pulse pounds under the grip of her fingers. In the second her focus shifts to me, Jace appears in front of her. Her head snaps to him and her eyes widen.

He slips his blade, almost gently, between her ribs. Inda grabs his wrist as if she can yank the blade out and heal herself. Maybe she could. Jace leans his whole weight into the blade. The hand on my throat releases and I land on my rump again, the shock rattling my teeth. Inda hisses at Jace. The knife twists and she slowly, almost peacefully, crumbles to ash.

Everyone freezes.

In the silence, a tiny, tear-drenched voice says, "Mum?"

43

Ellie gently shakes her mother's shoulders. The humans watch her while the demons stare at Inda's ashes sifting through the air and soaking into the mud, the expressions of both groups identical in their grief. Jace spares a glance for the blood- and soot-stippled blade in his hand. He wipes it on his sleeve and tucks it into his combats, conflicting emotions flashing across his face—anger, guilt, satisfaction, sorrow.

Another of Ellie's soft pleas to her mother sinks talons into my heart. I scramble to my feet before Jace can assist me and we kneel opposite Ellie, Rose's body between us. Claw marks stripe the material of her thick leather jacket that hides a grey t-shirt with the slogan 'If zombies chase us, I'm tripping you.'

Her fashion choices may be growing on me.

I reach for Rose.

"Don't touch her," Ellie snaps.

Tears fill her green eyes. Mud streaks her face and clumps in her pale hair.

"She can help," Jace says without his usual bite whenever he's talking to Ellie. His voice catches as he turns to me. "You can help her, right?"

I focus on Rose. Her beatha is depleted, her chest still, but a spark of life flickers deep. I ease out a breath.

She's not my favourite person in the world, but she means a lot to Jace. And I'd do anything for him.

"She's not gone, but she's fading," I say.

Jace swallows hard. "Do it. Take whatever you need from me."

I lean closer to Rose. Jace shifts to give me room.

I doubt I'll need any of his energy given the cocktail from the Diviners still swirling inside me. They can all help to heal their leader.

"What the fuck is she doing?" Ellie says as I press my mouth to Rose's cold lips.

"Just let her work," Jace says, somewhat strained.

I peek out of one eye. His tall frame is arched over me and Rose, his hands braced on Ellie's shoulders. Ellie slaps at him, looking like she wants to shove me away from her mother. I close my eyes and trust Jace to keep her at bay.

Sharing beatha gets easier every time I do it. The snap and sizzle of energy flows from me to Rose. I guide it to the places it's needed most—head, heart, lungs. Rose twitches under my hands, my fingers splayed on her ribs. Her mouth opens wide, and I sit back on my haunches while she sucks in a huge gulp of air. It takes a few blinks and throat clearings for her to climb back into her unruffled persona, especially as she's still sprawled on her back. Ellie sobs and buries her face in her mother's chest, her fingers bunching in the leather of her jacket.

"What happened?" Rose croaks, one hand awkwardly patting Ellie's hair.

Jace throws a protective arm around my shoulders, and I cuddle into his side. "Seraphina saved your life."

"I replaced the energy Inda stole."

Rose nods, and rubs her free, shaking hand over her face. "Thank you, Seraphina."

"Uh, guys," a voice says behind us. "Oliver isn't doing so good."

Since a crying Ellie seems to have no intention of moving off her mother, we leave Rose to comfort her. Oliver lies amongst the churned pine needles where he collapsed after Zev rammed his claws into him. His breaths come in short gasps, his face slicked in sweat. Another Diviner presses bloody fingers to the wounds in his gut, the clothes around it stained red. Oliver's glassy blue eyes stare off into the canopy above.

The stocky male seems smaller on the ground, pale and in pain.

I remember him drawing the torture ward on my arm. His detached curiosity at my agony. No hesitation when he drew it again and again and again.

I shiver, and Jace squeezes me tighter.

"Well, I did say he had a date with something sharp. Who knew it'd be a demon's claws and not the pointy end of his own pencil." Jace crouches next to the wounded Diviner, his brethren tossing him strange looks. "Hey, Olly, if you survive this, I'll let you off for abusing my girlfriend, but you will owe her. Big time."

Oliver blinks and pants and doesn't appear to have heard. Jace holds a hand out to me and I let him guide me down next to him. The metallic scent of human blood hits my nose.

"You all right with this?" he says quietly.

"I can't let him die. Just like I couldn't let you die, even after you tried to kill me." I peek at Jace. "Though I'm not sad that Oliver is feeling a little pain right now."

Jace grins. "Vindictive, princess. I like it."

I place my hands above and below Oliver's wounds, shutting my eyes to concentrate. The flares of his beatha show me the rents in his skin, his muscle, and deeper into his liver. Zev's talons were a whisper away from perforating his stomach. I guide my energy into knitting the delicate tissues together. The last of the Diviner's glut of power drains from me, taking mine with it.

I sway on my knees, my back aching. Strong arms scoop me against a firm chest and replace the smell of blood with blackberries and cloves.

"Easy there, princess. That's enough."

"How the fuck did she do that?" someone hisses, but I'm too tired to open my eyes.

"Get him on a stretcher and back to the house." Rose's voice is commanding once more, and closer. "He'll need a blood transfusion."

"Is she okay?" Ellie says, her words rough from crying.

"She will be." Jace's voice rumbles beneath my ear. "Drink from me, princess."

I sip his beatha with my eyes shut, revelling in the electric ice water thrill of it. The coldness zings to my belly yet flares in a burst of heat. I squirm in Jace's lap and purr into his throat.

"I like how you taste," I whisper. Or try to. It seems to come out louder than I intended.

Jace chuckles. "Maybe keep that to yourself until we don't have an audience."

I peer out from the warm curve of his neck. Two Diviners fashion a stretcher from branches fastened together by rain-coats. An unconscious but steadier-breathing Oliver is placed onto it and carted away between the pine trees. Rose tracks their progress, Ellie standing close enough to merge at the hip. The demons have clumped together in the clearing with Felecior at their head, the surrounding Diviners regarding them warily, as if ready to draw a knife should one of them so much as sneeze.

Zev and Kalyan are nowhere to be seen.

I straighten in Jace's lap, content to remain in his arms while his energy buzzes under my skin and something hard presses into my rump, especially when I wiggle a little. He growls in my ear, and I wriggle some more.

"Stop squirming, princess," he says in his husky, sexy voice, "unless you want to take us home right now."

"I want that," I gasp, "but there's something I need to do first."

Jace stands easily with me in his lap—such a strong male—and puts me on my feet. My first couple of steps wobble, but my stride is firm by the time I reach Felecior and his waiting demons.

"What would you have of us, Seraphina?" he says with a tip of his head.

"Gather everyone in the amphitheatre—males, females, younglings, elders. Everyone in the clan." I raise my chin to regard the males over Felecior's silver wings, and the Diviners beyond. "It's time everyone learned of our new way of life."

Epilogue

Four Months Later

"And this, younglings, is coffee. When you're mature, seek out where humans congregate to drink the stuff as it fuels their beatha and makes it easier to siphon without notice. Coffee shops will be your sanctuary."

Twenty eager little faces follow my every move, their claws clasped on the desktops. Various wings and horns and tails bristle in excitement.

Six years ago when I fled my clan, I never would have guessed I'd become a teacher. The youngest teacher in history. I'm not even an infertile female. I can very much be bred but, now that I have a choice, I have no interest in reproduction. I would rather teach the children of others how to live a peaceful life than have any myself. And Jace feels the same, though sometimes I wonder what our young would have been like. Half-Diviner, half-demon.

I lift my gaze to the rear of the classroom. A smile tugs at Jace's lips where he's sprawled in a chair, his lean warrior's body tucked under the desk. No doubt he's remembering the first time we met—when he invaded *my* sanctuary.

I miss my coffee shop. The smell of freshly ground beans, the hiss of the machine, watching the trees outside and the lazy flow of the River Ness while Harmony chattered in the background.

Before my homesickness can get too great, Harmony blows me a kiss from her seat next to Jace, her hair in a braid over her shoulder.

She's travelled out here every time she can wrangle extra cover for a few days off. Her first visit after things settled was a real test of my brethren, young and old, to be on their best behaviour.

She was not to be another Father Benjamin. There would never be one again.

I drag my focus from my best friend and my boyfriend. "Who would like a taste?"

Little hands shoot up. I cradle the warm mug between my palms and cross to the side of the classroom. The male youngling ducks his head at my approach and curls his raised arm into his chest. Silky red hair slides forward to hide his face.

My heart always aches at the sight of it. He takes after his mother.

"Here you go, Daire," I say softly. "Have a sip."

He accepts the mug carefully, though his talons clink on the ceramic. They're trimmed often, but still curve, long and black, from his fingers and toes. Daire sniffs the steam, then slurps a mouthful of brown liquid. His nose wrinkles, and I laugh.

"It's an acquired taste."

I pass the mug around the room until it's empty.

I told Daire all about Deirdre. How much she'd wanted to raise him. How excited she was. How she'd been my only friend in the clan. I told Daire it wasn't his fault that she died giving birth to him.

That blame lay with the elders.

I beckon to Jace and Harmony. They weave between the desks to join me at the front of the classroom. Jace sweeps his eyes over the gathered younglings, and most of them shiver beneath his attention.

He turns a grin on me. "I still can't believe I'm a demon's assistant, princess."

"Yet how many knives do you have on you at this moment?"

"Three," he smirks.

Harmony slaps his bicep. "You brought knives into a roomful of children?"

"I bring knives everywhere," he says.

My perfect, terrifying male.

"Who would like to see?" I say.

Enthusiastic hands wave at the ceiling, mostly the younger ones. The older children have had more lessons to ingrain the fear of Diviners.

They're still to be feared, but only for those who refuse to change.

Four months ago, I stood on the cold marble of the amphitheatre in front of my entire clan. The place where so much death and pain had occurred, excluding the birthing hospital, of course. I gave them an ultimatum—they stop feeding on human deaths or the Diviners continue to kill them. It was an effective threat with a troupe of armed and menacing Diviners at my back. Felecior took the lead on organising groups to spread the new rules to other clans, both in the UK and internationally. Now, emissaries of demons and Diviners travel together to where they're needed since, sometimes, you just need to see it to believe it.

As I predicted, there are those of my brethren outwith my clan who want to continue the old ways. The human-killing ways. The Diviners spend the rest of their time policing and hunting them. Ellie and Rose are still tracking Zev and Kalyan. Last I heard, they were getting closer, with a sighting reported by a clan in Cornwall.

Felecior met a male when he was on a diplomatic visit in Sweden. Their pairing caused more shockwaves than the news of demons and Diviners working together. I was introduced to his Chosen on a video call a month ago, overseen by Harmony since technology still confuses me. He and Felecior were adorable together.

Jace draws a knife from his hoodie pocket. The younglings stare at the black, swirling blade with expressions of wonder and apprehension.

"Now, what would happen if Harmony were to touch it?" I say.

Glances flick between the children. Rumps shift on seats.

"Nothing," Daire mumbles from under a curtain of his hair.

I nod at Jace. He passes the knife to Harmony, who pinches it between her thumb and forefinger as if it might cut her.

"And what would happen if I touched it?"

"It would burn," pipes a high voice near the back of the room.

"That's right. With demons and Diviners mixing amicably now, we still have to be careful around their weapons. But let's get back to the main subject of our lesson—beatha. Jace and Harmony have kindly volunteered to let you practise on them. So what do we say?"

"Thank you, Jace and Harmony," the younglings chorus.

"Some of us had to be bribed," Jace whispers.

His bronze eyes flash before he schools his face to something more child-appropriate, and disappears the knife back into his pocket.

He gets to tell me what he wants and I have to do it. It's no hardship for me. Jace knows everything about how humans make love. And my Diviner is kinky.

That's a new word I've learned. I like it. *A lot.*

Harmony clears her throat. "Uh, Phin, your drool is showing."

Heat flares in my cheeks. I bustle around herding the younglings into two groups while Jace chuckles low and husky. It doesn't help my overheating problem.

"When you're mature," I say, ignoring my burning face, "you'll need to feed on small amounts of beatha to survive. It's not a requirement until then, but you can still drink it. We've just never been taught how before."

I stand beside Jace and can't resist touching him. A hand on the firm curve of muscle at the small of his back. Nothing too risqué, though the older children have seen mating ceremonies already.

But no longer.

"Focus on Jace. Feel his beatha, his life force. I want you to take a tiny sip and tell me what his energy tastes like. But remember, females—you have to be careful. Unlike males, you can drain a human to death without touching them. And we don't do that anymore."

The younglings gaze up at Jace with wide eyes. His face is calm, but there's a tiny quiver beneath my hand. I rub his back. My chest swells with love for my mate.

Daire gasps. "He tastes like putting your tongue on a battery."

The children titter and nod, offering up more descriptions of 'cold' and 'buzzy' while I try not to laugh.

"And how do you feel, Jace?"

He eases out a slow, deep breath. "Not any different."

"Well done, everyone! That's all there is to it when you reach maturity—take small sips of beatha from humans as and when you need it. They won't even miss it."

I give Jace a pat and cross to Harmony's group, going through the same process. She smiles fondly at the kids when they tell her she tastes like coffee and oranges. Everyone takes their seats, the younglings bright with joy and pride.

Marrichar has also become a teacher. She trains the children and mature females on maintaining their glamour no matter the situation. Our rivalry growing up pushed her to succeed. I suspect that's also the reason why she's suddenly decided she wants a Diviner for a mate. Poor Oliver seems bemused at her attention, though at least he's sturdy enough to withstand her advances. For a while.

I clap to get everyone's attention. "As well as preserving human life, and, therefore, our own, what is the other benefit of changing our feeding habits?"

The younglings fidget and focus, not-so-subtly, on Daire. He raises a trembling, talon-tipped hand.

"To protect females when they have babies," he says, his eyes big and sad.

I give him an encouraging smile. "We coddled our females, but not where it really mattered. Restrictive feeding will produce fewer demon characteristics in the next generations and lead to easier births, meaning fewer lives lost. It's too early to see a difference yet, but we're monitoring the pregnancy of all our females from now on to make sure they get the care they need. To make sure they're still around to raise their young after the birth, the way they're meant to be."

Daire bows his head, but not before I glimpse the shine of tears.

Caesarean—that's another new word I've learned. The medical term for cutting the young out of the mother. I can understand why it was never performed by demons, the shock and blood loss too great for even a female's healing ability to keep up with. The lack of advanced surgical knowledge would also have affected the youngling.

But the Diviners have their own medical facilities and staff since they often suffered wounds that would be difficult to explain in normal, human hospitals. And they opened their doors to us.

I glance at the clock above the blackboard. "Okay, everyone—off you go to Marrichar to practise your glamour."

The younglings file and flap out the entrance in a burst of chatter, their voices fading down the corridor. Jace scoops me into a kiss.

"You were amazing today," he says against my lips, each word deepening to a purr. "But it's time to pay up. I have lots of ideas, princess. You might not be able to walk after."

Harmony rolls her eyes, but can't hide her grin. "You pair of sex maniacs. I bloody love it. When you need me, I'll be at the playground, ogling the warriors while they do their fitness and self-defence classes. I really like how demon males wear such few clothes."

She gives us a cheery wave as she skips out the door.

Jace chuckles, wrapping his arms tighter around me. "And

she calls us the sex maniacs."

He dips his head to nuzzle my neck. His warm breath scatters goosebumps down my torso, my nipples hardening against his firm chest. His hands glide down to cup my rump, and knead.

"I want you to bend over that desk, princess," he growls into my throat.

"But, Jace... Marrichar... the younglings, next door—"

"Then I guess I'll have to gag you to keep you quiet."

He helps me on my way with a swat to the rump. I stagger to the desk and flop across it, my knees already trembling, my core hot. The door clicks shut. I turn my head to watch Jace, my cheek pressed to the wood. He prowls towards me, every inch the predator.

"Lift your skirt and spread your legs," he says in his danger-ous, husky voice.

The wickedness on his face is enough to make my thighs clench, but I force them apart and lift my skirt, baring my underpants to the room.

Jace licks his lips. "Fucking beautiful."

He disappears behind me where I can't see him unless I strain my neck. Gentle hands peel my underwear to mid-thigh, and I gasp at the caress of cool air.

Jace makes a pained noise. "Fuck me, princess, you're dripping."

His fingers swipe between my legs, curling into the core of me. My moan slips out before I can stuff my fist in my mouth. My wings, completely limp, hang off either side of the desk.

"Open," Jace says.

I open my mouth and he slips his fingers in. I taste myself on his skin, and whimper around him, wiggling desperately.

Jace leans over me, his erection nestling between my bared buttocks.

"You can suck on something else later when I get you back to the cabin. Where you're going to do *all* the good screaming until you pass out."

I suckle on his fingers, brushing my tongue around them and earning myself a soft and frantic, "Fucking Christ."

I love my Diviner, especially when he loses control for me.

He tilts my hips with his free hand, his delicious weight pinning me to the desk. Kisses brand the nape of my neck. His erection glides lower between my legs and Jace pauses for a long, tortured second.

"I choose you, princess," he breathes in my ear. "Every time."

And he claims me, though I'm already his.

Free Bonus Scene

Thank you for reading my book! For a bonus scene from *Better the Devil You Know*, book 1 in the *Divine Demons* series, exclusive only to members of my mailing list, join at nadinelittle.com/bonus-scene by scanning the QR code below:

Who was your favourite character—Seraphina or Jace? I'm quite partial to Harmony, myself. Leave me a review and let me know. Every review brings new readers and gladdens the heart of this little author.

Can't wait to hear from you :)

Buy the First Book in the Series:
Better the Devil You Know
Reiley MacEwen can see demons. When she meets Kade, a

treacherous yet tempting incubus, her life takes a dangerous turn. Especially when one touch is all it takes to ignite a passion that could save or destroy them both.

About the Author

Nadine Little lives in Scotland and is an ecologist who loves botany. She should probably stop writing a different biography for every book series, but it's kinda fun.

Working four days a week, she spends her Fridays having brunch adventures and sunny walks. Weekends are for writing. When she's not scribbling away, you can find her in her hammock or out sniffing the flowers.

For more on her books and a peek behind the scenes, sign up to her mailing list and follow her on social media.

You can connect with me on:
- https://nadinelittle.com
- https://twitter.com/Nadine_Little_
- https://www.facebook.com/nadinelittleauthor

Subscribe to my newsletter:
- https://nadinelittle.com/bonus-scene